AF207289

Shy Girls
CAN'T DATE
Billionaires

First Published by Halo & Claws Publishing 2022

SHY GIRLS CAN'T DATE BILLIONAIRES
Shy Girls Sweet Romances – Book 1

Copyright © Milly Rose 2022

All rights reserved. No part of this book may be used or reproduced in any manner whatsoever without written permission except in the case of brief quotations embodied in critical articles or reviews.
This book is a work of fiction. Names, characters, businesses, organizations, places, events, and incidents are the product of the author's imagination or are used fictitiously. Any resemblance to actual persons, living or dead, events, or locales is entirely coincidental.

For information contact: https://www.hcpbooks.com

Cover Design by Emily Bourne
Copy Edit by Jenny Sims
ISBN: 978-1-925990-21-8

Shy Girls
CAN'T DATE
Billionaires

SHY GIRLS SWEET ROMANCES

MILLY ROSE

One

I've never felt pain like this. My heart is like shattered glass, and the sharp edges cut my insides, leaving me raw and bleeding. Tears stream from my eyes as I scrunch the canvas pouch which holds my paintbrushes and pencils. It was the only thing I grabbed in the panic, making me feel so stupid. Many important things were inside the house. My mother wails into my father's arms over the loss of her wedding dress, our family photos, and the memorabilia from my childhood.

I can't think about anything except my artwork. It's a part of me... and now it's gone. Everything I've spent years working on has vanished in flames.

I grabbed my utensils without conscious thought. I was preparing to start again. But how can I start over after this chaos? Our fire alarm woke me up in the middle of the night. As the smoke hit my nostrils, my dad yelled from across the house. My heart was in my throat and beating like I'd run a marathon in my sleep.

When I launched out of bed, I hit the floor. The house was pitch black, but the thick smoke was overwhelming. I'd learned as a kid what to do in a house fire. *Stop, drop, and roll.* Snatching my artist's pouch off my desk, I belly crawled out of my bedroom. The heat in the hall was incredible. Through the smoke, I saw the glow of flames. The scariest light anyone could see.

A raging fire grew in our dining room, spreading through our living room, and was headed in my direction. I screamed for my parents and then covered my head with my hands, stashing my canvas pouch under my chin. The noise was like nothing I could dream about. It crackled and hissed, with miniature explosions in the roof and walls. As my face buried in the carpet, I suddenly felt my body lifted into the air.

My dad had me in his arms, carrying me through the smoke-ravished house. I screamed as heat encircled us. The ceiling fell in chunks, and charcoal embers flew up, covering our hair and clothing.

Choking and coughing, we made it out alive. Dad fell to his knees, and I collapsed in our front yard beside him. My canvas art pouch tumbled off my belly, and seeing it on the grass was like seeing my fifth limb unscathed. My mother's arms swept me up, and her tears washed against the soot caked on my face.

"I was petrified," Mom said as she held me against her heaving chest. "I didn't want to leave the house without you. I'm so sorry, Christie."

I held her tight and told her it was okay. We're all alive. If she had hesitated, that might not be the case. I'm thankful we're together now.

An hour ago, this was our house. Now fire hoses blast at the smoldering remains. How can everything be destroyed?

I stand under a streetlight, looking at our house's broken and burned frame. Emergency crews have set up lights that shine through the house. The interior of my bedroom no longer exists. My mind flashes through all my artwork. The scorching flames have stripped them to nothing more than embers and cinders.

As the flashing blue and red lights of fire, ambulance, and police vehicles light up our street, we become a spectacle to our neighbors. The gossiping whispers have become louder, and a news crew sets up behind the police cars. My knees knock from the adrenaline, and my shoulders hunch from being everyone's primary focus. I'm a background character, always shying away from the spotlight.

They say the news never sleeps. It's four in the morning. The morning shows air in two hours, and they need a good story. It's mortifying. Thankfully, the police hold them back. There's no way I want my face on television. Not that anyone would recognize me. Even at sixteen, I still haven't mastered the art of making and maintaining friendships. Someone seeing a news clip and worrying about me won't be a factor. Except for maybe my teachers.

I clutch the foil blanket given to me by a paramedic and wrap it around me like a snug hug. Something made the fire start at three o'clock in the morning, and the forensics team will work to find out the cause. The lead agent told my parents they assumed it was an electrical fault, but they couldn't be certain until they thoroughly investigated.

Mom holds on to Dad as she attempts to stop her whimpers. I see it in her face. She blames herself as her mind races through all the appliances she had in the kitchen.

Dad soothes her, saying, "It's no one's fault. It was a freak accident. We just need to remember we're stronger together."

"Mom? Dad?" I ask, "Wha… Wha… What are we going to do?"

I shiver under my foil blanket. Seeing the fear in their eyes scares me beyond belief. They've always been my strong and dependable parents. They are never afraid of anything.

But this is unknown. Terrifying and unworldly. Never would I expect that when I went to bed yesterday evening, I'd wake up to literal hell.

"Sweetheart, we'll be fine," Mom says. Her strained smile shows

3

she's being strong to combat my fears. How can she be brave after seeing what I saw?

"We'll figure this out," Dad says, smoothing back my hair. "Don't worry, Christie. We will get through this. We're a family who always gets through things together."

My heart pounds, and my brain is fuzzy. How am I even standing right now? I clutch the foil blanket and take in our surroundings. Everyone is talking about the house, not the people who crawled out.

We're fine. We're all covered in ash and soot, but we're fine. We're wearing charcoal-stained pajamas... but we're fine.

As I attempt to console myself, more of the house collapses. The fire department extinguishes the flames, and the smoke dissipates as the walls and framing break and crumble. The house is a glowing coal version of Swiss cheese.

"Mr. Klein," a police officer says, joining us. "Thomas Ashworth is arranging accommodation for you and your family."

"Thomas Ashworth?" Dad replies in a splutter. His mouth hangs open in shock.

The officer nods. "Dispatch said he's arranged transport, which should arrive in fifteen minutes."

"Thank you," Dad manages to say, still stunned.

The officer pats Dad's shoulder. "You and your family will be okay."

When the officer walks away, Mom whispers, "Thomas Ashworth? He's helping us?"

"I've only met him once or twice," Dad says, shaking his head as his brow furrows. "Not enough to make a lasting impression. This makes no sense."

"How did he know about the fire?" Mom asks.

Dad nods to the media, who are nudging their way closer. "He's a powerful man. He has resources."

"Who is Thomas Ashworth?" I ask, feeling very out of the loop.

"He's your father's boss," Mom replies, and Dad flips a hand up like a stop sign.

"Whoa, whoa," he says. "Mr. Ashworth is not my boss. There are a few positions between us. He is the head of the company. Not only the company I work for, but he owns many companies."

My eyes pop. "He has an empire?"

Dad mumbles a laugh, and then admits, "Thomas Ashworth is a billionaire."

"Billionaire?" I choke. "Billion with a B?"

Mom's eyes well with tears. "And he's so generous to help us."

Time seems to pass without me noticing. Perhaps I had an out-of-body experience. I must have looked like a zombie. Standing by my parents, I'm motionless and expressionless. Waiting for our savior to arrive, I didn't want to look at the house wreckage. I was so out of it I probably drooled.

As a band of reporters breaks through the police barricade, the officers call them back and wave in a shiny black limousine.

A limo... In our neighborhood... How bizarre.

The loud whispers of our neighbors have died, but this raises the volume again. I'm surprised some of their heads don't pop off like Pez dispensers the way they're craning their necks and stretching on tippy-toes.

The limousine pulls up in front of us, and the driver emerges.

"Mr. Klein," the driver says with a gentlemanly nod.

"Yes?" Dad says, awestruck.

"My name is Roger. Mr. Ashworth has sent me here to collect you and your family," the driver replies.

"Yes," Dad says with a catch in his throat. His hand presses into my back, and he nudges Mom and me forward.

"You will all be okay," the driver says. He opens the passenger side door and gestures to the interior of the limo. "Please, climb on in. You're on your way to safety."

5

Over my shoulder, I take one last look at our family home. I don't know where we're headed, but I'm certain we aren't coming back here. Even if we rebuild, what we had is gone forever.

"This is extraordinary," Dad says. He gives Mom and me a squeeze, and we pile into the limousine.

I discard my fireside foil blanket and upgrade to the cashmere throw I find in the limo. Under a strip of neon lighting, I spy a bar fridge. What other goodies are in here?

This is crazy.

We were just in a blazing fire, watching our house disintegrate, and now we're in a limo because my dad's billionaire boss sent it for us.

And accommodation. What does this mean? A crappy motel? One of his investment apartments? Where are we going? Even if this guy has loads of money, how did he learn about the fire so quickly? Does he keep tabs on his employees?

"Dad?" I ask, sitting on the most comfortable car seat ever. Seriously, am I on a plush couch right now?

"Yes, Christie?"

"Shouldn't we know where we're going?"

"If Mr. Ashworth has made the arrangements," Dad says, "it'll be the best of the best. We should be thankful we're here."

I nod in agreement. "Yes, I'm glad we're no longer standing in front of the house for everyone to ogle us. But this is weird, isn't it?"

A tear slips from Mom's eye, and she puts a hand on my knee. "Everything about tonight is weird," she says. "Please, just be grateful to be here."

"Do I really sound ungrateful?" I ask. "I'm just confused, and I'm scared. And..."

"We know," Mom and Dad say at once.

I pull the cashmere throw higher to my chin. My stomach cramps at the notion of dirtying the beige material with charcoal soot, but I remove the thought from my mind. Thomas Ashworth is aware we were in a fire. He knows we come with a cleaning cost.

I sink into the seat and stare out the dark-tinted window. The sun hasn't broken, but the streetlights brighten the view. That is until the suburbs disappear, and we travel along the highway.

The screen between the driver and us lowers. "Everyone okay back there?" the driver asks.

"Yes, fine, thank you," Dad answers. "May I ask where we are headed?"

"Ashworth Estate, sir."

Confusion muddles Dad's expression. "Excuse me?" he asks.

The driver nods, taking a quick glance over his shoulder. "Mr. Ashworth will have your suites ready for your arrival."

"Ashworth Estate?" Mom questions. "Does that mean...?"

Dad nods. "Yes. It's the Ashworth's family home."

"Wait," I say, breathless as I pivot between Dad and Mom. "He's a billionaire, right? Are we staying in a mansion?"

Dad shrugs with a chuckle. "I've never seen the Ashworth Estate," he says, "but I hear it's enormous. A mega-mansion."

"Why would he take us in?" I whisper, inadequacy rising inside me. "How far from home is it?"

Dad peers out the window. "He lives in the mountains. He has acres of land and commutes to work by helicopter."

"What does that mean for school?" I ask, feeling an imminent panic attack.

Mom pats my knee. "Take a breath, Christie. We don't need to worry about this stuff right this minute. I have insurance and mortgage repayments bouncing around in my head, but we have to eliminate the thoughts until the shock wears off."

"So we just sit here, in our ash and soot, and wait?" I ask dryly.

"Yes, Christie," Dad says. "We just wait."

By seven in the morning, the sun has risen, and the brilliant awe-inspiring views of the mountains mesmerize us. The vehicle slows to a stop at tall wrought-iron gates, which open before us.

With the early sun sparkling against the dewy grass, acres of land stretch out in vibrant greens. The car strolls along the winding path to the house, and as we get closer, I realize "house" is the wrong word to use. It's grotesquely enormous, with wealth oozing from the inside out. A building perfect for make-believe but too ridiculous for reality.

This is one family's home. Dad said the Ashworths only have two kids. Even though I'm an only child, it's reasonably close to our number of family members. Our three-bedroom house had enough room. We had a living room, dining room, and kitchen; the third bedroom was Dad's home office. I primarily lived in my bedroom, which doubled as my art studio.

This three-story, gothic Tudor manor is monstrously obtrusive. Built with two-toned stonework and framed stained glass windows, it's topped with steep gable roofs and several elaborate chimneys. Oh my goodness, is that ivy growing on the walls? This is too much. I feel tiny and insignificant staring up at it. My teeth chatter as I ready myself to leave the limousine because my knees might give way from the sheer grandeur.

What will this family be like? Is there a sliver of a chance we'll get along? Please tell me they have extended family with their own wings. This behemoth shouldn't house only four people. And what happens when their kids graduate? Will the parents live somewhere that could house hundreds of people? Okay, they might have staff living on the grounds, like gardeners and housekeepers. I doubt they live in the main house. There's probably a servants' quarters at the rear of the property.

The driver, Roger, opens the door, and I motion for my parents to exit first. When I step outside the vehicle, a crisp freshness hits my nose. The air feels cleaner than back home. I take in the surrounding mountains and the pollution-free sky and smile.

Maybe this won't be so bad after all.

The large and heavy front door of the mansion opens, and a man in a white suit jacket and pressed black trousers walks toward us. His pointed black shoes look shiny enough to be a mirror.

Oh boy. Is he a butler?

Two

"Mr. and Mrs. Klein," the man in white and black says, "Miss Klein. Welcome to Ashworth Estate. My name is Murphy, and I'm the head of the household staff. I'm here to ensure you're as comfortable as possible. Please, follow me into the manor, and we'll get you settled."

"Thank you so much," Mom says. "We can't believe we're here."

"When Mr. Ashworth heard about your troubling situation," Murphy says, "he asked me to arrange everything immediately." He smiles kindly at Dad. "Mr. Klein, you're a very important part of Mr. Ashworth's work."

"Ah, ah. Really?" Dad says, stuttering.

"You all must be frightfully exhausted and in need of showers and clean clothes." Murphy gestures toward the mansion. "Allow me to show you to your suites and where you can get refreshed."

"Suites?" I whisper, clutching Mom's hand.

Mom shakes her head with wonder in her eyes. "I can't fathom this either."

We walk past the manicured hedges and large stone sculptures toward the ornate front door. My legs quiver as we enter the foyer of the mansion. The light reflects off the sandstone tiles, revealing veins of gold in individual tiles.

The artwork on the walls is astonishing. I recognize some of the hand-painted autographs. They give me a sense of the amount of money displayed in the frames. Eclectic handcrafted side tables with Swarovski crystal ornaments and vases ripped from the Ming Dynasty. The wealth engulfing the hall sends me dizzy.

My happy place is in art galleries and examining prized pieces. I want to take everything in, but it is unbelievable people call this home. They hang out here after work and school. When I came home from school, our house felt like nothing special, and it felt normal. How can living with stuff be normal?

We pass an expansive living room where floor-to-ceiling windows shed light on the staggering opulence. My eyes run over the chaise lounges, elongated glass coffee tables, and the long marble bar on the back wall. I swear this one room is three times the size of our little house.

That house no longer exists. We are here because Mr. Ashworth thinks my dad is special. But why? How did it lead to Mr. Ashworth monitoring him? Should I be worried about this?

My head throbs with questions. I rub between my eyebrows and hang my head low. I cannot tolerate any more of this insanity.

"Are you okay, Christie?" Mom asks, rubbing my back as we continue behind Murphy.

"Yeah, I'm fine. I'm just tired."

Murphy takes us up a winding set of stairs and then shows us to a suite.

"Mr. and Mrs. Klein, this is where you will lodge," he says, opening the heavy door.

It's massive. Like four times the size of a normal bedroom. Oh wait, it keeps going. Whoa.

"Peter, thank God you're here," says a man striding down the hall.

"Mr. Ashworth," Dad says, trying to keep his cool.

They extend their arms and meet in a handshake.

Mr. Ashworth smooths back his hair and lets out a quick breath. "I'm so glad you're here. I was so worried about you all. Is your family okay?" he says, looking past Dad to Mom and me.

"We're all fine," Dad replies. "Thank you for bringing us, but this is too much."

"Nonsense, nonsense," Mr. Ashworth says, swatting a hand. "Have you seen this place? We have plenty of bedrooms. You're hardly an inconvenience. I need to know you're okay."

"Thank you so much, Mr. Ashworth," Mom says. She steps forward and extends her hand. "This room is lovely. I'm Mary, Peter's wife."

"Yes, of course," Mr. Ashworth says, "and, please, call me Tom."

Mom places her hands on my shoulders, telling Mr. Ashworth, "This is our daughter, Christie."

"Wonderful to meet you, Christie," Mr. Ashworth says. "I can show you to your room. I need to see my son before I leave. It will be on the way."

"Where will her room be?" my mom asks, fear in her eyes like she wants to keep her baby close.

"I thought she might want to stay in the kids' wing," Mr. Ashworth says. "My son's and daughter's rooms are there." He looks at me and smiles. "Maybe some kids your own age will make you more at home."

This guy doesn't know me. I'd rather just sleep on the floor by my parents' bed.

"Are you okay with that, Christie?" Mom asks, knowing me too well.

"Yes," I say quietly. "Wherever I need to be is fine."

"I'll let you two get settled and washed up," Mr. Ashworth says to my parents. He turns to me with a clap of his hands. "All right. I'll show you where you're staying."

He's far too enthusiastic. Does he not fathom that he's talking to a girl literally covered in the remains of her house?

I follow him across the landing, and he's jabbering about something. Maybe about work or the house, but it's not computing. It's like he forgot we're here because of a traumatic ordeal because he moves in a hurried stride. I keep up as best I can, knowing I'm rid of him as soon as I get to a bedroom or bathroom.

"This is my daughter Vanessa's bedroom. She'll be nice and close to you, but she is away from home. She's visiting Switzerland with her mother."

"Wow, Switzerland," I murmur. Seriously, who are these people?

"Your room is just up here." As he says that, the door to the neighboring room opens.

A boy about my age walks out. He's wearing a blue blazer, crisp white dress shirt, and a navy-striped tie. A hand slips into the pocket of his pressed trousers. Once I lift my gaze from his shiny black shoes, I fixate on the broadness of his shoulders. I almost smile when noticing his chiseled jawline. That is until a scowl crosses his face.

"What's this?" he says, somewhat annoyed.

"There was some excitement overnight while you were sleeping," Mr. Ashworth says.

Excitement isn't exactly how I would put it.

"This is Christie Klein. She and her family are staying with us."

His son's face creases further. "What? You've moved a family into our home?"

Wait, this guy is offended I'm here?

"Christie, this is my son, Thomas Ashworth the third." Mr. Ashworth looks me up and down with a smirk. "Or, ironically, you can call him—"

13

His son cuts him off. "Dad, are you serious right now? Have you talked to Mother about this?"

"Son, we have plenty of space. They don't have a house, and we have the resources."

"So you're taking care of another family? After everything that's happened?" Thomas throws a pointed finger in my direction. "We don't even know these people. Do you know these people, Dad? Because I sure don't."

I take in my clothing and my arms. No matter how much I rubbed the cashmere throw over me, I'm still blackened. Does he think I'm poor? Is that what insults him? Sure, my parents aren't even close to millionaires, but there's nothing wrong with being middle-class.

The panic rippling through Thomas Ashworth III's expression gives me pause. Does he think I'll steal from him? Is that what terrifies him about not knowing me? My whole life, no one has acknowledged I exist. It's never led me to steal. Even when I can identify the most valuable items in this mansion.

"Forget this," Thomas mutters. "I have to get ready for school."

Mr. Ashworth's son marches toward us, and when he slides by us, he sends me a filthy look.

I feel lower than low after the massive contempt thrown my way. Like I'm nothing but dirt. By standing in the hallway, I've offended this precious boy. I'm supposed to stay in the room next to him, and he already hates my guts.

"Claudia," Mr. Ashworth calls to a woman waddling up the hall with a pile of fresh towels. "This is Miss Klein. Will you show her to her suite and where her bathroom is located?"

"Of course, Mr. Ashworth," Claudia says with a bright smile.

"Splendid." Mr. Ashworth claps. "I'm off to work. I hope you get some much-needed rest."

His tone is ultra chipper. Take away the fact I'm a hot mess. Didn't the argument with his son faze him? He didn't run after him to sort out what was bothering him, as either of my parents would. He just let him walk off and ruin the start of his school day. I would hate to go to school in such a sour mood.

Claudia is a short yet delightful woman with light-olive skin and thick black hair rolled into a neat bun. She shows me to my bedroom, and my jaw is ready to smack the floor. It's gorgeous in shades of blush, tan, and nude. It's like something from a style magazine. A plush throw blanket and too many pillows to count cover the king-sized bed. The furniture is delicate with French sophistication, and the windows frame the pristine landscaped gardens.

"You can use Miss Ashworth's bathroom in her absence," Claudia says, gesturing to the hall. "The guest bathrooms are farther away, and her bathroom is the closest."

I follow her out, and she takes me to the bathroom. The fresh scent of lavender and lemon lightens my mood. The gold hardware dazzles against the sparkling white marble tiles, which have rivers of black running through them. A large oval-shaped soaking tub sits in the back corner, and a large shower takes up the opposing wall, with a large rain shower hanging from the ceiling.

"Wow," I whisper.

Claudia sets a towel by the tub and then walks to a closet. She opens it and says, "In here, you'll find a nightgown, robe, slippers, and undergarments. Would you like me to draw you a bath?"

"Oh no." I raise my hands. "No, I'll be fine. I need a shower to wash away all this grime."

Claudia nods. "Of course, Miss Klein. Will you need anything else?"

"No." I'm quick to respond. "I'll manage. I think I'll hit the pillow as soon as I'm out of the shower."

"I work in this wing. If you need anything, you call for me," Claudia says, making her way to the door. "We'll supply you with new clothes and any other supplies you may need."

15

"Thank you," I whisper, disbelief washing over me.

Claudia smiles and closes the door behind her.

I strip off my tattered pajamas and throw them in the trash. I never need to see them again. I notice how bad they smell once they're off and realize I must reek of smoke myself.

I turn on the hot water and slide into the shower. As the water reaches the perfect temperature, I let it glide over my hair and down my body. I close my eyes as everything washes away. I don't need to see the scummy dark gray hitting the formerly sparkling white shower base at my feet.

Flames fill my third eye, and when the images get too real, I blink my eyes open. After a few ragged breaths, Thomas's face appears in front of me. His disgusted expression.

I've gone my whole life being invisible. No friends. And honestly, I'm now glad about that. Thomas giving me that look is not worth being seen.

Invisibility is better than contempt.

We lost everything. Our house burned down. All that remained was what we could carry. And this guy has zero empathy.

He doesn't want people he doesn't know living in his house. Because I look a certain way, I might steal.

Well, I have zero interest in getting to know this guy. If he has no compassion or kindness in his body, he's not worth my time.

I uncoil my hands from tight fists. I lift my palms and see half moons where my nails have pierced my flesh.

I didn't realize he made me this angry.

I shampoo my hair three times before it feels clean. I scrub my face with a cleanser, and it's meltingly soft and luscious. I wash my entire body five times over. My skin crawls like the smoke and stains will never come off. I only stop because I'm conscious of rubbing my skin raw.

After the shower, I towel off and put on the sleepwear Claudia had prepared. My eyes feel ready to pop out of my skull. Trudging back into the hall, I pick out which room I think is mine. When I'm greeted with the subtle shades from earlier, I flop down, face-first, onto the bed.

Heaven.

Claudia enters the room, mumbling a sweet tune as she draws the curtains closed. As I fade into dreamland, she tucks the bed covers around me. I cough twice, hard like the smoke is taking over again. Claudia strokes a circle on my back, and my chest relaxes.

I'm scared of what will appear in my dreams.

Three

I don't know how long I slept. Thanks to the fire, I no longer have a phone, which is my usual time-telling device.

Pulling the covers back, I stretch my arms over my head. They look squeaky clean, and this makes me smile. I turn my head to a nearby window, and even though the curtains are drawn, I spy a sliver of the outside. There's no daylight, so it must be dusk.

Oh boy. Did I sleep all day?

I sit in bed and look around. There's a large clock in a handcrafted wooden frame facing the bed. The time is nearing seven o'clock in the evening.

I wonder if my parents are worried about me. Or maybe they're still asleep themselves.

I can't believe I slept so long and that I pushed through the adrenaline and knocked myself out. My heart has never raced faster, so I'm not surprised I took advantage of the rest.

I slide out of bed, pull on the dressing gown Claudia provided, and move to the bedroom door with the fluffy slippers on my feet.

I feel super weird about walking around someone else's home in pajamas so late in the day, but I don't know where I'm supposed to find extra clothes. Maybe I should rummage through the bedroom furniture or check the bathroom. Perhaps Claudia has restocked the cupboard my pajamas came from.

I creep into the hall, dreading someone finding me, wandering around lost. I make my way to the bathroom, and as my fingertips touch the doorknob, a bedroom door opens.

It's him. Thomas Ashworth III.

My heart races in panic. One, he's keel-over-clutching-your-heart gorgeous. And two, I know he hates me.

Annoyance steams off him, and his eyes narrow in deep focus.

I'm the last person he wants to see. He must feel like his space is being invaded. His sister is gone, so this wing is supposed to be his. And now I'm here, taking up space where I'm not wanted.

"What are you doing?" he asks.

His hands slide into the pockets of his trousers. He's wearing a dress shirt, and the top two buttons are undone, giving him a casual look. After a long day at school, his hair is tousled. With this house surrounded by acreage, I'm assuming it takes a while for him to get to school, wherever it is.

"Um... I'm going to the bathroom," I reply.

"That's my sister's bathroom," he says flatly.

"Yes, I know," I say with a mortifying squeak to my voice. "I was told I could use it while she's away."

"You're just taking over?" he accuses, standing tall like confrontation is no issue for him.

As I keep a hold of the doorknob, my shoulders hunch forward.

When it comes to talking to people, I'm never assertive or confident. And with this guy, I feel minuscule. There's just something about his eyes, his jawline, his hair. I've never felt attracted to someone who I can't stand.

He just stares at me.

Why can't he just walk past and leave me alone? Please, stop looking at me.

I've never hated enduring eye contact so much. I never thought becoming visible to someone could make me feel worse about myself.

"I just want to find some clothes," I mumble at the floorboards.

"You'd better hurry up," Thomas says, walking toward me. "Dinner will be ready soon, and you shouldn't be late." He continues past me, and as he turns the corner into the next wing, he says, "I'll send Claudia down to help you."

Without a moment's thought, I blow out a hard breath. I lean forward, holding the door for support, and breathe long and slow until my pulse steadies. Being around Thomas makes me feel an inch tall and still covered in soot and reeking of smoke. I've been homeless for a day, but he looks at me like it's been eons.

The only people I communicate with are my parents, my teachers, and the librarians. None ever made me uncomfortable. Despite this gigantic house sending me dizzy, Thomas is the one factor making this stay a nightmare. And I've spent five minutes with him. I hope we can get a new house soon. How can I survive another day with Thomas Ashworth III treating me like a piece of human garbage?

Claudia hurries up the hall like she's on a mission. Her eyes are wide like she's in trouble.

"I'm so sorry, Miss Klein," she says, puffing. "I should've been here when you woke up. Please, let me help you with some fresh clothes."

"You don't need to apologize," I say, but she's already pushing past me to get into the bathroom.

20

I follow her inside, and she opens the closet, which held the pajamas.

"Tell me if this fits," Claudia says, pulling out a lilac dress with a conservative neckline and capped sleeves.

She hangs the dress on the three-piece divider by the bathtub. I slip behind the divider. It's not see-through, but I'm awkward about undressing while she's in the room. Claudia doesn't need to help me get dressed or anything. I can manage and wish Thomas hadn't fetched her. I would have figured this out. I was on the way to the bathroom before he stopped me.

I slip out of the pajamas and pull on the dress. It is the most gorgeous and smooth fabric I've ever felt. As I pull it over my body, it fits like a glove.

"Oh my gosh," I whisper.

"Everything okay, Miss Klein?" Claudia asks.

"Yes, it is," I say, loud and chipper. "I'm in love with this dress. It's amazing."

"Oh, I'm so glad to hear it," Claudia says. "Let me see."

Walking out from past the divider, I'm met with Claudia's warm smile.

"Would you like me to help you with your hair?" Claudia offers.

I grasp my hair. Oops. I haven't looked in a mirror since my shower earlier. Is my hair a disaster? Oh my gosh! Thomas was staring at me! No wonder he thinks I'm a freak.

"It's no problem," Claudia says. "I help Miss Ashworth every day."

"I don't want to be late for dinner," I say, fidgeting my feet in an awkward stance. "Thomas said it was soon."

"You have plenty of time," Claudia says, reassuring me with a pat on the shoulder. "Don't worry about being late. I will escort you to the dining room myself."

"Okay," I say, with nothing to lose.

Claudia taps the stool by the bathtub, smiling. "Please, sit."

Claudia easily combs through my hair after the multiple washes I gave it this morning. She twists and pins pieces of my hair and then ties the rest of my hair in a neat and low ponytail.

She holds up a small mirror. "What do you think?"

I grin at my reflection, feeling nurtured. "It's lovely. Thank you."

Claudia moves to the closet and pulls out white sandals with a low heel. "Try these on," she says, placing the shoes at my feet.

There's something unpleasant about Claudia buckling the ankle straps on my behalf. Is this what it's like being a rich kid? Never upgrading from childhood because someone is always around to spoon-feed you?

Oh my gosh... Someone won't cut up my food for me at dinner, will they?

"You look delightful, Miss Klein," Claudia says, standing and moving to the door. "Shall we make our way to the dining room?"

With a nod, I stand and follow Claudia into the hall. I want to tell her to just call me Christie, but my voice sticks in my throat. My neck is bowing from wanting to say it, but my fear of saying the wrong thing prohibits me. I don't want to offend her. She calls me Miss Klein because formality is part of her job description. What if she got in trouble with Mr. Ashworth because she called me by my first name without his permission? I'd never have the guts to tell Mr. Ashworth it was my call. After the way his son glares at me, I don't need another Ashworth loathing me.

I fall behind Claudia's brisk pace, distracted by the beautiful pieces hung in golden frames against the antique wallpaper. Everything on our walk appears more striking now than during our hazy arrival.

Claudia gestures to a flight of stairs. "Down this way."

I hold the wooden railing as I take my steps down. The staircase turns as we descend to the floor below. This is a different route from the one we took with Mr. Ashworth because we land at the rear of the luxurious living room I spied earlier.

22

We don't go into the living room and instead move into another hallway. The delicious smell of cooking food wafts toward my nostrils, giving me the sense the kitchen is nearby. I don't see it on our walk. The path ends in a large room.

From the doorway, I spy a crystal chandelier hanging overhead, long candlesticks for the table's centerpiece, and exquisite bone china dinnerware. White linen dresses the elongated table, which houses too many chairs to count.

At the head of the table sits Mr. Ashworth. My parents sit beside him, and on the opposite side is his son, Thomas Ashworth III.

"Good evening, Miss Klein," Murphy says, greeting me at the doorway.

Claudia turns around and walks back into the hall. It's like having my safety blanket taken away. I like Claudia and wish she could sit beside me at dinner.

"Right this way," Murphy says, and as I follow him, he's not taking me to my parents, which is where I want to sit. Murphy is taking me toward Thomas.

Oh my goodness. I have to sit next to him for the entirety of dinner. My stomach spasms with dread. This will not go well.

Thomas looks up from his phone and locks eyes with me. I duck behind Murphy to avoid his glare.

"Did you sleep well, Christie?" Mom asks as Murphy slides my seat in and under me.

Mom and Dad are dressed more sophisticated than I've ever seen them.

"Yes, I did," I say, brushing back a loose curl by my face. "I can't believe I slept so long."

"We were out like logs too," Dad says with a light chuckle.

"I'm glad you all took advantage of the time and slept," Mr. Ashworth says, lifting a glass of wine. "You are all welcome to stay as long as needed."

At that, Thomas agitatedly shifts in his seat. Doesn't he get why we're here? Didn't his dad explain that our house burned down?

Mom sighs. "I'm dreading the paperwork and the phone calls I have to make to our insurance company regarding the house."

Mr. Ashworth snaps his fingers. "Murphy, get those phones I had you prepare."

Murphy comes back with a silver tray and three iPhones sitting on top of it. He hands one to me, and one each to Mom and Dad.

"It's one small gesture to get you on your way," Mr. Ashworth says.

"We could have gotten replacements ourselves," Dad says modestly.

"Nonsense," Mr. Ashworth says with a shrug. "And besides, Peter, I need to get in contact with you at work."

"You would need direct contact with me?" Dad asks, confused.

"After dinner, we'll have a bit of a chat," Mr. Ashworth says. "I was getting things prepared, but circumstances have brought the timing up a notch."

Dad's face is a mix of bewilderment and eagerness.

Mom smiles at the phone lying by her plate. "Thank you, Mr. Ashworth, for the kind gestures. This keeps getting too much. We do appreciate it."

"Not a problem. And remember, it's Tom," Mr. Ashworth then turns to me. "Christie, I bet you're glad to have a phone again. I know how precious phones are to you young people."

Yeah, so I can go back to texting my mom, like usual.

Even though I'm looking down, I sense Thomas turning in my direction. He taps his armrest to a frustrated beat. I must seem like a total charity case to him, but his dad just keeps giving us things.

We didn't ask to end up here. I take in the elegance and wealth decorating the room. Is Thomas jealous because he's not the only one being handed gifts? For me, a heavenly soft mattress, a new dress, and a phone have made my year. I wonder how much stuff it takes to make

Thomas happy. If he's ever happy.

Two men wearing black caps, crisp white chef jackets, and black and white tartan pants serve our dinner. So it's not that they have their own cooks, but they staff gourmet chefs.

A delectable meal of pan-seared Wagyu beef with red wine sauce, steamed greens, and smashed baked potatoes sits before me. The smell alone has my mouth watering. The presentation is to die for, and it's still unfathomable that the Ashworths consider this a family dinner at home.

"So how long will your wife and daughter be overseas?" Mom asks, making conversation as everyone busies themselves eating.

Mr. Ashworth checks his watch as if his family were due at any moment.

"You know, I'm not sure." Mr. Ashworth chuckles. "Perhaps they will be a week away."

"I'm sure they will bring home many stories to share," Dad says with a polite nod.

I've never seen my dad this nervous. Mr. Ashworth has him on edge. It would be surreal to live with the man who signs your paychecks.

Thomas sinks into his chair and rolls his head in his father's direction. The glazed look he gives his father is one of utter boredom. The way their eyes twitch at each other, I swear he is telepathically talking to his dad. Maybe rich people have their own language.

Small talk between the parents plays out for the rest of dinner. On my side of the table, I display my fidgety awkwardness while Thomas shows off his fidgety boredom.

After a dessert of raspberry sorbet with blueberries and crushed walnuts, we follow Mr. Ashworth into the living room. He slips behind the bar, picking between brown and clear liquors as Mom and Dad take in the exquisite room.

When I move closer to my parents, Thomas announces to his dad, "Okay, see you later. I'm heading to the theater."

"Wait a minute," Mr. Ashworth says, leaning on the bar to glimpse his son. "Take Christie with you."

No, no, no. Please, don't make me go with him. I'll just sit in the corner. I'll go back to my room. I want to avoid more awkwardness shifting between us.

Thomas backtracks after his father's words.

"Christie doesn't want to hang out with us old fogies," Mr. Ashworth says. He smiles and winks at me. "Son, take her to the theater with you. She'll have a lot more fun with you than sitting around listening to the adults drone on."

Again, this guy has no idea who I am.

Thomas huffs and then beckons me to follow. "Come on, then."

I tug on my dress as my stomach spins.

Mom and Dad wave at me, with Mom saying, "Have fun, dear."

Her giddy smile is beaming. Like she's excited about me making my first friend. But she's seen this guy, right? The annoyance that billowed off him during dinner. She has to realize this won't go well.

"Bye," I say, waving to the three parents. Begrudgingly, I follow Thomas into the hall.

He's already a fair way ahead, a signal for me not to follow. I don't want to, but where else will I go? I don't remember how to get to my room. It'd be super convenient to go back upstairs with him. Just so I know where to go.

Thomas stops when the hall turns. He folds his arms as he waits for me.

It's nice that he's waiting, but the hostility is palpable. Why didn't he just keep walking and let me get lost?

When I'm a few steps away from him, he continues around the corner. Does going to the theater mean leaving this mansion? Movies and stage shows spring to mind. Wait. Is this a home theater situation? Like an actual cinema in their home? Let me guess, there's a freaking bowling alley in this building?

Thomas leads me to a heavy door, and as he tugs it open, he says,

"The theater is downstairs."

The door opens to a darkened space, and as my eyes dip down, neon strip lighting frames black carpeted steps. Yep, it's a cinema in their home. Whoa.

I follow Thomas down the steps when Murphy's voice sounds behind us. "Can I get you two anything?"

Thomas lifts a hand in a disinterested motion. "I'm good," he says.

I turn around to give Murphy a gracious smile. "Me too. I'm fine, thanks."

"Very well," Murphy says, and closes the door on us.

I panic at the darkness cloaking our surroundings until dim overhead lights shine above us as if on a sensor. To my left are four stacked rows of comfy, reclining seats. Thomas moves to the third row, and I notice power cords running between two seats of the first row up to where Thomas sits. Reclining, he grabs a controller and throws on a headset.

Oh man, he's here to play video games. I fold my arms and turn to the enormous screen, which powers up a game. I pray it's not super violent and gory.

I take an aisle seat in the second row and turn on the phone Mr. Ashworth gave me. At least I can distract myself from whatever ends up playing on the screen. Perhaps a new ebook will help teleport me from here.

Thomas boasts into his headset, continuing loud chatter with whoever plays the game alongside him. It's a shoot 'em up action game that I have zero interest in. Listening to the egomaniacal words coming out of his mouth makes leaving, with the risk of getting lost, worth it.

I check the contacts on the phone and see Peter Klein and Mary Klein. I grin and change the names to Dad and Mom. Should I text Mom? Maybe she's sick of politely listening to Mr. Ashworth talk about business and wants to curl up on a sofa and chat about future design projects like our usual Friday nights.

"Christie," Thomas says, and I'm so surprised I jolt in my seat. I turn around, and Thomas holds a controller in the air as he asks, "Do you want a turn?"

I shy away, waving my hands in my face. "Ah, no, thank you."

He shrugs. "Suit yourself."

He pulls his headset back on and looks at the screen like a well-dressed zombie.

I play with the buttons on my armrest and find the perfect angle to recline my head and feet. I open an article, "A Day in the Life of Picasso," and tune out the speaker blasts.

I tap on my phone as Thomas says, "So where are you from?"

I wait out Thomas, hearing the answer through his headset, by skimming the article. When the room grows quiet, I glance up from my phone. Across the giant screen is the word "paused."

"Christie," Thomas blurts.

"Huh?" I say, turning in his direction.

He smirks. "Yeah, I'm talking to you."

"Oh," I say.

"Where are you from? I don't think I've ever seen you at school."

I shake my head. "Yeah, I'm not from here."

"So where are you from?" he asks, his smirk growing bigger.

"I'm from Thornton."

"What? Isn't that near the city? What are you doing here?"

I shrug. "I don't know. Our house burned down. We were waiting for the emergency teams to do their thing. The police officers were taking our statements. And then one of them tells us your dad arranged a limo to pick us up. Next minute, we're here."

Thomas frowns. "So what? Is Dad going to chopper you to school every day?"

I swallow with discomfort, and my stomach whirls. "Geez. Well, I hope not."

He hits play on the game and slides down in his seat. "What? Afraid

28

of flying?"

"A helicopter is like a deathtrap." I turn to the screen and view the portrayal of violence. "Yeah, a little something like this."

"You don't like video games, either?" Thomas asks.

I sigh. "No, not really."

"Oh, whoa!" Thomas yells at the screen, flinging his controller high. "Did you seriously just do that?"

And that's it. He's back in the headset conversation. *Phew.* Back to the safety of invisibility.

I can't believe an hour has passed, and I don't excuse myself. But I'd hate for him to flip out and give me an awful glare. I can't take another hit of direct eye contact.

Thomas shuts off the game, then bounds off his seat and into the aisle.

He stops by my chair. "What are your plans for the rest of the evening?"

I look up, but my eyes only manage to land on his collar. "Um, to sleep."

"Do you remember how to get to your bedroom?"

I lower my head and shake my head with shame.

An airy laugh slips out of Thomas as he jogs his way down the steps. "Well, come on," he calls. "I'll show you upstairs."

I hurry out as Thomas heads for the exit. Just like going to the theater, he's strides ahead. It makes it really hard to commit objects to memory, find my bearings, and form a map in my head.

This mansion is equivalent to wandering around a museum unsupervised. We take a winding staircase, which I'm not sure I've taken before, and somehow we're back in the kids' wing. Yep, I'm still clueless.

"Well, good night," Thomas says, continuing along the hall.

"Good night," I say with an involuntary squeak.

Thomas turns his door handle and looks back at me. "You actually look nice tonight."

"Oh, um…" I can't finish the thought as a sweltering heat localizes in my cheeks from the surprise compliment.

His expression is flat. "Amazing what can happen when you're not covered in mud or whatever that stuff was."

I fidget in place, far too tongue-tied to explain it was remnants of the house fire.

"But I don't suppose we'll be seeing much more of each other," Thomas says, pushing open his door. "Dad can't keep giving handouts. You've gotta go home at some point."

He walks into his suite, closing the door behind him, and my mouth hangs open. What home? Didn't he listen when I said our house burned down? Is he that careless? There's no home left.

Ouch!

I uncoil my hands and see a new imprint of half moons.

Geez. Thomas Ashworth III, you make me livid!

Four

I wake in a hot sweat after flames dance under my eyelids. Even though I witnessed the fire department extinguish it, the fire in our house is still alive in my dreams. My chest is heavy. It's like I'm still choking from the thick smoke. I sit up in the darkened room and snatch my phone from beside the bed.

2:00 a.m.

The phone falls to my lap, and I brush back the sweaty hair from my clammy face. I peel my T-shirt off my chest and grimace from the way it sticks to my skin.

I can't go back to sleep. I don't want to see the fire again. A chill runs down my spine, and I shiver in bed. The silent darkness in this room is more comforting than my dreams.

I pick up my phone to look for a distraction. I search through podcasts, skim ebooks, and when my desperate level spikes, I scroll through mindless clickbait articles. Nothing works because the flames explode into my third eye.

In frustration, I throw the covers off and slip out of bed. With the flashlight from my phone, I pace the bedroom. I've never looked around this room. I run a hand over the wooden embellishments on the antique wardrobe, rub the fabric of the curtains through my fingers, and open a chest of drawers. Nothing super appealing is inside. A few notebooks, loose photographs, and some sweaters and scarves.

My pulse slows as I walk around the room. I shake out my arms and roll my shoulders. Perhaps a walk around the manor will help calm me.

Lamps light the hall, but I keep my flashlight to the floor for peace of mind. My steps are small and careful because I don't know my way around, and I don't want to wake anyone up. The looming hallway is cast in shadowy darkness. Before I get to the corner, I look back at my bedroom. Perhaps I should stay inside because the complete darkness is less scary than these shadows. The orange tinge from the lamps sends upsetting quivers through my stomach.

I swallow hard and continue around the corner. It seems darker down this way. I keep the light by my feet and gingerly step into the next wing. My breaths seem maximized in the silence. If anyone was awake, they'd be sure to hear me.

A light is on above the staircase. I step toward it, place a hand on the banister, and consider my options. If I stay on this floor, I could wake someone up. I'd never forgive myself for interrupting someone's sleep. I pat my stomach. I could go downstairs and find food. The problem is finding my way back.

I doubt I'll be back to sleep anytime soon, so I take my chances and descend the staircase. On the ground floor, the air is crisp. I find the hall and shine the flashlight. I recognize where the food smell hit me before getting to the dining room and assume the Ashworths don't want their guests going into the kitchen. They'd think kitchens are only for "the help," but I miss rummaging through our kitchen for a midnight snack. There's no harm because no one will be around.

I sneak into the hall and press along the walls, looking for a door. I move away from the dining room and discover a swing door. Eureka. Two windows let in light from outside, which reflects off the stainless-steel countertops. I shine my flashlight around my immediate area, searching for light switches.

Before I find the switch, a door opens, and someone enters from the outside.

A voice asks, "How could you do this to me?"

Without seeing him clearly, I know it's Thomas.

He groans and flicks on some lights. He has a phone to his ear and hasn't noticed me.

"Don't say that, Ness," he says, hunching over as he talks. "No, don't." He pauses, listening to a reply. His face is strained, and his mouth drags downward.

"Don't you understand what it's like for me?" he continues. "Can't you just…?"

He groans again, pulling the phone away from his ear.

"Did you seriously just hang up on me?" he says, staring at the phone.

It's like there is a solid block of ice around me. I'm frozen in place. A small voice in the back of my head tells me to leave the room.

It's impossible to move. His focus is on me.

"What are you doing here?" he grumbles with a stern look.

"I… I…" Geez. I'm about to pee my pants.

He tosses his phone on a counter, huffs, and moves toward the fridge.

"Couldn't sleep?" Thomas mutters, opening the fridge door.

I stammer some words in trepidation. None of them a proper reply.

"Did Murphy tell you about the phone?" Thomas asks as he pulls a drink from the fridge. He moves toward a phone, which hangs on the wall between us. He lifts the phone, saying, "If you want someone to make you something, he'll come right away. Hey, Murphy," he says into the phone.

"No, don't," I blurt.

"Yes, sir?" Murphy replies through the speaker, breathless and hiding a yawn.

"Don't wake him up. I'm fine," I reply, waving my hands in a rush.

Thomas lowers the phone from his ear and gestures it at me. "You're sure?"

I nod, wide-eyed. "Positive."

"False alarm, sorry," Thomas blurts into the phone, then hangs it up.

How rude. It's two o'clock in the morning, and he woke Murphy for nothing. These rich kids do act like helpless children.

Thomas throws a thumb over his shoulder, pointing at the fridge. "Well, help yourself, then."

As he moves back toward his phone, I take a step forward.

My legs are like jelly. I can't rummage through his kitchen. It would be different if I were alone. I could take my time and find something no one would miss. I don't want him watching or judging me. Or thinking I'm a charity case who's looking for more free stuff.

"Mmm, I'm okay," I say, taking a step back.

"You can just grab something," he says, and his tone is littered with severity. "It's no big deal."

He picks up his phone and frowns. Anger billows off him the more he stares at the screen. I don't care what he says. With the way he's acting now, he will lose whatever cool he has left if I go near that fridge.

Thomas shoves his phone into his pocket and moves toward me. His heavy steps make the floor jolt. The aggression sends me cowering, fearing the possibility he might throw a punch.

He pushes past me and out the door. Just like that, I'm alone again.

In the silence, I note how hard my heart is beating. I wish I hadn't walked in on that phone call. Who was he calling in the middle of the night? It didn't sound friendly.

I move toward the fridge and scan the overstocked contents. A waft of fresh herbs hits me first. There are rows of canned bubbly drinks, a shelf of fresh fruit, and below that are stacks of clear containers.

I pull a container out and lift the lid. Inside are segments of julienne carrots and cucumbers, sliced cheese, deli meats, and a small pot of hummus. Wow, the perfect little snack pack ready to go. Murphy must read minds.

My late-night rummages at home didn't come with this level of convenience. This place brings a wealth of privilege, which should make me grateful. As I walk out of the kitchen with the container in hand, I can't help missing my home.

I move into the hall, still trembling from my encounter with Thomas. My palms slip across the container, sleek with more sweat than when I woke up from the nightmare. My whole body convulses. I don't understand Thomas's way of life. There's no way for me to predict what he's thinking. He acts in ways I could never imagine.

His reactions after that phone call make one thing clear. I never want to be in his bad books.

Five

It took me an hour to find my room. Feeling lost in this place makes me long for home. For something familiar and comforting.

I ate on my bedroom floor, and I'm unsure how much I drifted off to sleep. It wasn't enough to count as rest.

As morning creeps into the sky, I glance around the bedroom in the daylight. I kneel on the carpet, and it all looks alien. A pain deep in my gut aches and will not go away. As I gaze around the room, my mind drifts to what I'm missing. My bedroom, my art supplies, my canvases, my artwork. Everything I held dear went up in flames.

This building has everything a person could desire, yet I feel nothing. I would sell every item in the manor if it meant I could regain what I've lost.

My eyes fill with tears, and the pain ricochets through my heart.

My bedroom was nothing grand, but it held what I valued the most. Whenever this kind of inner pain wrecks me, I would paint to work through it. Escaping this pain is unfathomable because I've lost my tools. I'm mourning my lost possessions, and those possessions help me deal with my grief. How will this cycle ever end?

I lean over, plant my face between my knees, and let it out. The sobs are raw and ugly, but I don't care. They need to come out because I'm breaking inside.

"Miss Klein," Claudia says with a gasp as she opens my door. "My goodness, are you okay?"

She rushes to the ground and wraps her arms around me.

I push my hands hard into my face. I don't want her to see me like this. I'd hate for it to upset her. But these tears are long overdue, and it's futile to hold them back.

Claudia strokes my hair and soothes me with a gentle hum.

"Can I get you anything?" she asks. "Are you hungry? Or cold? Or is it just sadness?"

I nod because I have no strength to answer her with words.

"Did you get enough sleep?" she asks.

Vociferous sobs fire out of me, and I shake my head against her shoulder.

She brushes back my hair, and it feels like she kisses my forehead. Now, I just want my mom. Something about Claudia's hugs says she understands.

"Do you want me to show you to your parents' room?" she whispers, hugging me close. "Do you remember the way?"

I rub my eyes and cough as my whimpering simmers.

"No, I don't remember," I say with a croak.

"Why don't you get yourself cleaned up, and I'll show you the way."

I nod and whisper, "Thank you."

My life is small compared to the Ashworths'. How I prefer it. My hand glides through the air as I wash, holding a phantom paintbrush. My eyes fall closed, and I envision the piece I wish to work on.

I don't want to be alone anymore. I can't wait to see my parents.

Stepping out of the bathroom, I meet Claudia in the hall. I've tied my hair in a ponytail because I don't want her to help me. I just need my mom.

Claudia takes me into the next wing and down a long hallway. She stops by a door that's ajar and knocks.

"Yes?" says my mother's voice, and relief spreads through my chest.

"Mrs. Klein, it is Claudia, and I'm with your daughter."

The door pulls open. Mom springs through the doorway and latches on to me.

"Hi, sweetheart. Good morning. How are you?"

I give Claudia a side-glance, who nods and walks away. I embrace Mom tighter, saying, "I'm better now."

Mom strokes my back and finds my eyes. She frowns. "You've been crying?"

"Just a little," I say.

In her room, I notice an open notepad on the desk.

"I'm working out what to do about the house. All I've done is jot down the police reports. The fire department hasn't determined the cause of the fire. We're still in limbo."

"So we just have to wait here?"

Mom looks around the room and out at the breathtaking view, smiling. "It's not a bad place to wait."

"How long will it be until we're back in our house?" I ask.

"Christie, our house isn't there anymore."

I shake my head. "No, I know that. I mean, back in a house of our own. Like, out of here."

"You don't like it here?" she asks.

"Sure. It has everything we could possibly want. But it's not our

38

home. We're still living with people we don't know."

I think of Thomas, and my fists curl.

"I understand," Mom says, "but how lucky are we that they helped us? Of all the people to take an interest in us. We're not an imposition because the family doesn't need to take care of us. They employ people who do that. This is crazy, but it's wonderful."

I pull a skeptical face. "You like having people take care of you?"

"I wouldn't have it all the time, but I guess it's a nice vacation."

She plonks on the bed, and I sit beside her.

"I just miss our home. My stuff," I say, looking at my hands. "I wish I were painting."

"I can imagine how much you miss that," Mom says, clutching my hand. "I guess it feels like having a limb removed."

I nod. "It feels exactly like that."

"I don't want to make any more phone calls," Mom says. "Why don't we take a walk? The grounds are huge, and I haven't explored them yet."

"Is Dad here?" I ask.

"No. He went to work with Mr. Ashworth." Mom gives a playful grin. "He left by helicopter today."

My mouth falls open. "What?"

Mom giggles. "I know. Isn't that crazy?"

"I didn't think he was involved with Mr. Ashworth."

"Well, he wasn't," Mom replies. "But last night, they got to talking. It seems your dad is moving up in the company."

"But Dad said there are lots of positions between him and Mr. Ashworth. Did he get promoted?"

"He has a new role. Your father has skills Mr. Ashworth wants to use, so he created a new position."

"That's crazy. I mean, I'm happy they have promoted him, but what does this all mean? Will we have to move closer to the city or—?"

"Christie, I don't have all the details yet. Your dad didn't have answers when he left. But he and Mr. Ashworth will discuss it in the office."

At that, my stomach rumbles.

Mom laughs, patting her stomach. "I haven't had breakfast yet either. What shall we do? Do they serve breakfast at any time? We slept through it yesterday."

"I should have asked Claudia," I say, hoping she's nearby.

"Murphy is close by," Mom says. "I'm sure he organizes breakfast."

Mom moves into the hall, and when I join her, she gains Murphy's attention when he exits a nearby room. Mom is a bundle of nerves when she stammers our need for breakfast.

"Happy to oblige, ladies," Murphy says. "Please follow me to the dining room."

When we reach the ground floor, Mom asks, "How was last night for you? You went to the theater with Thomas?"

"Yeah, a home cinema. It's kind of bonkers. It's down in the basement."

"Don't tell me they have a bowling alley next door."

"That's what I was thinking!" I say with a laugh.

We continue down the hall behind Murphy. I don't want to say anything rude about Thomas with Murphy in earshot, but I'm desperate to tell Mom how rude he is. I need to get it off my chest because I don't think my palms can take my nails piercing them anymore. I should ask Claudia for a nail file later to save the pain. No, I should check the bathroom first. I don't want to prove Thomas right by asking for a handout.

As we approach the dining room, Thomas walks out, having finished his breakfast. When I left my bedroom, it was ten o'clock, so I assumed he was at school.

"What day is it?" I ask Mom.

"Saturday. Can you believe it? I don't know how we will keep track

40

of the days."

"It's Saturday, and Dad went to work?" I question.

Mom shrugs. "They had a lot to discuss and a time crunch."

Thomas strides out of the dining room and into the hall. I shrink against the wall. After his verbal jabs at me and our midnight kitchen encounter, I don't want to get in his way.

"Can I get you anything else, sir?" Murphy asks Thomas.

He shakes his head. "Nah, I'm good."

Thomas moves past us, and I let out a sharp breath. Phew!

"Right this way, ladies," Murphy says.

As we make our way to the dining table, he pulls out our chairs for us.

"I could get used to this," Mom says with a giggle.

I give her a disapproving look.

Mom shakes her head. "Not really. It's like a fancy hotel with a butler."

"Mrs. Klein," Murphy says, "I am a butler."

Mom clasps a hand over her lips, giggling to herself.

Okay, I'm glad she's enjoying our stay here. I don't want her deep in despair about everything that's happened. Making the phone calls to the insurance company has her down in the dumps. Having mortgage payments for a house that no longer exists is stressful.

"What would you like for breakfast today?" Murphy asks.

"Christie? What do you feel like?" Mom asks.

"Wh-Wh-What do you have?" I stutter with overwhelm.

"We can prepare anything your heart desires," Murphy replies. "A fruit platter, eggs Benedict, eggs Florentine, a short stack of pancakes... You name it."

My eyes widen. "Did you say pancakes?"

Mom grins. "Christie's favorite."

"Pancakes it is. We'll get that started right away," he says. "And for you, Mrs. Klein?"

41

"You had me at eggs Benedict."

"Splendid," Murphy replies, and leaves for the kitchen.

"How was Mr. Ashworth last night?" I ask, hoping Mom's gonna say he's a rude, pretentious man, and that will be a nice segue into talking about Thomas.

"I have to admit, I did get a little bored," Mom says. "But then I relaxed because I had a cocktail in my hand. And when the glass emptied, it replenished, and so it went on."

"Mom, did you get drunk last night?" I ask in a hushed tone.

"I wouldn't say drunk," she says. "I mean, yes, I did get up much later than I normally would. The alcohol helped ease my mind before getting to sleep."

"Rub it in," I say, folding my arms.

"Are you sleeping okay, honey?" she asks, concerned. "We can get you to a doctor for some sleep aids."

"No. I don't want to take pills," I say. "But it is tough getting to sleep. Well… staying asleep."

"Are you dreaming about the fire?"

"Sometimes," I say. "I think it's the fact that it happened at night. It makes going to bed anxiety-inducing."

"I understand," she replies. "Are you okay with sleeping so far away from us? I can ask Murphy about moving you closer to our room."

"No. I don't want to be any trouble," I say. "I'll stay where I am."

"Okay, but make sure you let me know if you want to move rooms."

"I will. Plus, Claudia is easy to talk to."

"I'm glad," she says.

"What will I do about school? Will I commute every day?"

Mom sighs out hard. "That's on my list of calls for Monday. Perhaps an option is for you to do distance learning."

I grin. "That would be fine by me."

After all, I'm a loner at heart.

Mom frowns. "You know, I don't like the idea of you hiding and not socializing with your peers. We will find other options to discuss. Perhaps tutoring sessions."

"I can study on my own."

"I don't like you isolating yourself from others. You need more friends than just your father and me."

I sink into the plush dining chair and settle into silence. I don't need friends, but she doesn't want to hear it. Mom knows what I'm thinking, so we take advantage of the quiet and take in the magnificent objects decorating the room.

It's not long until Murphy is back, serving our breakfast. From the scrumptious smell to the mind-blowing taste, they're the best pancakes ever.

"Mmm," I say with a mouthful. "I could get used to this."

"Nuh-uh," Mom says, shaking her head. "Just because we're living in a mansion doesn't mean you get to eat pancakes every day."

I put on my best bratty voice. "But Mommm!"

We giggle through every bite.

After breakfast, Mom asks Murphy to show us how to get to the grounds. I'm glad this place seems like a maze to Mom as well.

He takes us out to the back deck. It sits on a high elevation, and we look out at the sweeping green land with beautiful hedges and magnificent sculptures.

"Would you like me to escort you?" Murphy asks.

"No, thank you," Mom says, linking her arm with mine. "I'm sure we'll manage. I have my phone in my pocket in case we get lost. But we can find our way back."

I grin at the house. "It's big enough that I think we'll see it wherever we go."

Murphy smiles. "Very good, ladies. See you when you return."

We begin our stroll, descending the stairs that lead into the garden. We follow the stone steps and view the majestic, grassy hills in the distance.

43

"So tell me about this basement cinema," Mom says with curiosity. "Did you watch a fun movie?"

"I wish. Thomas was playing video games and talking with people through a headset."

"Video games? I know how you love those."

"What can I say? I'm a board games person. I like to physically see a board when I play a game."

Mom laughs, rubbing my shoulder. "Did you at least give the game a try?"

"Thomas did offer, but I declined. Mr. Ashworth had just given me my phone, so I was busy setting it up with apps and finding new ebooks to download."

"Please tell me you made an effort with Thomas," Mom says, a stern expression hardening her face. "I would like to see you making a friend. Considering there's one kid here, it would be easy to try."

My segue has arrived. "It's not easy to make an effort with him. He's despicable."

"How can you say that?" Mom asks, placing a hand on her chest over her heart.

"I don't think you've heard how he speaks. Did you not notice how he sulked his way through dinner?" There go the angry fists at my sides. "When we first met, it disgusted him that our family had moved in. He fought with his dad about it, and his dad didn't care. He just left for work, leaving Thomas to stew on it. Mr. Ashworth encourages Thomas's bad attitude because he doesn't talk to him about his feelings. Which leaves him glaring at me. I didn't even do anything wrong, but he hates me!"

"He doesn't hate you," Mom says, exasperated. "He doesn't know you."

"Exactly. He hated me the moment he saw me. He thinks we're poor and total charity cases. I can't stand him."

"Don't you think you're judging him too harshly? You don't know him very well. It may be difficult for him to get to know people. He might seem rude, but maybe he's shy."

I scoff with an indignant look. "Thomas Ashworth the third is not shy. He struts around the mansion like he's a king. He talks to his dad and their staff like he's better than them. He told me we have to hurry up and move out because his dad can't give handouts any longer."

"Are you paraphrasing, Christie? It sounds like you're paraphrasing."

I stomp my foot against a stone step. "Mom, would you take me seriously?"

I'm cut off by the sound of revving motors. The "yahoos" of testosterone-filled boys boom from a distance. Mom and I stop in our tracks and watch two ATVs jump over the rolling hills. One driven by Thomas and the other by a friend of his.

They skid and slide across the grass. I cross my fingers, hoping they don't see us and use us as target practice.

"See what I mean?" I say, deadpanning at the pair.

"Christie, they're having fun. Which is something you, a sixteen-year-old girl, should try."

"I do have fun. But that," I say, pointing a finger at the pair, "is not my idea of fun."

"If Thomas has friends over, you should hang out with them. If you get comfortable in this home, it will help give you the confidence to make some friends."

"I'm not changing my personality to befriend people who think this kind of wealth is normal."

"It's not Thomas's fault that his father has acquired wealth. Well, his father's father. Or was it… his father's father's father?"

"I have nothing in common with Thomas Ashworth the third. You can quit trying to push me toward him."

"At least be friendly to him while you're in the kids' wing. This is his home. You are his guest, and I would like you to be more courteous."

"I don't prompt him to say anything to me. He just lashes out."

"Why would he be rude without you prompting him? I'm sure you are just misreading the situation. You get so tongue-tied around people your own age. Maybe he thought you didn't like him."

"You need to stop being so optimistic about him. Please, just watch him at dinner. You'll see."

"I'll keep an eye on him," Mom says. "Of course, I don't want you around anyone who is indeed rude or nasty to you. But I won't stop being enthusiastic about the opportunity for you to make a friend. I'm not letting it go."

"You are so annoying," I grizzle. "You're lucky I love you so much."

She cuddles into me, wrapping her arms comfortingly around me. "I love you too, sweetie. I'm just trying to look out for you."

"I know."

Mom needs to wake up because I'm never going to like Thomas. He and his friend hurl insults at each other in that "boys will be boys" way people always excuse.

Why would she insist I befriend this person? She's so desperate for her daughter to have a friend that she doesn't care who it is. Why bother with him? We're leaving the Ashworth Estate soon, anyway.

Aren't we?

Six

Mom asked Murphy for a pad and a pencil for me. This allowed me to sketch the ideas floating around in my head. I spent the day in my parents' suite. Mom sat at the desk, making phone calls and taking notes. I reclined on their balcony, looking at the green grounds below. Now and then, Thomas and his friend would ruin the serenity.

At one point, they were clay shooting. I didn't know people shot clay in real life. I had thought it was movie magic nonsense. Something they claimed the rich and elite do. But there it was. Clay shooting, followed by the boisterous laughter of snobby rich boys.

I sketched the memory of my bedroom. It is so crazy we don't own photos now. I can sync my cloud storage to my new phone, but there's still so much lost forever.

I'm halfway through the sketch of my bedroom when I stop. My fingers started drawing flames and smoke, and it's something I don't want to remember. I want my room before the fire, but the fire keeps infesting my memories.

I put the pad down and close my eyes. I can't wait for Dad to come home. I need to know about his promotion. I can't believe he went in a helicopter with Mr. Ashworth. But it's also unbelievable that I'm sitting in his mansion right now, so I guess anything is possible.

Murphy announces dinner will be ready in forty minutes, and Mom suggests we get changed.

I gesture at the jeans and T-shirt I found. "Why?"

Mom says, "Because it's what they expect."

I raise an eyebrow. "Do we have to dress up every night? It's just dinner."

"They've provided the clothes," Mom says. "It's not a problem."

"Okay," I say, moving into the hall. "If I remember how to get to my room…"

Claudia appears in the hall, thwarting my attempt at an excuse. It's her job to look after me. And Thomas, poor her.

When I reach the bathroom, I find a light pink floral dress Claudia has hung out. It drapes below the knees, and the sleeves fall just below my elbows. It's a perfect fit. Wearing the dress makes my smile hurt my cheeks.

Because the dress is so beautiful, I let Claudia do my hair. She did a great job last night, and this dress deserves the best.

I'm annoyed we won't see Dad until dinner. It gives us no time to talk in private.

Claudia and I leave the bathroom when Thomas is in the hall. I frown, wishing he'd already left.

He keeps moving, and I don't know if I'm supposed to follow him or if Claudia will walk with me. It's a huge sigh of relief when she continues walking with me. I'm so awkward I would have jogged to keep up with Thomas instead of embarrassing myself by asking a simple question.

We meet Mom in the hall, and Dad follows out of their suite behind her.

"Hi, Dad. How was work?" I ask, bouncing with enthusiasm.

"Very interesting," he says, rubbing his hands together. "I'm still spinning from all the new information."

Mom nods. "I haven't gotten a lot out of him yet."

We continue along the hall, and Claudia turns around as soon as we make it to the dining room. I wish she could eat with us. She's so nice.

Mr. Ashworth takes his seat at the head of the table. Thomas stands by his chair with a strained look on his face.

Between the candle centerpieces, a laptop sits on the table. Odd.

Mr. Ashworth beams a grin and gestures at the laptop. "We have an extra guest this evening," he says.

My lips purse as I wonder what that means. I move forward with my mom and dad to the top of the table. On the screen, an impeccably dressed and highly sophisticated woman grins at us.

"Hello, everyone," she says, and before we can answer, Mr. Ashworth says, "This is my wife. Hilda Ashworth."

"Oh, Mrs. Ashworth," Mom says, clasping her hands together in front of her. "So lovely to meet you. Thank you for letting us be guests in your home."

"Not a problem. I'm so glad you're settling in," she says.

"I'm grateful we can extend our thanks to you in person," Dad says. "Well, as close as we can get."

"I'm so happy we can help," Mrs. Ashworth says. "I'm saddened not to be there in person. Please know, you are welcome to stay as long as you like."

Mr. Ashworth asks everyone to take their seats, and I notice Thomas is especially moody. He half turns toward the screen, and an angered expression hardens his features. I didn't think his jawline could become more chiseled. No, Christie, what are you thinking? He's not

49

handsome. Stop it!

Something about his demeanor is off-putting. Is he mad at his mother? Did he want to travel with her? Why didn't he go when his sister did?

"Is there a big time difference between us and Switzerland?" Dad asks, looking at the laptop screen.

"We are eight hours ahead," Mrs. Ashworth replies. "Good thing I'm a night owl. It's three o'clock in the morning here."

"Oh my goodness," Mom gasps. "You didn't need to talk to us so late."

"It's typical," Mrs. Ashworth says, and she almost glares in Mr. Ashworth's direction. "I wait until midnight to talk with Tom."

"Most of my days are too full," Mr. Ashworth replies with a tight jaw. "I want to make time to include Vanessa."

"Yes, she won't stay awake all night for a video chat," Mrs. Ashworth says. "Christie, it's a shame you two haven't met. I'm sure you have much in common."

"Mm-hmm," I mumble, nodding. Mrs. Ashworth is so glamorous that my words stick in my throat. I can't imagine what her daughter would be like. I'd be too far out of her league to ever be her friend.

The girl who never made a friend befriends a billionaire's daughter. I don't think so.

"Son, have you been making sure Christie is comfortable?" Mrs. Ashworth asks.

Thomas shrugs beside me. "Sure."

"Everyone is still settling in," Mr. Ashworth says. "It was quite the ordeal they came from."

Mrs. Ashworth frowns, nodding. "I agree. I'm so sorry you have had to deal with that. We want to ease the burden for you." She looks at my parents and then at me. "We'd like to take care of Christie's education."

"What?" Mom and Dad gasp.

I'm light-headed at the thought of the Ashworths even thinking about me.

Mr. Ashworth laughs under his breath. He turns to my dad, smiling. "Seems I have one more surprise for you. We've enrolled Christie in the Ashworth Academy. For you, there's no expense."

"You can't be serious," Dad says with a smile filled with shock and awe.

"This can't be," Mom says, tearing up. "You've already done so much for us."

"It's one thing we can do to take some of the burden off you," Mrs. Ashworth says. "We're happy to oblige."

"What good is a school named after your family," Mr. Ashworth says, "if you can't use it to your advantage?"

My heart pounds in my chest. My mouth runs dry, and I seem unable to blink.

Is putting me in school an advantage for Mr. Ashworth? A way to keep my dad around? What skill set does my dad have that makes Mr. Ashworth so eager to suck up to him?

"Son," Mrs. Ashworth pipes up, "you will escort Christie into school on her first day. Ensure she's comfortable and finds her way around."

Thomas slides in his chair with his head dipping low. "Sure, whatever."

Even though he's agitated, he doesn't argue with his mother. Their relationship is odd. He is agreeable yet aloof with his mother and brash and opposing with his father.

"What if we move back to our neighborhood?" Mom asks, her head shaking like too many thoughts are spiraling through her head. "I don't want you going to any trouble. We might have to change her school again."

"Mary, please," Mr. Ashworth says in a soothing tone. "Don't stress about this. Christie can stay at the school as long or short as needed. All you have to worry about is finalizing the house details. The company will take care of Peter, meaning you can move to wherever feels right for your family. We hope it is here in Victoria Falls."

"I've arranged for a tailor to come by the manor tomorrow to fit her for her school uniform," Mrs. Ashworth adds.

Mom's hands clasp over her mouth, and Dad loops an arm around her.

"Thank you both from the bottom of our hearts," Dad says to the Ashworths. "We are eternally grateful."

Thomas exhales with impatience, fidgeting beside me. Is he annoyed that dinner is delayed or that the conversation is about me?

Realization dawns on me. I'm going to school with Thomas Ashworth III. A school named after his family. This won't be an easy transition.

Mrs. Ashworth bids us all a good night and ends her video link with us. Dinner proceeds with one-dimensional conversation by the parents, discussing the weather, recent news headlines, and vacation destinations. It's all wildly superficial, and I'm glad I'm not involved. The school discussion was enough to suffocate me in shyness.

I'm itching for dinner to be over so Dad can give us the details about his day. After dessert, we vacate the dining room as a group. It's dismaying when Mr. Ashworth encourages my parents to have a nightcap.

"Are you kids going back to the theater tonight?" Mr. Ashworth asks, hinting at the minors to leave the room.

Thomas shakes his head, looking at his phone. "Nah, I'm headed to Luke's."

"Take Christie with you," Mr. Ashworth suggests.

No! No way. Don't do it.

Thomas turns to me, raising an eyebrow. His lips twist as if asking me if I want to go while simultaneously telling me to stay away.

I rub my temples and turn to my parents. "Actually, my head is throbbing. I haven't been getting much sleep."

"We should take you to a doctor," Mom says, placing a hand on my back.

"A doctor?" Mr. Ashworth says as if he's about to summon one who has an office on the ground floor.

It wouldn't surprise me.

I shake my head, lowering my hand. "No, I'm okay. I just need some extra sleep."

Mom kisses my forehead. "Okay, honey. Have a good night's sleep."

"Thanks," I say, and hug her and then Dad. "Good night."

"Good night," they reply.

"All right," Thomas says with a wave. "See you all later."

When he leaves the room, I wave to Mr. Ashworth and then to my parents. "Thanks for dinner."

"Good night, Christie," Mr. Ashworth replies, standing behind the bar.

I move into the hall, and Thomas circles back. He points at me. "Do you need help to find your way upstairs?"

My shoulders bunch to my ears, and I shake my head. "No, I'll manage," I say with that annoying squeak.

He nods. "Okay, have a good night."

He continues along the hall, and I whisper in shock, "Bye."

That was actually nice of him. Perhaps talking with his mother tonight brought out something thoughtful in him.

I turn to the staircase, which I'm thankful starts right by the living room. At least I won't get lost on the ground floor. As I ascend the stairs, I reassure myself that I only need to find my parents' room. From there, I continue to follow the hall to my room.

My heart flutters at the notion Thomas offered to walk me upstairs before leaving the house. One random act of kindness doesn't cut it. He's still a selfish, spoiled brat. Throughout the day, it became increasingly

53

obvious we had nothing in common. I bet he's at a friend's house to party with booze. That's what rich kids do on a Saturday night, isn't it? So far, the movies haven't led me astray with my assumptions.

Mr. Ashworth is determined to keep my father close. I hate having distance from my parents. Our usual nights were sitting on the couch, discussing our days and the upcoming week. I hate being kept out of the loop. Mom told me she doesn't want me to become isolated, yet she's allowing Mr. Ashworth to isolate me from them. Just because he doesn't have a close relationship with his kids is no reason to separate me from my parents.

Without paying attention and stomping my way through the hall, I pass my parents' suite.

Phew! That was easy. I guess not paying attention helps sometimes. Although, I wish the distraction hadn't come because I feel cheated. I rub the ache from my chest. At least I know the rest of the way to my bedroom.

As long as we stay here, I'm going to stay fit. The walks throughout this mansion are like epic journeys. I wonder how long that will be since I'm enrolled in Ashworth Academy. It's bonkers that Thomas attends a school that shares his last name.

I jog the rest of the way, wanting to grab my phone. When I locate it by my bed, I google the Ashworth Academy to discover what I'm up against.

My phone fills with images of students in neat, pressed uniforms, which include blazers and ties. Oh boy, I have to wear that stuff? The images alone are intimidating. Is it an entire school of Thomases? There's no way I could handle a full school day. I'll be a stammering, uncoordinated, unpopular mess.

I flop on the bed, wrapping my arms around my head. I just want to go back home. I want to reverse time and find the source of the fire. If only I could extinguish it before it grows out of hand.

I hate it here. And I already know I will hate it at Ashworth

Academy.

Seven

I expected to spend my Sunday by my parents' side. However, Mr. Ashworth invited them to a long lunch at a cliffside restaurant. I've had no chance to speak with Dad, and it's killing me. What's the deal with him and Mr. Ashworth?

I spent the morning googling Mr. Ashworth's companies. His empire revolves around manufacturing, from metalwork to chemicals and plastics to computers and technology. The latter being the area where my dad works. He's a computer programmer, and something he created must have sent Mr. Ashworth over the moon. Is that why he's so infatuated with my dad?

One day, I'll explore the mountain area where my parents dined out. I'll discover if everything is glitz and glamour like life in the manor. Or perhaps regular people live here. When I imagine the students who fill Ashworth Academy, I picture offspring from rich parents.

I wasn't able to go to lunch because it clashed with the tailor's arrival. My parents felt bad about leaving me alone, but I eased their guilt by complaining about another headache. Plus, staying behind had to be better than listening to Mr. Ashworth drone on. He wouldn't say anything interesting with me around. He gives off a vibe that children are not worth talking to.

Having a professional tailor measure me for a school uniform was utterly ridiculous. Now it's Monday morning, and I'm dressed in layers of uniform. I have a pressed white blouse and a navy neckerchief, covered by a fitted navy blazer adorned with the school crest. Below, I wear a cobalt and navy tartan skirt, knee-high socks, and shiny black shoes.

In the mirror, it looks kind of cute despite being constricting. Do they really wear the blazer all year round, even when the weather warms? I guess it doesn't get especially hot in the mountains. I hope I'm not around long enough to find out.

I meet Mom for breakfast and find Thomas seated at the dining table. He was told to be my escort and is less than impressed. Claudia told me he takes a limousine to school, which would draw a spotlight. Fingers crossed, all eyes stay on Thomas. I won't be okay unless I remain the overlooked shadow walking behind him.

"Are you nervous, sweetheart?" Mom asks as Murphy arranges our usual breakfasts.

I bite into my lip and give a timid shrug. "I'll be okay," I whisper.

Mom nods at Thomas, smiling. "At least you'll already have a friend at school."

Thomas lifts his head to take us in. He smiles through an apprehensive expression and then returns his focus to his phone.

He'll ditch me as soon as he can. I just know it.

After breakfast, Murphy leads Thomas and me to the limousine. A driver waits by the open passenger door and introduces himself as Sam.

It's ludicrous. Mr. Ashworth and his son have their own personal drivers.

Murphy packed our school bags for us, which are cobalt blue and sporting a large school crest, and hands them to the driver. It's the first time I've gone to school with zero idea of what's inside my backpack.

Mom kisses my cheek and squeezes me in a hug. "Have a great day, honey."

"I'll try," I murmur, hugging her back.

The thought of being stuck with Thomas wrecks my nerves. I didn't sleep a wink for a whole new reason. I'll be glad if he continues ignoring me while we're off the Ashworth Estate.

I climb into the limo, and Thomas sits behind the driver, facing the back seat. As I sit on the back seat, my stomach flips. What would be worse; him sitting right next to me, or him staring at me the entire journey? I've sat through his pouting at dinner, so I guess we're trying something new for the ride to school.

But Thomas doesn't stare at me. He rests his elbow against the door and sits his chin in his palm. He stares out the window with deep intensity in his eyes.

I settle into the plush seating, ready for an easy ride to school. Oops. There goes the queasy stomach again. I press hard into my gut, lowering my head and pursing my lips hard as saliva fills my mouth.

"Are you okay?" Thomas asks.

I can't look up. This is beyond embarrassing. My stomach has always betrayed me when I'm bashful, awkward, or nervous. Usually, I deal with this alone or with my parents. No one my age has ever paid attention to how I act. If they have, they never showed any concern.

I swallow hard, push my palm against my stomach, and sit back against the seat. I nod at Thomas's tie. I have no courage to look at his gorgeous face.

Gorgeous?

Did I really just go there? Dang. Now my face is heating up. Ugh. Can this day get any worse?

"I'm okay," I whisper.

"You don't have to be nervous," Thomas says. "It's a big school, but it's easy to find your way around. It's spacious, not cluttered with stuff like at home."

I take in three rapid breaths. I wasn't even thinking about getting lost. Ugh. I was so worried about people staring at the freakshow new girl. It never occurred to me they would laugh because I keep getting lost. Everyone will know this homeless girl doesn't belong.

"Christie." Thomas's voice breaks through my panic. "Don't freak out. You'll be okay."

I blink hard and then look up, finding his big brown eyes. They're warm with little wrinkles on the outside because he's smiling at me.

I smile back and give him a thankful nod. All my words are lodged in my throat. I have no hope of speaking without the horrid squeakiness.

He flashes a quick smile and then turns to the window. His cheek slides into his palm as his eyes fixate on the changing view. I settle into the seat and turn to my window.

We stare out the same direction, with different perspectives, and have nothing but traveling car sounds to fill the void.

Thank goodness I don't have anyone to miss from my old school. If I have to make a fresh start, at least it'll be an easy transition. I'm used to hiding from people, staying in my head, and stealing time for creative outlets between classes. Well, sometimes in the middle of classes. Flowers, hands, eyes, lips, and hearts filled the margins of every notebook.

My stomach flips again, and I remind myself there's always time to draw. Time to escape the anxious moments by using my hands and closing my eyes.

The limousine slows, and through the tinted glass, I read a sign, "Welcome to Victoria Falls." We drive down the main street, and it appears to be a quaint town with log-style buildings. Along the rolling hills, I spy a smattering of houses. This is no village. There's a large, thriving population here.

The main street continues on for a long stretch. We pass boutique stores of women's and men's fashion, homewares and gifts, jewelry and crafts, and many eateries.

"This is the town you live in?" I ask, keeping my eyes glued to the scene outside the window.

"Yep," Thomas replies. "You haven't ventured out yet?"

I shake my head in response, hoping he'll look at me. Then my ears grow hot at the thought of him looking at me.

"Is it different from your town?" he asks in an uninterested tone.

"Nothing here has been like home," I say, still not meeting his eyes. "Like this ride. It's an upgrade from my old school bus."

A hushed laugh comes from Thomas. I glance at him, and he continues to look out the window.

I breathe out a slow sigh of relief. I pull a curl behind my ear, and my body temperature lowers.

The relief is short-lived when the limousine pulls up to a colossal building. A proud sign sits across the front of the building: "Ashworth Academy."

Oh boy. It's real.

When the driver opens the passenger door, I'm stuck to the seat. I know I'm staring at him, but it's like I'm not in my body. An opaque gray shrouds my surroundings.

Thomas slides off his seat and moves to the door before me. I regain my vision and realize my mouth hangs open. With relief that he's out of the car first, I follow suit. As I reach the path, I find Thomas staring at his smartwatch.

"Hmm," he mutters. "Umm. Okay, I'll take you to the administration building," Thomas says, scrolling his watch screen. "It's basically by the front door. I've just gotta get going. I have stuff to do."

He lowers his hand and slides it into his trouser pocket without acknowledging me for a reply. He tells the driver farewell, then takes his schoolbag and walks toward the school building.

I take my bag and hurry behind him.

It took forever to find my bearings in the manor. I assume it'll be the same way at school. Loads of students spread across the lawns and crowd the front steps. Again, I'm like a lost sheep. It's my doomed default as someone so out of her depth in this new wealth-driven world. I'm so rushed, anxious, and dizzy that I can't take in my surroundings. As Thomas pushes between a sea of navy blazers to reach the front door, fear clamps my body at the possibility I'll lose sight of him before getting inside the school.

When I reach the top step, he's waiting for me. Like usual, he impatiently huffs. Without a word spoken, he presses on and moves into the building.

It'll be awesome if we don't have any classes together because he is unbearable enough at dinner. Six hours without a fidgety, bored, and irritated Thomas will make going to school worthwhile.

"Okay, you need to go in here," Thomas says, gesturing inside a long-stretched room with a high counter running along one side.

I step into the doorway and then freeze. "And?" I murmur.

Thomas scrunches a hand through his hair and then steps into the office ahead of me. He looks over his shoulder, an annoyed flare to his nostrils, and beckons me to follow.

I push myself forward despite my feet suction-cupping to the timber floor.

Thomas leans against the counter, and a woman, mid-forties with a high bun and half glasses slid down her nose, moves toward him.

"Hello, Mr. Ashworth. What can we do for you?" she says.

He motions toward me. "This is Christie. She's new."

I step forward and give a shy wave. "Hi."

"Yes, I've been expecting you," she says, thumbing through paperwork. "I'm Ms. Thornesmith, head of administration here at Ashworth Academy. I'll be helping you with your orientation."

Thomas looks at Ms. Thornesmith and then at me. He turns back to Ms. Thornesmith and asks, "So you're good?"

"Yes, of course," Ms. Thornesmith says, angling her chin upward, accentuating her high cheekbones.

"All right," Thomas says, pushing off the counter. With a rough pat to my shoulder, he says, "I'll see you around."

So much for listening to his mother and being my escort. He is so predictable. I'm surprised he didn't ditch me back at the limo.

I watch him leave the room and spot three girls. They stand by the doorway, sharing harsh whispers behind cupped hands. The one in the middle has her eyes locked with mine, and a cold chill runs down my spine. The other two are watching Thomas.

Does everyone know I'm the new girl and live with him? I take in a sharp breath, and my chest constricts. When he went out on Saturday night, he probably told his friends about the horrid charity case staying with him. He hates me. He could have labeled me with the most vile names, leaving everyone wanting a glimpse of this ultimate loser.

I'm transported back into those blackened, sooty clothes and shrunk to one inch tall. I want to be invisible. I can't get through a whole day of every student staring at me. I'll panic attack myself into oblivion!

"Miss Klein?" Ms. Thornesmith calls, pulling me out of my spiraling thoughts.

I turn around, an ache compounding between my eyes. She stares at me, waiting for me to speak, but my voice box is sealed shut.

"Anything the matter?" she asks, adjusting her glasses against the bridge of her slender nose.

I shake my head, urging my lips to create a smile. But as my face grows cold and pale, my mouth sinks deeper into a frown.

Ms. Thornesmith purses her lips as she slides a piece of paper across the counter. "This is your class schedule," she says. "Do you have any issues understanding it?"

I blink three times at the paper. I know it's a timetable, yet the information isn't registering in my brain. I'm too flustered to see straight. The lines waver and blur. Can't she just push me toward my first classroom and tell me to go inside?

"Miss Fisher?" Ms. Thornesmith says, lifting her gaze to someone behind me. "Can I help you?"

I turn as the girl from earlier, who stared into my core, saunters her way over. She has long and sleek chestnut hair, piercing hazel eyes, and ruby-colored lips. She's a textbook definition of gorgeous, and I feel like I should kneel in front of her.

Why does she keep staring at me?

"I saw we have a new girl," she says, flicking her hair over her shoulder. "I was wondering if she needed a tour guide."

The girl greets me with a smile. Something about her reads as genuine, but my intuition says otherwise. I press my palm hard into my churning stomach.

"What wonderful initiative from a senior student," Ms. Thornesmith says and slides my schedule toward the girl. "It would be splendid if you could show Miss Klein where these classrooms are located. The tour should take you two periods. I'll mark you both down for attendance to save any tardies."

The girl takes the slip of paper and clutches it to her chest. "I'd be delighted to help." She holds out her hand toward me. "Hey there, I'm Hope."

"Christie," I say, clasping her hand.

"Nice to meet you," Hope says. With a bounce, she skips toward the doorway, waving me over. "Come on, silly. The bell will ring any minute."

Hope scans my schedule, sashaying her hips as she walks. "Okay, locker," she says, hastening her pace.

Clutching the straps of my backpack, I struggle to keep up with her between the mass of students. The first bell rings, and the students disappear into the classrooms.

63

Hope slows by a row of lockers. She tugs at a lock and works on the combination. When she opens the locker door, she rips my bag off my back and chucks it inside the locker.

"There," she says, slamming the locker door. "You won't be needing that."

Hope is quick on the move. In my rush, I didn't notice which locker was mine. Or if she did indeed shove my bag into my locker and not someone else's.

I hurry behind Hope, who glides in no particular direction. She neglects to point out any of the classrooms we pass. Maybe I need to stop fretting. Perhaps I don't have any classes in this wing.

"Hey, Hope," two girls say, waving. Were they the same girls from earlier?

"Who's the fresh meat?" one girl says, giving me the side-eye.

"Like, I dunno," Hope says, grimacing like the girl pointed out something foul. "Like, she just keeps following me around."

The girls laugh together, and sweat drenches my back. Maybe she's being sarcastic and will introduce me.

I also heard pigs fly...

Why doesn't she give me back my schedule and let me figure it out on my own?

"Get to class, ladies," a teacher says, moving into a nearby classroom.

The two sniggering girls wave goodbye to Hope. Their noses upturn at me like I'm roadkill. Hope pulls her phone from her skirt pocket and leans against a locker. She styles her hair in front of the screen, leaving me fidgety as she launches into selfie mode. Hope's facial expressions change as she repositions her hair and angles her posture.

Am I supposed to be watching this show? Why is she wasting time like this? She doesn't seem like a high achiever, so I'm guessing it was to get out of class.

I busy myself by straightening my neckerchief and blazer. Time seems to stand on end along a vacant corridor with Hope. My uniform squeezes the life from me, and I wish I'd faked an illness and stayed home.

"Why are you at this school?" Hope asks flatly. Her eyes stay on her phone, so I'm half sure she's asking me. She could be on a video chat.

Hope grumbles and glares in my direction. "Well?"

"Oh. Oh, umm," I splutter, moving closer to her. "I moved."

I don't want to tell her where I'm living. She has to be looking for ammunition. I don't need it going around school that the Ashworths are paying for my education. That kind of spotlight will crush me.

Hope slides her phone into her pocket. She's quiet as her calculating eyes run up and down me. Her jaw rocks as she works me out.

My stomach twists in on itself. I can't stand this. This is a whole new level of uncomfortable eye contact. I feel like an animal on display at the zoo.

"So how long have you known Ash?" Hope asks, eyes still searching me for clues.

I gulp and squeak, "Who?"

Hope huffs and plants her hands on her hips. "I don't like it when people aren't straight with me. Don't avoid the question."

"I'm... I don't... Umm..." Perspiration beads on my forehead as I frantically try to spit out an answer she wants.

"Oh my gosh," she says in a low tone, staring at me like a circus sideshow. "Are you slow or something?"

"Slow?" I say, choking on humiliation. "No."

Hope's eyebrows press together as her frown intensifies.

"My one and only Hope," a male voice calls out.

A bright smile lifts Hope's sour demeanor, and she swings around on tippy-toes. Her hands clasp together, and she looks around to find the voice. She rubs her lips together and arches her back when he approaches.

"Hey, babe," Hope says in a sultry voice. She kicks a heel into the air as she leans in to who I presume is her boyfriend.

As I get a better look at him, my heart drops to my gut. It's the boy who rode the ATVs with Thomas last weekend. The obscenities he shouted throughout the day circle in my head. My blood runs icy as the pair cuddle together.

The knowing sensation quivering in my gut begs me to turn and run away. But I'm stuck. Frozen in place like an ice sculpture. Except, I'm not melting from a rising temperature. I'm sweating as their demeanors turn sinister and the hum of mocking laughter rises in volume.

"Is this the girl?" he mutters to Hope while giving me the side-eye.

I gulp involuntarily. The girl?

Hope flicks her hair, stepping away from her boyfriend and into my personal space.

"You need to stay away from Ash," Hope says, jabbing a finger into my shoulder. "He's spoken for."

"Huh?" I squeak, stumbling over my feet as I stare into her menacing eyes.

"I'm watching you," she warns. "If I see you with him again, I'll make your life at the academy a living hell."

Fear widens my eyes, and my heart bats against my chest like a ping-pong ball connected to a paddle. Hate fills her eyes, although I'm sure I've never met her before. What did I do to turn her against me?

I want to tell her she's got the wrong person and that I don't know anyone in this school, but I'm tongue-tied. I jammer garbled nonsense, which sends Hope and her boyfriend into obnoxious laughter.

While laughing, Hope holds up my class schedule. A troublemaking smile curves her ruby lips as she tears the paper in two.

"Oops," she says, cupping a hand over her mouth. "Looks like you won't be using this."

"Looks like an accident to me," her boyfriend chimes in, taking the

66

two halves from Hope. He scrunches them in one palm and flings his other arm over Hope's shoulders. He steers her away from me, and they cuddle into each other as the next school bell rings.

A shiver runs over me from head to toe. My teeth chatter, and my knees knock. I swallow hard as my eyes prick with hot tears. My gaze shoots in all directions. Students move up and down the hall, and some barge into me like I'm nothing.

"Sorry," I mumble, stepping out of the way.

I press my back against a locker and breathe out hard. Do I go back to Ms. Thornesmith and tell her what happened? I don't want any heat from Hope and her boyfriend, so I can't rat them out. Ms. Thornesmith will think I'm an ignoramus if I go back so soon saying I lost the paper.

The hallway clears, and panic pulses through my veins. My hands press into the locker behind me as I'm cloaked in a weighted, smothering feeling. I grow short of breath and force my eyes closed. A lump balls in my throat as I battle the severe impulse to whimper.

Why did I agree to come here? I should have protested for my parents to arrange a tutor or distance learning from my old school. I knew I should have stayed home. The first person I meet at this school turns out to be like Thomas. I hate when I'm right. Although, I never predicted she'd be worse than him. Hope is callous. Thomas acts annoyed with me, but he's never threatened me like she did.

"Get to class, Miss," a man says, striding past me.

I open my eyes to see him in an impressive suit with his hands clasped behind his back.

"Truancy equals detention," he says, giving me zero eye contact. "Hurry along now."

Does he realize he's never met me before? I want him to look at me and offer help. Someone may as well glue me to this spot because my body is shutting down. Not to mention my voice box has gone on vacation.

Christie, please. Just move. Go back the way you came. Find the administration office. Tell Ms. Thornesmith you dropped your schedule in the bustle of students. Tell her you lost sight of Hope in all the commotion, and none of it is her fault.

Do it, Christie! Move!

With an urge to vomit, I push off the locker and move down the corridor. After retching three times, I veer into a bathroom.

I rush inside, burst into the nearest stall, and hurl my breakfast into the toilet.

Starting over shouldn't be this torturous. I enjoyed my life as a background player. At my old school, no one bullied me. I was so unmemorable that no one took notice. It was perfect. Now I live with a guy who glares at me with condemnation. At school, I'm harassed by the first kids who talk to me.

After I flush the toilet, I sink to the tiles. I rest my head against the stall divider and huff a sigh. I just want to go home. I want my old life. I wish the fire never happened and everything could be normal again.

I pull myself off the floor and move over to the washbasins. As I splash water on my face, I wonder if it's possible to hide out here all day. No one would miss me. I doubt it would get back to my parents. I'd have to lie and tell them I had a fun day.

Has it come to lying to my parents? They are the only people I can talk to without freezing up.

A tear rolls from my eye, and I cup more water into my hands. I take a long inhale, and on the exhale, I wash my face once more. When the tears have dried, I turn off the water.

It will be humiliating, but what else can I do? There's no other option than to find my way back to the administration office and ask Ms. Thornesmith for help.

I dry my face with a paper towel and push open the bathroom door. As I step outside, the adjacent male bathroom door swings open. Thomas steps out and stares into my eyes.

Great. Let's add another layer of pain to my morning.

Eight

"Hi," Thomas says, folding his arms across his chest. "What's your first class?"

I stare at him as bags pull under my eyes. My lack of sleep and the adrenaline from panicking have taken their toll.

He unfolds his arms and tilts his head. "What's up?" he asks.

I smooth my clammy palms over my blazer and fidget in my shoes.

"I told you, you don't need to panic," Thomas says, stepping closer to me. "This school is a piece of cake."

I run a hand over my hair and turn my face away from him. I'm gonna lose it again. My insides contort with another urge to launch over a toilet bowl.

"Hey, what's wrong?" he asks, placing a hand on my arm.

I jolt in surprise.

He removes his hand and takes a step back. "Sorry," he says.

I look away. "It's okay."

Thomas smiles. "Glad you got your voice back."

I blush and mumble, "Me too."

"Why do you look so freaked out?" he asks. "They showed you where to go, didn't they?"

I shake my head. "Not exactly."

"What happened when I left? Ms. Thornesmith usually handles everything, so I figured you wouldn't have an issue."

I fidget in my shoes again and turn my head in the other direction, staring at the closed bathroom door.

"A girl offered to show me around. Somewhere along the way, we kinda parted ways... I don't have my schedule, and I don't know where I'm going." Huffing, I pause my ramble to throw my arms in the air. "I don't know what classes I have... and I'm just lost again, like usual."

"Don't sweat it," he says. "I'll take you back to admin, and we'll get you a new schedule. Then I'll show you around."

I cross my arms and let out a tired, "*Humph.*"

"What?"

"You'll show me around?" I say, looking at the floor. It is as confrontational as I get. It's shocking the words have come out of my mouth.

I doubt he'd help me. Why would he?

"Christie, you need to know where you're going. I'll show you where to find your classrooms. It's not a big deal."

"It was a big deal earlier," I say.

It's baffling that I'm continuing with this conversation.

"Hey, I'm sorry," he says, taking another step back. "My parents kind of threw this on me. I already had plans for this morning that I needed to follow through on."

"Fine, whatever," I say, crossing my arms in frustration. "You could have at least told your parents or me that you couldn't show me

70

around. If you had said you couldn't help me, my mom would have come with me." I pull my arms tighter across my midsection. "It'd be better than being alone."

"I'm sorry you felt alone," he says, taking a step forward. "But, be honest, you don't exactly enjoy my company. I assumed you'd be relieved when I left."

His words surprised me. I look up to meet his eyes, finding them filled with sincerity.

"What do you mean?" I ask.

He puffs a laugh and slides his hand into his trouser pockets. "Don't act like you don't hate when I'm around."

I place a hand on my chest over my heart. "Me?"

"You're always judging me."

"I haven't said anything bad to you."

A nervous laugh seeps out of him. "You don't have to say it. It's in your eyes. I know you can't stand me."

My mouth falls open.

Has he thought this the whole time? Sure, I've thought badly about him, but I never thought he'd pick up on it. I didn't think he'd pay that much attention.

But, I guess if anyone is paying attention to me, it's Thomas Ashworth III. The guy who can't seem to let me stay invisible.

"So do you want me to show you around?" he asks, hanging a thumb over his shoulder.

A cringe-inducing heat sweeps across my cheeks, and I answer with a timid nod.

Thomas replies with a smirk, and my stomach somersaults as we walk toward the administration office.

"So who was this girl that offered to show you around?" he asks as we wander along the hallway.

I scratch behind my neck. Hope's laser focus still radiates in my pupils.

"Did she give you her name?" Thomas presses.

"Yeah," I mutter, looking at my feet. "Hope Fisher."

Thomas sucks in an apprehensive breath. "You were with Hope?"

"Briefly."

"That can't have been fun."

I bite into my bottom lip and find a tactful way to respond. "She wasn't the nicest."

"What did she say?"

I shake my head, still unsure of why she went on the attack. "Something about staying away from Ash. I don't know why she thought I knew anyone at this school."

Thomas laughs under his breath. "Is that all she said?"

I glance at him. "Yeah, why? Who is Ash?"

"I'm Ash," he says with a smirk.

I stare at his big brown eyes without comprehending his words.

In a mixture of mumbling and stuttering, I ask, "You're Ash? They don't call you Thomas here?"

"No one calls me Thomas," he says with a slight shake of his head. "It's weird to hear that name referring to me."

My mind rewinds from the moment I first met Thomas. Thomas's frustration cut the interaction short when his father tried introducing us. Mr. Ashworth had mentioned there was something ironic I could call Thomas. There was still ash in my hair.

"I saw the girls when I left admin," Thomas says. "I should have known they were up to something."

"I don't know why Hope lied about wanting to help me. Her plan was to tell me to stay away from you," I say. "I'm guessing your girlfriend feels jealous, and Hope was sticking up for her."

Thomas stops in place. "Girlfriend?"

I stop beside him, nodding. "Hope said you're spoken for."

Thomas's eyebrows lift, and then his face grows serious as a scowl strains his lips.

"What's wrong?"

He sighs. "I don't have a girlfriend, and I'm not pursuing anyone romantically."

"Oh." It's all I can say because now my interaction with Hope is more confusing.

"Was Hope with anyone else?"

I suck in a breath because he is one of Thomas's friends. I don't want to cause awkwardness. Thomas will ditch me again. But I've already ratted out Hope when I'd told myself to keep it quiet.

I nod and whisper, "Your friend."

"Which friend?"

"From the weekend," I say with a squeak. "The one who visited the manor and drove an ATV."

The answer riles him up. Thomas turns around and walks in the direction we just came from.

"Come with me," he says. "We'll get your schedule in a minute."

I hurry behind him, asking, "Where are we going?"

"To tell my alleged friends to back off."

"Back off?" I say, squeakier than ever. "I'm okay, really. You don't need to say anything. I'm sure they've forgotten I exist by now."

"That's not how things work around here," Thomas says, quickening his pace. "I let people know when I'm not happy."

Spots fill my line of sight as I follow him. What does he mean by that? What will he do?

Thomas paces along the corridor, and I hurry a few steps behind him. I don't want to lose track of him, but I'd rather not get into a confrontation. I'm sick to my stomach, and that's after already having sickness projectile out of me.

Thomas edges toward a classroom and slides by the window with his back against the wall. He throws a fist up and knocks on the glass.

Standing a few feet away, I'm clammy, pale, and out of breath.

The boy from the ATVs peers out the window and locks eyes with

Thomas. Thomas curls his index finger to signal the boy to join him.

And he does. The teacher doesn't ask why he's getting up or tell him to stay inside the classroom.

My heart hammers inside my chest. Is this a manipulation? Has Thomas lured me here so they can harass me as a team?

The boy meets Thomas by the window. He glances at me but quickly returns his focus to Thomas.

Thomas folds his arms as he leans against the wall, resting one foot up behind him. He talks to the boy in a low voice. I can't tell what he's saying. Halfway through a sentence, he nudges his head toward me. The boy turns his head in my direction, but as Thomas keeps talking, he pivots his head back.

My heart is in my throat.

When Thomas says, "Got it?" the boy nods his head and returns to class.

Thomas pushes himself off the wall and walks toward me.

I'm panting as I stammer, "Wha... Wha... What was that?"

Thomas shrugs. "I just told him to back off."

"Huh? Back off?"

He smirks. "You don't want them messing with you, do you?"

"No," I squeak.

"Well, they won't," he says. "Doesn't that make you happy?"

"I guess," I mumble, light-headed and confused.

Thomas throws a thumb toward the hallway. "Hope's classroom is up this way. We'll go see her next."

"No!" I yelp in panic. "She made it clear I shouldn't tell anyone about our altercation. I shouldn't have told you."

"Christie, I've told you a million times that you don't need to panic."

He turns and keeps moving up the corridor.

I hurry behind him out of sheer necessity.

A teacher walks down the hallway toward us, and I'm sure we're getting the "truancy equals detention" line again.

She nods at Thomas. "Good morning, Mr. Ashworth," she says, bright and bubbly.

"Morning," he says and keeps walking.

The teacher barely acknowledges my existence and continues past us.

"Why didn't we get into trouble?" I ask, catching up to him and looking over my shoulder at the careless teacher.

Thomas laughs under his breath. "You know I have the same name as the school, right?"

"What are you saying? Do you get away with breaking school rules?"

"Pretty much," he replies.

"Do you ever go to class?" I ask.

"Yeah, the ones I like."

I pull a curl behind my ear and blow out a hard breath.

"What are you gonna say to Hope?" I rush as goose bumps chill my arms. "I don't want her to be mad at me."

Thomas slows his pace and tilts his head to look me in the eye. "She won't be mad at you."

"How do you know that? You can't be inside her head."

"Yes, I can."

"What does that mean? Do you have so much money it's led you to believe you can manipulate people's way of thinking?"

"I know how Hope thinks. She listens when I tell her what is acceptable."

"I don't want you to tell her how to think," I protest. "You shouldn't tell anyone how to think."

He plants his hands on his hips and looks me up and down. "You don't want me to tell her to leave you alone?"

"Why do you care if they are mean to me or not?" I ask, looking at my shoes. "It's not like you're nice to me, anyway."

"They were mean to you because they saw you with me," he says, and it forces me to look up. "It's my fault they singled you out, and I can't let them take out their frustrations on you."

"I thought you were a god around here," I say. "Why would they be frustrated with you?"

He shakes his head, looking away. "It's complicated."

"Oh."

He looks back at me with sadness in his eyes. "Will you let me talk to Hope?"

Taking in the emotion in his eyes, my words evaporate, and I'm left nodding.

His pace slows to keep with my timid speed. "What happened to your bag?"

"Hope dumped it in a locker. I don't know which one or the combination."

Thomas nods. "We'll find it once we get back to Ms. Thornesmith for second copies of your information."

"Hi, Ash," two girls say in unison, walking out of a classroom and waving at him.

My fists squeeze in the pockets of my skirt. I don't recognize them, but I'm ready for the same level of aggression.

He waves back, saying, "Hey."

One girl looks at me and smiles. "Who's this?" she asks Thomas.

"This is Christie Klein," he replies. "Christie, this is Wendy and Callie."

"Oh, umm, yeah, uh, hi," I stutter, turning away and moving my face up, down, and away.

"Uh, yeah, okay," one girl says, sounding put off by my frenzied reaction.

"We'll see you around, Ash," the other girl says, and they both continue down the hall.

"Why do you act like that?" Thomas asks in a low tone.

"Huh?"

"You never give anyone the time of day," he replies. "Is it so hard to give someone eye contact or a proper reply?"

He thinks I'm rude?

My ears burn hot with embarrassment. Can't he see how painful talking with people is for me? Is nervousness beyond his comprehension?

"Why are you staring at me blankly?" he asks. "Do you really want to avoid making friends?"

I shake my head as shameful tears well in my eyes. "It's never worked out for me before," I whisper.

Thomas's demeanor lightens, and he takes a step back.

"Sorry," he whispers. "I shouldn't have said anything."

The sentence leaves me dumbfounded. As we move up the hall again, our pace is slackened. I keep up with him as he moves toward a classroom door. He knocks once and turns the handle without waiting for the teacher to answer.

"Is Hope Fisher in here?" he asks, taking one step inside the room.

Moments later, Hope joins us in the hallway. She smiles at Thomas and then shows me a horrendous frown.

When she looks back at Thomas, she flicks her hair over her shoulder and asks, "What's this about?"

"Don't threaten Christie," Thomas says bluntly.

Hope giggles and presses a hand against Thomas's bicep. "Oh my gosh, is that what she told you happened?"

Thomas's expression deadens as he replies, "Don't play with me. I've already talked to Luke."

Hope scowls and crosses her arms across her chest. "Look, whatever he apologized for, you know I do, too."

Thomas nods. "Good. So we're clear? You'll leave Christie alone?"

"Sure," she answers. "But I wasn't trying to be mean to her. We had a simple miscommunication."

"Just make sure it doesn't happen again," Thomas says firmly. "She has nothing to do with how you feel about me."

With an alluring smile, Hope caresses Thomas's cheek. "No one will change how I feel about you. Only you can."

Thomas takes her hand and pulls it down to her side. His voice is soft as he orders, "You should go back to class."

"Sure," she replies. She turns to me, winks and waves, and then walks back into her classroom.

I can't even hear my heartbeat anymore. My heart plummeted somewhere below my stomach. The dread of being near an apex predator like Hope is beyond unnerving. When the teachers let Thomas rule the school, it's scary to see Hope stand up to him. She has her own weapons, giving her an edge, and I'm terrified to find out what they are.

Her so-called apology was the opposite of genuine. Somehow, I think Thomas confronting her made things ten times worse.

"She just plays games," Thomas whispers, turning back the way we came. "Her bark is worse than her bite."

"Her bite scares me," I say, unable to muster more energy than a dawdle.

"Don't worry," Thomas says in a dispirited mood. "She won't come at you again. She knows I say what I mean."

The way he speaks has a forlorn tone. She got to him. Something she did sent his mood spiraling.

"Were you and Hope a couple?" I ask, surprising myself that I spat the words out.

"Nope," he says in a way that is flat and hard to read.

My stomach quirks. I move closer to Thomas as we can walk. I want to stay as close to him at school as possible because there isn't a shred of Hope I trust. I believe Thomas that she won't do anything that he can hear or see. But I don't trust her not to come after me when I'm alone.

By the time we're back at the administration office, the next school bell rings.

"Oh no," I squeak.

Thomas shakes his head. "Don't worry, it's your first day. You need a proper orientation. None of the teachers expect you to be in class."

"But it is the first day. Isn't it important that I'm in class?"

"No. It's not the first day of school. It's only your first day. The lessons are already partway through."

Thomas enters the office and talks to Ms. Thornesmith for me. I stand behind him as he takes the paperwork, saying, "So this one is her locker, these are her classes, and this one is the latest newsletter?"

"Correct," Ms. Thornesmith says. She looks over his shoulder and asks me, "Have you got that this time?"

The loudest gulp echoes out of me. I nod, crippled by her glare.

Thomas turns, papers in hand, and gestures for me to follow him out.

I sigh as we leave the office and shake out my hands in relief. "Thank you for your help, Thomas."

"Ash," he replies, and he pauses for a beat as we gaze into each other's eyes. "Call me Ash, remember?"

I smile. "Okay, Ash."

He waves the papers. "I'll show you how to get to your locker and these classrooms. It looks like we have at least two classes together. You won't get rid of me for the whole day like you wanted."

"Yeah," I say as a warm feeling spills out from my reappearing heart. "More time with you. Bummer."

The way Ash smiles at my words sparks a new layer of warmth through me. I want him around to save me from Hope. But this new feeling is something else. Thomas Ashworth III is despicable. A bratty rich kid with whom I have nothing in common.

But this isn't Thomas. He's Ash. I'm curious to find the differences.

Nine

Ash shows me to my locker and helps me figure out the combination. He suggests I leave everything inside while we tour the school.

"I really did think someone would walk around with you today," he says as we move to my next classroom. "I thought someone else would have a better approach than me."

"It's okay," I say. "You were right. I was looking forward to not seeing you."

"Am I annoying you now?" he asks.

"No, you're a great tour guide. Thank you."

He smiles and shows me into the next corridor.

Ash takes the time to point out different things to help me remember the location of my classrooms. From the ceiling hangs signs with directional arrows and classroom numbers. It's perfect because this school is the size of a hotel.

I fidget with my neckerchief and sigh. "How do you stay in this stuff all day?"

Ash smooths a hand over his tie and says, "I don't know. I'm used to it. I basically wear a suit at home."

"I couldn't get used to a life that's always formal."

"Well, you have to," he says. "You're living at the manor and attending this school. Formal is your life now."

"Oh boy." Before the dread takes over, I change the subject. "So where did the name Ash come from?"

"Well, I'm the third Thomas Ashworth, so it gets confusing. My grandfather is Thomas, and my dad has always gone by Tom. When I was born, my grandfather nicknamed me Little Ash. Over the years, the name Ash stuck."

"I like it," I say. There's something different in his demeanor. "It suits you."

Looking at him as Ash, he doesn't seem rigid or serious. There's something lighter and more casual and fun about him. How the kids at school see him.

Maybe I have been too judgmental.

"What was your old school like?" he asks.

"Nothing like this," I say. "No uniform. It was a tenth of the size. Small enough to remember everyone's names. But I was invisible there. I can't believe people have already singled me out on my first day. I've never had this much eye contact in my life."

"Really?" he asks with a level of shock in his tone.

"Yeah. Why does that surprise you?"

His eyebrows have lifted, and his eyes are round. "I just can't imagine anyone not paying attention to you."

I don't know how to respond.

What does that mean? Because I'm hideous and weird? Is there something repugnant about me that makes me stand out?

But he doesn't look at me like I'm hideous.

My heartbeat slows, and everything around me pauses.

I haven't had anyone look at me like this. No one's stare has ever made me feel this good.

After we've finished our school tour, Ash leans against a wall and hands me back my schedule.

"You want to get out of here?" he asks.

"What are you talking about? School isn't even halfway through."

"Yeah, but it's your first day. We should play hooky."

"I've never done that in my life. I can't."

"Don't tell me you're a rule follower."

"I don't like getting into trouble."

"Remember, I told you, you don't have to panic?" he says with a charismatic smile. "It is because you're with me. I don't get into trouble. The people I'm with don't get into trouble."

"Is that why you tell people how to think? It's easier to keep your story straight."

He pushes off the wall, stepping in close to me. "You catch on pretty quick, Christie Klein."

A blush lights up my cheeks, and I laugh. "Thanks."

"So what do you say?" he asks, tilting his head toward a door. "Wanna skip out? You haven't even seen Victoria Falls yet. You should get settled in properly."

"Do you want to show me around? Or do you want someone to tag along so you're not bored?"

"Are you asking if I'm using you?"

"You told me you don't go to classes," I say, taking a step back so there's some daylight between us. "It has to get boring hanging around doing nothing all day."

"Who says I do nothing?" he says, staring into my eyes in a way that keeps me glued to his. "You need to stop judging me before you know me."

82

With that, I hate to admit it, but I'm intrigued. "Okay," I sigh. "Let's go. Show me the town."

"That's a better attitude," he says with a clap.

"You clap like your father does."

Ash's smile drops. "Eww. Okay, I'm never doing that again."

"You don't want to act like your father?"

"My future is set up to be like his," Ash replies."That's why I take opportunities to have fun. I know I won't have it once I finish school."

I frown. "I'm sorry. Are you really expected to follow in his footsteps?"

"I got the name to get his title and take over his companies."

"You're still your own person."

"The Ashworth family doesn't have individuals."

Ash calls his driver, and by the time we reach the front of the school, the limousine is waiting for us.

I giggle at the sight. "Isn't there usually sneaking around when kids ditch school?"

Ash laughs and gestures to the car. "Anywhere, in particular, you want to go?"

I look back at the school building, cowering with fear that Ms. Thornesmith will rampage outside and drag me back in for a month of detention.

"No idea. I'm a homebody."

"There's one other thing I do like my father," Ash says as the driver opens the passenger door for us. "I'm good at organizing a long lunch."

"Oh… Yeah…" I mumble.

"Are you panicking again?" Ash asks, sliding into the limo.

I stand at the open door. "I… I can't…"

Ash leans toward me and stares into my eyes. "You can," he whispers. "You can live a little."

Knots tie around my spine, and my knees quake.

"We can go back to school if you want," Ash offers.

I look back at the school and grow dizzy. My stomach flips because I don't want to disappoint Ash. He's already called his driver. I don't want to be a further annoyance for him. But I don't want to disappoint my parents. They can't find out I didn't attend a single class.

"Sam," Ash calls to the driver. "Keep the car here. I'm just stepping out."

"Yes, sir," the driver replies.

Ash steps out of the car, puts a hand on my shoulder, and spins me around.

"There's a bench seat over here. Why don't we take a seat, and you can catch your breath?"

I nod and follow him toward the bench.

We take a seat and sit in silence. It's embarrassing how loud I'm breathing. But he doesn't fidget and huff like he does in the manor. He's kind and patient.

"Sorry," I whisper.

He shrugs. "It's no big deal."

"I don't want my parents to get mad."

Ash sits back with a slow exhale. "You and your parents are tight?"

"They're my best friends," I admit.

"So what happened at your old school?" Ash asks. "You said making friends hasn't worked out for you in the past."

I shrug as I sink into the seat. "I just haven't made friends before. I never learned the skill."

"But you can talk to people," Ash replies. "You're talking to me now. That's how you make friends."

"Maybe for you. I'm not confident."

"Why don't you feel confident?"

My shoulders rise to my earlobes, and I withdraw. "I don't know."

"Something must have scared you when you were a kid."

"No, I was just born this way. Nothing has scared me like the fire did."

84

"I haven't said it, but I am sorry about your house and what you went through," Ash says with a strained voice. "It's just... When you first came to the house, it was bad timing. I was mad at my dad. I didn't mean to be rude to you. You came in like another distraction. A reason for Dad not to deal with the family stuff."

"What is going with your family?"

Ash shakes his head, looking down. "I don't want to talk about it. Probably like you don't want to talk about the fire."

"It's hard to process it all. I'm not good at talking things out. That's why I paint."

Ash lifts his head with an intrigued smile. "You paint?"

I nod, smiling. "My bedroom back home was my studio. I was always collecting more colors, brushes, and materials. I love creating. I miss it so much."

"That's awesome. I wish I could be creative like that."

"You could. It just takes practice and patience." I sigh and gaze out at the green sports ovals nearby. "My artist's pouch was the only thing I grabbed during the fire. It's this canvas pouch that holds my favorite paint brushes and pens. I'm so dumb. I could have grabbed something more important."

"That's not dumb. It's important to you," Ash says, and I move my gaze back to him. "I don't know what I'd grab in a fire."

"Adrenaline kinda takes over, and you don't think about it."

A delicate smile tugs at Ash's lips. "Actually, I know. There's a photo by my bed of me, my sister, and my parents. We were on a skiing vacation, and it was the most fun I remember having with my family."

"That's great," I say with a big grin.

Ash's gaze dips low again. "I miss them," he whispers.

I don't push. He's already said he doesn't want to talk about his family problems.

He looks up at me and smiles. "Thanks."

"For what?"

"I appreciate you not prying."

"I might jumble my words, but I'm a good listener."

He nods. "I need a good listener in my life."

I suck in a tight breath. When I let it out, I force myself to say, "Maybe I do need a friend."

He places his hand over mine. "I'll be your friend."

I quiver from his touch. "Even if I don't skip school with you?"

He moves his hands back to his lap and laughs under his breath. "We don't have to leave school. We can stay."

"Thanks. I think my heart would leave my body if I ditched classes."

"Geez. You want to stay at school and go to classes?"

I blush, nodding.

Ash holds out his hand. "Show me your schedule again."

I hand it to him.

He taps the paper. "This one, economics. I'm in this class too. We're focusing on ethics, and it's boring."

"I can't imagine how ethics in economics are taught in this school. I'm guessing it will differ massively compared to my last school."

"Maybe we should head to our lockers and get ready for class?" Ash suggests, getting up from the seat.

I stand beside him and utter, "Are you sure you want to go to class?"

"I'm not looking forward to being bored out of my mind," Ash says, walking back to the school's front door and giving his driver a wave. "But I'll do what my mother asked and escort you. Plus, after class, you might beg to ditch school with me."

"I'd only ditch if I get to spend the whole day at home. I tried to convince my parents to homeschool me."

"I wanted to do homeschooling too."

At that, I laugh. "Yeah, right."

He stops walking. "What?"

"You would rather stay home than rule the entire school? Hard to believe."

Ash continues to walk, saying, "There you go, judging me again."

I don't follow him. I stay still, mouth hanging open. The one time I try to be friendly leads to me offending someone. I need to keep my mouth shut because I can't afford to have Ash make life unbearable.

He is right. I don't know him. Even if we get to know each other, what are the chances we will like what we find? We come from different worlds, and his world turns me off.

Maybe getting to know Ash will be a big mistake.

Ten

I didn't sit next to Ash in any of my classes, yet his being in the room gave me peace of mind. I just needed some distance from him.

At lunch, I found my way to the library. The cafeteria was too noisy for my anxiety to handle. Plus, I didn't want to run into any of Ash's friends who think I'm an easy target. It was difficult to know if Ash was in school. I figured he may have met his driver without care of where I was.

At the end of the day, it takes a while to find my locker. When I retrieve my bag, a tap on my shoulder makes me jump out of my skin.

"Good lord, Klein. Why are you so jumpy?" Ash asks.

I plant a hand over my heart as I turn around. He smirks while I pant for air.

"Ready to go?" he asks, holding back a laugh.

I nod, still catching my breath.

Ash gestures toward the front of the school. "Come on. Sam will be ready for us out front."

With my backpack on, I grasp the straps and follow Ash. He slings his bag over one shoulder, and there's a casual gracefulness to his stride. People seem to pass for him. As I follow him, it is obvious he never swerves his path. He walks in one continuous direction, and it's everyone else's problem to get out of his way.

The limousine parks directly in front of the school steps. I bet it's Ash's reserved space. The driver opens the passenger door, and when I get in behind Ash, whispers grow louder around us. If anyone didn't notice me during classes, they are now very aware of the new girl hanging around the god of their school.

As I sit in the back seat, my blood is icy. Please don't let there be any more Hope Fishers in this school. I don't need other girls telling me to leave Ash alone. Especially if they have boyfriends backing them up too.

I shake off the dread and sink into the plush seating as the limousine pulls out of the school gates. We drive into the main street of Victoria Falls, and I gaze out the window at the shops I missed earlier.

"Hey, Sam," Ash calls, knocking on the divider. The divider lowers, and Ash says, "Pull over here, would ya?"

Does this guy ever say please?

"Right away, sir," the driver says, and the car stops by the curb.

"Where are you going?" I ask. My heart is in my stomach, apprehensive that one of his friends will jump in the car with us.

Ash bounces off his seat and opens the car door. "Check this out," he says, a ball of enthusiasm.

I follow out of sheer surprise. For the past few days, I've only known him as sullen and bored, and now something has him excited.

"This will have to be your favorite shop in Victoria Falls," Ash says, pointing out a nearby store.

I look at the front signage and fall into an easy smile. It's an art supplies shop. Moving closer, I gaze at the window display. A forty-by-forty-inch canvas hangs in the center, sporting a watercolor design of a striding peacock. The rest of the display houses acrylic, oil, watercolor paint selections, and an array of brushes from long handle to flat tip.

"You want to go in?" Ash asks, his arm extended to open the door.

I look past the display and into the store. It's filled with my dream supplies, and I'm overwhelmed by its immensity.

I step backward, waving my hands in front of me. "No. No, I can't."

Ash drops his arm by his side and tilts his head at me. "Why not?"

"Sorry," I mumble, turning back to the car. "I'm ready to go home."

"Fine," Ash mutters, walking toward the limo. "Just thought you'd like it."

I do. I want to say it, but it's clogged in my throat. My nose grows stuffy, and heavy suffocation hits me again.

How can he possibly understand? He's from a world where he can buy anything his heart desires. My collection took years. Buying took research and care. Starting over with new tools is a reminder of losing everything.

I'm just not ready to look at brand new art supplies.

The rest of the trip to the Ashworth Estate is stony and silent. Ash taps at his phone, and I fumble with the buttons on my blazer sleeve. It's a relief to see the manor.

Murphy greets us by the limousine to collect our school bags. Inside the foyer, Mom is giddy with excitement.

"How was your first day, sweetheart?" Mom asks, grinning as she opens her arms wide to hug me.

"Eventful," I say, leaning into her.

Mom cuddles me, asking, "Did you make any new friends?"

Ash walks past us, and I say, "One." He glances at me, and I add, "I think."

Ash continues into the manor, and I close my eyes to soak up more of Mom's hug.

"So it wasn't as unbearable as you imagined?" Mom asks with a teasing inflection in her voice.

I pull out of the hug and smile. "It was a mixed bag."

"Well, you're not saying it was worse than the bubonic plague," Mom says with a giggle. "I call that a win."

The trials of my first day leave me wanting to shower. Between the sweating and the vomiting, I'm surprised I'm not more of a mess.

In the bathroom, I puzzle out the best way to apologize to Ash. I never want to offend anyone because I even find apologizing confrontational. Getting tongue-tied when trying to make amends can often lead to more misunderstandings.

It was incredibly sweet that he showed me the art supplies store. It meant he listened to me and took an interest. I think I came off as rude and dismissive.

I leave the bathroom with an eager smile when I find him in the hall. I lift a hand to wave, but he's on a phone call and wearing a rigid expression. He glimpses at me, and his expression doesn't waver. I drop my hand, and he turns his back on me.

I am as deflated as a week-old balloon.

Why did he waste his time with me at school? Was he looking for ammo against my family to have us kicked out? The panic sweeps over me, and I dash toward the nearest staircase. Ash may have moments of kindness, but I need to keep my guard up. At heart, he is still a selfish and careless boy.

My cheeks are plump from puffing as I reach the dining room. I shake out my hands and force my breathing to slow. I enter the room to find Mom at the table.

"Where's Dad?" I ask, taking my seat.

"Not back yet," Mom says.

I ask Mom about her day, and her expression is sorrowful when she talks about waiting in limbo for her phone calls to be returned. Her smile pushes through when her subject changes to exploring the manor.

"Murphy showed me where the theater was, and I had a rom-com marathon," Mom says in a chipper tone.

"That sounds like fun," I say, grinning. "I wish I could have stayed with you."

"Too bad you're a teenager and have to stay in school," Mom replies with a thick hint for me to drop it.

I slouch in my seat. If Dad were here, I could totally suck up to him.

After more small talk, Dad and Mr. Ashworth finally enter the dining room. Phew. I'm starving.

Mr. Ashworth is quick to drone on, dominating the table in conversation. Seriously, dude. Can't I have a minute to ask my dad how his day was?

It's another ten minutes before Ash walks into the room.

"Nice of you to grace us with your presence, Son," Mr. Ashworth says, eyeing Ash as he takes his seat.

Ash is unimpressed and doesn't acknowledge his father's words.

"Are you going to say hello to me?" his father pushes.

Ash doesn't look at him, but there is a subtle roll in his eyes. "Hello," he mutters.

"Did you ensure Christie settled in at school?" Mr. Ashworth asks with solid skepticism.

"Yep," Ash replies, fidgeting with a linen napkin.

Mr. Ashworth clears his throat, then looks at me. "So everything went well on your first day?"

"Yes," I reply, taking in the belligerence between father and son. "Thomas was a great help."

We glance at each other, and I smile, adding, "Sorry, Ash was a great help."

Ash smiles with appreciation. His father seems appeased and turns to my father, starting a new conversation. Ash sinks into his dining chair with relaxed relief, now that his father is off his back.

Dang. This boy can twist my emotions like no other. He's handsome, charming, and deceptively observant. I want to hate him, but is it even possible to hate this guy?

I rub my lips together, trying to downplay my smile. Across the table, I spy Mom grinning at me. She steals a look at Ash and then flicks her eyes back to me. Her mouth begs to laugh, but she holds it back.

Geez. She is so embarrassing.

The rest of dinner runs smoothly. Ash scoots uncomfortably in his chair when his dad acknowledges him. Thankfully, his frustrations don't turn in my direction. I'm at ease by the time dessert rolls around. Ash even makes small talk, asking if I like the food.

When everyone stands to leave the table, Ash taps my shoulder.

"Yeah?"

"You know they're headed to the bar, and they'll dismiss us," he says with a smirk.

"Mmm. That's kinda the routine at night, isn't it?"

"Do you want to go to the theater with me?" Ash asks. "I can find a less violent game."

"Ah, no, thank you," I say, awkwardly turning away from him. "I don't think you'll find any games at my speed."

"Come on. You have to do something for fun."

"Puzzles." I turn back in time to see Ash's face screw up. I laugh, questioning, "What?"

"Puzzles? Seriously, Nanna?"

"Yeah, I like puzzles. Board games too. I'm old-school."

Ash rubs his chin. "Okay, maybe I can find something. My sister likes board games too. I'm sure Claudia knows where they are."

I giggle nervously. "You don't have to play a board game with me."

"I need something to pass the time."

"You can play video games with your friends," I suggest, shrinking into bashfulness.

"I thought you were my friend," he says with a gorgeous,

93

charismatic smile.

I'm a puddle right now.

I rub behind my neck, and my skin is red hot. "Umm, okay," I babble. "If Claudia can find a game, I'll play it with you."

His eyes captivate me with a twinkle as he replies, "Cool."

I take a big breath and then force out, "I'm sorry for not being excited about the art supplies store."

Ash stops, taken aback by my blurted apology. He blinks at me and smiles. "That's okay."

"I just didn't expect it, and losing everything is still raw..."

"Christie, it's cool. You don't need to apologize. You might want to go another time?"

I nod. "Sure."

Ash and I go upstairs and find Claudia in the kids' wing. Ash asks her for his sister's board games, and Claudia replies they are kept in the family room on the third floor. Claudia drops the pile of laundry she was busy with and turns to leave the wing for the third floor.

"Claudia, wait," Ash says. "You don't have to go. We can manage."

"No, it's okay, Master Ashworth," Claudia says with her cheery grin. "I'll get them for you."

"You were busy," Ash replies. "Christie and I will hang out upstairs."

"Are you sure?" Claudia persists.

"Thank you for your help," I chime in. "We will be okay."

Claudia smiles at me. "Okay. You two have fun."

"Ever been up to the third floor?" Ash asks me.

"No. Two floors and a basement already had me lost."

Ash takes me up the next flight of stairs, and we pass many rooms until we come to oversized double doors. Inside is a cozy family room filled with overstuffed bookshelves. Two Chesterfield lounges face each other on a plush rug, centered by a heavy wooden coffee table and next to an open fireplace.

Ash pulls three board games off a shelf as I stare at the fireplace. I notice ash and charcoal at the base, and memories of our house falling to bits flash in my mind. I suck in a ragged breath and try to look away. It's like a vise is holding my head because I'm unable to move.

"I should ask Murphy to get that started," Ash says, placing the games on the coffee table. His voice breaks me free, and he nods at the fireplace.

"No," I murmur. The thought of roaring flames sitting beside me is frightening enough.

A match striking pricks my ears. On the table between us, Ash lights a candle. The flame is bright orange. The same bright orange that consumes my nightmares.

A clammy sweat coats the sides of my face and neck. I kneel on the rug by the coffee table and rub my palms over my skirt.

"What is it?" Ash asks.

I can't answer. I'm hypnotized by the dancing flame.

"Wait. Is it this?" Ash asks, pointing at the candle.

I summon my courage and nod my head.

"Oops. Sorry," he says and hastily blows out the candle.

Smoke floats through the air and toward my nostrils. Any hope of keeping it together fades away. I clutch the edge of the table as my body convulses. My shoulders jolt up and down as the panic intensifies.

"Whoa, Christie!" Ash exclaims, skidding around the table to sit beside me.

He takes my arms and tilts his head until our eyes meet. Taking in those big, beautiful brown eyes, I note the concern rounding them. I move my breath in sync with his.

My puffing and panting eases, and he lets out a relieved sigh.

"Are you okay?" he asks.

I nod my head, still without the energy to speak.

"I'm sorry, that was so dumb," Ash says, lowering his head with shame.

I shake my head, wanting to say it's okay, but the words still won't come out.

He lets go of my arms, frustrated with himself.

"I don't think about other people," he mutters. "I'm sorry."

I pat my hand against my chest, and strain to say, "You couldn't have known it would trigger me."

"I'm sorry," his voice falters.

"It's okay. How about we play a game?" I ask, hoping to put his mind at ease.

I don't want him to feel bad. It's not his fault. He was trying to do something nice. He doesn't know I'm having nightmares about fires.

Ash moves the extinguished candle off the table and places it on the windowsill. As he walks back over, I pick between the board game boxes.

"Did you want to talk about the fire?" Ash offers.

I shake my head and select the second box. "No, I'd prefer to whoop your butt at this game."

Ash laughs under his breath and moves the other two boxes to the ground.

"We'll see about that," he teases. "I'm usually good at everything."

"You've never gone against me before," I joke, and as I giggle, the confidence radiating through me has me shook.

We skim over the rules and set up the board. We have the dice, game pieces, and chance cards ready to go. Our conversation revolves around the game, and I settle into a small feeling of normality.

"I have to admit," Ash says, leaning back on his elbows. "This is kind of nice."

"See. You don't have to shoot things to have fun."

"I didn't realize I needed to slow down and unwind," he says. "I enjoy living at a fast pace because it doesn't give me time to dwell on anything."

"Do you avoid the thoughts in your head?"

"Yeah, pretty much," Ash says with an exhausted sigh. "My dad already tries to involve me in his companies. He's figuring out which one I should run. It's his choice, not mine. Arguing with him about it is tiring."

I roll the dice and move my game piece, letting Ash talk without interruption.

"That's why, if someone wants me to jump online and play a game, or ride a quad bike, or make an appearance at their party, I do it." He sits up and scratches his head. "Because, right now, being in school lets me avoid the responsibilities. I don't know if I'm good enough to do what my dad does."

"I'm sure you'll be good at it," I say. "I mean, it's your dad and granddad's companies, right?"

"It just sucks," he says with a sigh. "They gave me the same name. Therefore, I'll live the same life."

"You don't know what you want?"

"No. I shouldn't have to figure it out now."

"That makes sense," I say. "I like doing my art, but I've never thought about making it a career. I don't think about having a showing or owning a gallery. For now, it's a hobby. It takes up my time and frees my mind. I don't know what I'd want for an actual career."

"We should be allowed time to figure it out."

"I agree," I say.

"I feel like I'm self-involved on purpose," Ash admits. "But… I'm not doing anything I want to do. It passes the time, but I'm not sure it's real fun." He flicks a finger at a game piece. "I mean, I never thought I'd enjoy this, but it is fun."

A blush sparks in my cheeks. "I guess it's about trying something new."

"I try new things all the time," he says, raising his gaze to my eye level. "Maybe it's the company that makes tonight more enjoyable."

I suck in a breath and have an urge to dance. An intensity surges through me, and I'm drawn to him more than ever. His eyes are gentle and purposeful. My eyes dip to his lips, which have transformed into an irresistible shape. I hadn't noticed until now the plumpness of his bottom lip.

I gulp, blink hard, and sit back against the couch.

"Uh, umm," I stammer. "It's your turn."

He grins and picks up the dice. "Thanks, Christie. You're so easy to talk to."

I laugh disbelievingly.

"Sure, you're quiet," Ash says. "That doesn't make you inferior."

My laughter stops as I stare into his sparkling brown eyes. "Really?"

"Don't feel bad for being shy," he whispers. "People should work to know the real you."

I pull a curl behind my ear and raise my shoulder to my earlobe. "Is that what you do?"

"Make people work for it?" he asks, rolling the dice. "Sure, but most people don't work hard. It's been a long time since I opened up like this."

"It's a first for me."

Ash grins. "Then I should feel special."

I smile, and my eyes fall to the board because I'll most likely keel over if I continue making eye contact with him.

"Were you just being modest when you said you were invisible at your last school?"

My eyes follow his fingers as he moves his game piece. "No, why?"

He places his game piece on a square. He's silent for a long beat. His eyes are delicate as his smile creeps upward.

He clears his throat. "I'm not buying it. How could anyone not notice you?"

I grasp the edge of the table with trembling hands.

He stares at me for another beat. "It's your turn, Christie."

It's hard to breathe, so I don't reply. I mouth the word, "Okay," and pick up the dice.

My thoughts bounce out of my head as I make my next game move.

I rest my back against the lounge and breathe again.

Wow.

Thomas Ashworth III.

Ash...

A warm feeling spreads inside me. Spending more time with this open and kind-hearted boy is a blessing. We part ways after we finish the game, yet I'm walking on clouds until my head hits the pillow.

Eleven

Ash walks me into school the next day, and he escorts me to my first class. We compared schedules on the ride to school and found that today we have one class together.

There's an energy to Ash as we walk through the school hallways. I have faith that no one will say anything nasty to me because he'll keep me safe. Even knowing he's in the building fills me with security.

Throughout my first class, there is a hum of whispers. Out of the corner of my eye, I spy a group of girls who point me out with the pens they twirl.

It's a relief when the bell rings. However, being the new girl glued to Ash's side, every class has whispers aimed at me.

I let the other students push ahead before leaving the classroom. Once I get to the doorway, I trip on my own feet when I see Ash standing there.

Girls from my class walk backward, trying to gain his attention. Yet his eyes fixate on me.

Wow.

"How was class?" Ash asks with a big smile.

"It was fine," I say, joining him in the hallway. "You got over here super fast. Did you not go to class?"

"I might have," he says, which doesn't answer the question. He shrugs and adds, "I just thought I'd walk you to your next class."

My cheeks flush with heat. I don't have the bravery to reply.

I'm smiling as we walk and then am overcome with a massive yawn.

"You've been yawing since breakfast," Ash says. "Are you still feeling tired?"

"I barely slept last night."

Ash laughs. "I thought raucous board game playing would have tuckered you out."

I laugh, nodding. "Sure, it was an action-packed game."

I leave it at that. I don't want to dwell on the nightmares. I want to forget about them in the daylight. Plus, I don't want him to stew on the candle incident. He shouldn't feel bad about it. Imagine how romantic it could have been, sitting together by candlelight.

Romantic? Did I really just go there? We're just friends. I can't start drooling over him.

"Here you are," Ash says as we reach my next classroom. "I'll catch up with you at the next bell."

"Okay. Thank you for walking with me."

Ash gives me a wave and continues along the corridor.

My heart flutters. Dang. I cannot wait for the bell to ring.

Before I walk into the classroom, a familiar voice chills my spine. "Hi, Christie."

I search the hallway and see Hope Fisher waving at me. Her

boyfriend Luke drapes over her.

Great.

I hurry inside, ignoring the pair. Ash will be on the other side of the door when class finishes. That is, if he doesn't get bored and call his driver. Oh boy. Was I wrong to put so much faith in him?

No, Christie. Remember what Ash said. I don't have to panic. Plus, he knows Hope and Luke's classes. I'm sure he's aware of how close my classroom is to theirs.

I wonder what else Ash keeps tabs on. He is like his father, who scooped us up after our house fire without prompting. The mystery of the Ashworths just keeps growing.

The next bell is like music to my ears. When I reach the corridor, Hope and Luke corner Ash.

"Ash, are you going to hang with us at lunch?" Hope asks, batting her extended lashes at him.

I hold on to my breath as Ash takes a beat to answer.

"I would," he says, "but I'm hanging with Christie today."

He slings an arm around my shoulders, and I'm heavy with the weight of Hope's gaze on me.

Daggers fill Hope's eyes, and I cower beside Ash.

What is her problem with me? She's told me to stay away from Ash because he's spoken for. Hope is with Luke, so she can't be jealous of me spending time with Ash. Is Hope standing up for another girl? Oh geez. I'm in big trouble if a girl, worse than Hope, is waiting to get me alone.

"I'll be okay," I squeak. "You don't have to hang out with me."

"No, I do," Ash says in a nonchalant way. He squeezes his arm around me tighter, and says to Hope and Luke, "Anyway, guys, we'll see you later."

Ash swivels me away from the pair, and I force my legs to follow his pace.

It's like bullets fire into my back as Hope's fiery glare follows us all the way along the hallway.

"Are you okay with going straight home after school?" Ash asks, peeling his arm off me once we turn the corner into a new corridor.

"Sure."

"Cool. I've just got something planned, that's all."

"You know, you don't have to babysit me between classes," I say, struggling to keep my heartbeat in check. "If you have plans with your friends, you can go with them. I can go to the library during lunch."

"If you want to go to the library later, I'll go with you."

"You don't have to."

"Did it ever occur to you that I want to hang out with you?"

I blush and dip my gaze in nervous embarrassment.

Ash laughs and points out a nearby classroom. "Here. It's your favorite part of the day. A class with me."

I rub my lips together, trying to minimize my smile. I can't believe I actually enjoy Ash's company now.

Ash was fidgety and bored in class, which made the fact he's drawn to me a drag. He shouldn't sit through classes if they agitate him. Maybe he wouldn't feel behind if he didn't skip so many.

At lunch, I didn't have to hide because Ash was by my side. Instead, we walked through the grounds towards the football field while everyone we passed wanted to steal him away. The boys want to hang out at Ashworth Estate, and the girls flirt their hearts out.

Ash didn't give them much of his time. The disruptions made the day slip away. After the last bell, we took the limo back to the manor.

"We have some time before dinner," Ash says, looking at his watch as we walk through the first floor. He lowers his hand and nudges his head toward the stairs. "Do you want to go to the third floor?"

"What, are you now addicted to board games?" I joke.

"Mmm. I might have another place I want to show you."

I shrug with a beaming smile. "Okay."

I follow Ash upstairs, take a hallway, and then up another flight of stairs.

"I think you'll get a kick out of this," Ash says, taking the lead.

He opens heavy double doors, and streams of natural light greet us through three floor-to-ceiling windows. I gasp as I step into the room. It's filled with canvases, drop cloths, easels, paints, and brushes.

"What do you think?" he asks. He steps aside, allowing me to take it in.

"What is all this?" I whisper as my mind whirs to compute what I'm viewing.

"It's all yours."

I stand in place, wide-eyed and mouth open. As I scan the scene, my limbs shiver, and my emotions fracture.

"I know you weren't ready to find new supplies," Ash says behind me. "But it's obvious how much you miss painting. I wanted you to have the space to create something."

"You brought all this here... for me?" I stammer.

"I called the shop in Victoria Falls," Ash replies. "I asked them for everything a professional artist would need. That's why I was late for dinner last night. I was on the phone with the owner. I arranged everything to arrive while we were at school."

My mind flashes back to him on the phone yesterday evening. Oh my gosh. He didn't want me to hear his phone conversation because he was planning a surprise for me.

I step back, waving my hands. "Ash, I can't accept this."

"Sure you can," he says, clutching my wrist and tugging me forward. "Take your time. You can go through it, bit by bit. If there's anything you don't like, Murphy will return it. And if you need anything else, I'll call the shop to bring it over."

"This is too much," I murmur, shivering. "I'm used to getting things myself, not having people run my errands."

"Christie, it's a gift." Ash walks around a canvas and rests an elbow on an easel. "At last count, my dad's net worth is eighty billion. We've got money lying around."

"Do you splash cash as a way of giving gifts?"

Ash shakes his head. "I don't give gifts often." He laughs nervously. "I only give gifts to people I like. And I don't like many people."

I blink hard and pull at my neckerchief. I unravel it from my neck and also slide off my blazer. I'm way too frazzled to keep on all these layers. A gradual exhale seeps out of me as I step farther into the room. I rest my blazer and neckerchief by the paint selections. The colors catch my eye.

"You've already had to move and change schools," Ash says softly. "I just want something to make you feel at home."

I shiver, keeping my gaze low. "You want me to feel at home here?"

"Yeah, I don't want you to be sad."

I raise my head to find his eyes. Sadness circles his pupils. Something is hurting him, and he doesn't want me hurting.

My heart swells. "Thanks, Ash. I love it."

He lifts a cream-colored smock. "Why don't you test out some of the gear before dinner?"

"I wouldn't know where to begin," I admit.

"There's no pressure," he says. He holds the smock at the perfect height for my arms.

I slide my arms into the sleeves, and Ash moves behind me to tie the back.

"I'll leave you alone to work. Unless you want me to hang around and pose for you?" he teases.

"No, no." I giggle. "It's okay."

I turn around and face him, and any sadness in Ash's expression has disappeared.

"Are you sure it's okay that I stay here alone?" I ask.

"Yeah, have fun."

My heart pounds like it's about to explode into fireworks. "I will."

When Ash leaves the room, I rub my palm over my heart. He did all this for me? Did the word "romantic" fall into his thoughts, too? Does he want more than a friendship, or is he just a billionaire throwing cash around?

The thoughts in my head sour. At school, he told me he's not pursuing anyone romantically. Deep down, he sees me as beneath him. He's placating me while we're under the same roof. Once my family finds a new house, I'll be out of his thoughts.

I pick up a mixing board and place it next to the paints. I pick out a shade of blue, red, and yellow and squirt a splodge of each onto the board. I select a brush and take my time mixing the colors. I appreciate the mass selection of brushes. Although, as soon as I come back here, I'm bringing my artist's pouch and using my trusted favorites.

As I sketch on the canvas, Ash's eyes never leave my mind. I glide brown paint into curved angles. With the help of black, white, and a gorgeous peachy tone, I work on creating beauty on the canvas by paying homage to Ash's eyes.

Even if he doesn't feel the same way about me, my heart can't stop fluttering.

"Wow," Mom says in awe as she walks into the room. "This is amazing."

"I know," I reply. "It's too much."

"It's very generous." Mom steps behind me and strokes my hair. "You must feel whole again, being able to paint."

I shrug with an involuntary frown. "I'm getting there."

"It's okay not to be okay," Mom says gently. "I told you I've been occupying my days with rom-coms, but that's just masking my devastation. We lost everything, Christie. We should talk about not being okay."

I nod at the canvas. "This will help me channel my emotions like it always does."

"Well, I'm choosing to be busy, too. I spoke to Mrs. Ashworth and

106

confided in her about feeling lost. She made a suggestion," Mom says. "She is part of a society group, and her place needs to be filled while she's abroad. She's contacting the new chairperson about inviting me to the next meeting."

There's a twinkle in Mom's eye I haven't seen in days. I smile and stand to hug her. "You look excited. I'm so happy for you."

"Thank you, honey. I feel better just seeing you at an easel. I hope things are looking up for us."

"I'm all in favor of bringing on positive thoughts."

"I'll let you get back to your art."

"Thanks. My head already felt lighter when I mixed the paint."

I look back at the eye on my canvas, and my heart swells.

This boy is magic.

Twelve

After dinner, Ash said he was going to a friend's house. I tried not to let the jealousy or hurt show on my face. He wished me a good night and left the manor.

I get why people fawn over him during school. Being around him is intoxicating. When he leaves, you feel like an addict wanting more.

I tossed and turned in bed, wrestling with my mixed emotions. Ash has driven me mad and sent me gaga. He spent most of the school day by my side. Now, left without an invitation, I'm woefully alone.

And then there's the art studio…

Oh my gosh… My heart and my head have never warred like this. From the moment we met, I wanted to hate him. However, at first glance, I noticed his attractiveness. He has layers, and I doubt half of them have been revealed.

It took an eternity to get to sleep, yet only nanoseconds for the flames to invade my dreams. The nightmare isn't set in our old house. It's here in the manor. The flames encircle my bedroom, and the walls grow hot. I launch out of bed and bang on the adjacent wall. I scream for Ash. I'm terrified he's trapped in the fire. My heart launches in my throat, and I'm drenched in sweat.

I scream again, and this time, I'm sitting up in bed. The room is no longer orange from the flames and heat. I'm awake and panting. My throat is raw, and I worry I was screaming in my sleep. I pull myself out of bed and consider a midnight shower because the thick sweat is real. I reach for my phone to check the time.

2:00 a.m.

I sit on the edge of the bed and fan out my nightshirt. I huff hard and sling my head in my hands. I wish these dreams would stop. Living in a wooded area has scattered my nerves because the possibility of fires is always higher. I remind myself of the cleared land surrounding the Ashworth Estate. Plus, there's a helipad on the grounds, so it may actually be the safest place to live.

I leave the bedroom for the bathroom. If not a shower, at least spraying cold water on my face will help. At the sink, running the water, my eyes become itchy. I'm deprived of sleep and overcome with emotion. The sadness fills my chest, and a sob croaks out of me. I splash water on my face, and tears roll from my eyes.

I can't take more nights like this.

I dry my face, pull a robe around me, and leave the bathroom. At night, I try not to leave my bed because of the orange tinge. As I enter the hall, I keep my head down and steady my breath.

"Ness, I'm not arguing with you." Ash's stern tone cuts through the air.

I look up to find him pacing the hall with his phone to his ear.

"Can't you just listen?" he asks. "We should be able to talk about it."

He continues to pace, his posture hunched and defeated.

"I can't believe you're shutting off like this," Ash says, his voice strained and quieter. "Fine. I've had enough of you."

He lowers his phone and paces in the opposite direction toward me.

I grasp the bathroom doorframe, hoping it'll keep me upright.

"I'm sorry," I croak, and without being able to catch it, a tear rolls from my eye.

Ash's expression softens, and he walks toward me. "What's the matter?"

I rub away the tears and suppress a sob. "Nothing. Are you okay? That sounded heated."

He stashes his phone by a vase on a side table. "Don't worry about that. Why are you crying? What happened?"

His worrisome eyes cause my heart to swell. Besides my parents, no one has shown such intense concern about me. The deluge of emotion renders me speechless, and tears and sobs splutter out of me.

"Aw, Christie," Ash whispers, and his hand caresses my face.

I plant my hands over my face, and our fingers touch. His hands move to my back. He stands two inches from me, and his arms loop me in a hug.

"Wanna come downstairs with me?" he asks in a whisper. "Murphy makes a killer hot cocoa."

I shake my head in my hands.

"Don't worry about waking him up," Ash says. "If he knew you were this upset and wasn't up to make you the ultimate drink that cures sadness, he'd be beside himself."

I sniffle into my hands and step back so Ash's hands drop from around me. I sneak into the bathroom, leaving the door open. I move to the sink and wash my face again.

Ash leans against the doorframe, watching me. Usually, this would send me down a shame spiral, but his gaze gives me security.

I dry my face and meet Ash with a nod. He smiles and places his hand on my back. We make our way to the kitchen in silence.

In the kitchen, Ash reaches for the phone on the wall.

"Wait," I say, grabbing his hand.

As I press on his hand, he turns, staring at me blankly.

I search the back corner of the kitchen. "There's a door leading outside, right?"

"Yeah, over there."

"Can we go out?" I ask. "I need to cool down."

"Sure. Follow me."

As soon as we step outside, the cool breeze swirls around me, and my body temperature dwindles. With purpose, I steady my breaths, grateful for this crisp mountain air.

"If you want to cool down, we could head to the pool," Ash suggests.

"There's a pool here?" I ask, but I don't know why I'm surprised.

Ash raises two fingers. "Two. An outdoor and an indoor."

"Geez. How much of this mansion haven't I seen yet?"

"Have you seen the bowling alley?"

My jaw drops. "There's seriously a bowling alley here?"

Ash bursts into laughter. He waves his hands in front of him, saying, "No, there's not, but the look on your face was priceless."

I laugh, shaking my head. "I would have believed you."

"You look happier. I hope I can take your mind off whatever is bothering you."

"I always feel better when I'm awake," I admit.

Ash frowns. "Are you having nightmares?"

The visions from tonight's dreams reform in my mind. The tears well in my eyes, and I reply with a nod.

"I'm so sorry, Christie. Is there anything I can do?"

"If you keep me company, it is more than I could ask for."

Ash shrugs. "I won't be getting to sleep, so I'm more than happy to stay with you."

As we walk toward the pool, I say, "That phone call sounded intense. Like the one a few nights ago. I'm sorry about walking in on both of them."

"Don't be. If I wanted them kept private, I wouldn't walk around the manor."

"Do you want to talk about it?" I ask, and then glowing blue lights distract me.

A long-stretched topaz pool illuminates from within. The surrounding deck is lit with angled lights, styled by deck chairs, and leads to a cabana.

"Do you want to get in?" Ash asks, opening the glass pool gate.

I pull my robe tighter as I walk through the gate. "I don't have any swimwear."

Ash points out a building on the opposite side of the pool. "There will be something in the pool house you can change into."

"I'd be happy just to sit on the edge," I reply.

Ash pulls two towels out of the cabana. He hands them to me and then tugs off his shirt.

Something nonsensical yammers out of me as I turn my head away. I got a peek at his abs, and now I'm overheating in this robe.

"You can get your pj's wet," Ash says, "but I'm stripping off my clothes."

When a splash sounds, I turn my face back. Cradling the towels, I spy his linen trousers by my feet. With another garbled non-word, I look at the water as Ash emerges from below.

I place the towels on the tiles beside me and remove the robe. Ensuring my night shirt doesn't bunch and hangs to my thighs, I move toward the water's edge and dangle my feet into the pool. The renewing sensation cools my temperature, and relief swirls within.

Ash swims toward me, and through the rippling water, I spy his black underwear. *Phew.* I'd jump out of my skin if he were skinny-dipping.

112

A surge of water hits the pool's edge as he lands by me. I yap out a small squeak when the water hits my thighs and rushes past my butt.

"Oh, oops," Ash says with a smirk. "You okay?"

I smile. "Yeah. I'm fine. Just wetter than I expected."

"You should just hop in."

"Maybe I'm just easing in."

Ash rests his arms on the edge with bent elbows. His chin sits on his hands, and his hair is slicked back from the water. Beads of water collect over his shoulders. He is a masterpiece I can't look away from.

"I've been staying up late to talk to my sister," he says, followed by a heavy sigh.

I bite into my lip and wait for him to continue. In case he decides not to share, I don't want to seem like I'm prying.

Ash moves a hand through the water, and I notice his frown. "We disagree about the situation with our parents."

I wait for a beat for him to keep talking. When his gaze stays low, I ask, "What's happening with your parents?"

Ash looks up at me, asking, "You haven't picked up on it?"

I shake my head.

"They separated," Ash reveals. "That's why my mom left for Switzerland. She left my dad."

"Whoa," I gasp. I place my hand on Ash's arm, slipping against the water. "I'm so sorry."

Ash pulls himself out of the water and sits beside me. "She wanted me to go with her." His voice lowers, and he hugs his middle. "But I wanted her to fight for our family. I refused to go in hopes she would stay. But she left, and Vanessa went with her."

I grab a towel from behind me and hand it to Ash. "Is your sister siding with your mom?"

Ash rolls his eyes and then pats his face dry with the towel and discards it by his side. "Vanessa does what she's told. If Dad had got to her first and told her not to board the plane, she'd still be here."

He pauses, staring at the water with deep thought.

"Aren't you cold?" I say, cutting the silence.

At that, Ash grins. "Not if I get back in."

The next moment, Ash slides into the pool and wades into the center.

"Why don't you come in with me?" he calls.

I bunch my nightshirt across my chest. I'm not wearing a bra. I don't want to get out of the water with my shirt clinging to my body.

Ash nods his head toward the pool house. "You can go in there and change."

I glimpse over my shoulder at my robe, and my hand glides over the rolled towel.

What the hell?

Keeping my shirt snug against my body, I slip into the water.

"*Woo*, Klein, getting wild," Ash cheers.

"Do you often go for a midnight swim?" I ask, wading toward him.

"Not at all. Sometimes I'll swim laps if I'm up early." He smiles at me. "It's been ages since I've come out here just for fun."

"No crazy pool parties?"

A handsome grin slides across his face. "Only in the summer."

"I can only imagine how crazy a pool party could get at a billionaire's estate."

"Maybe you'll stick around and see for yourself."

"I doubt we'll still be here by then. I mean, I hope it doesn't take months to get a new house."

"Dad would speed it up if he wanted you guys to leave."

His wording strikes me, and I almost suck in water. "What do you mean?"

"He'd have arranged a new house for your family if he didn't want to keep you at the manor."

It never occurred to me that Mr. Ashworth could help speed up the process. It is true. Mr. Ashworth never offers to help or lift the burden

114

when Mom complains about phone calls or paperwork. He's always distracted us with more offers to make our stay here more comfortable. And it works. He always leaves Mom giddy.

"Christie?" Ash asks, pulling me out of my head. "Are you okay?"

"Mm-hmm," I mutter and busy myself with swimming to the edge.

I rest by the edge, gazing at the legs of deck chairs instead of focusing on the thoughts in my head. The water waves and splashes as Ash glides through the water behind me. I plant my hands on the tiles and make small ripples in the water. My nightshirt balloons around me, and after a few minutes, I turn around and press my back against the pool's edge.

Ash reclines against the opposite side of the pool with his elbow bent against the edge tiles. He brushes a hand against his drenched hair, and deep inside me, I wish it were my hand. Before I can think twice, I push off the edge and swim toward him.

He grins. "Doing better?"

"Yep," I reply, stopping my momentum when I land in front of him.

His elbows remain bent against the tiles. My eyes run along his arms, and I envision him wrapping his arms around me and pulling me close. I bite my lip and find his melancholy eyes.

"Is your mind still on your family?" I ask.

"Sorry, I'm trying to take my mind off it."

"Don't apologize. I'm here to listen."

"I just want Vanessa to see my point of view," Ash blurts. "It's irritating. She's so worried about stepping on anyone's toes, she's refusing to do anything."

I move to the edge next to him. "I wish I could do something."

A breeze blows past us, sending a shiver through me.

Ash runs his hand along my arm and onto my shoulder. "You're cold?"

I smile, shrinking in the water. "I wasn't."

Ash pulls himself out of the water, and I'm flushed with heat as his abs glisten against the water and lights. With embarrassment, I dip my gaze to the tiles and watch his feet move to a towel.

"I won't look," Ash says.

I look up as I reply, "Huh?"

Ash stands by the pool steps, a towel wrapped around his hips, and holds the other towel out wide.

"I'll look away," Ash says and turns his head to the side.

"Oh, umm," I stutter.

He stands like a statue. As I clutch my chest, I wish he'd just left the towel on the tiles and walked away. He continues to stand there. Silent. Hurry up, Christie. He's waiting, and it's got to be cold in the breeze.

I force myself up the steps and step into the towel.

"Thanks." I grasp the towel, and Ash loosens his grip.

I wrap the towel around my body-hugging, heavy, and dripping nightshirt.

Ash's eyes run up and down my body, and he grins. "All good?"

Even though I'm blushing with red-hot cheeks, I shiver as I reply, "Yes."

Ash scoops up my robe and drapes it around me.

"Aren't you cold?" I ask with chattering teeth.

"Not for long," Ash replies, pressing his hand into my back. "Come to the pool house with me."

The pool house is stark white with floor-to-ceiling windows and large French doors. Inside, the oversized lounges, with overstuffed cushions, occupy the front room. Glass tables scatter around the lounges, and we approach a marble-topped kitchenette. It's easy to imagine cocktails being prepped during lazy afternoons and relaxing after a swim.

"There are two bathrooms," Ash asks, leading the way. "Do you want to take a shower? Get warmed up and rid of the chlorine smell."

"Sounds like a good idea."

Ash shows me to a bathroom, which houses carved stonework that

116

shrouds the shower. He runs the hot water and shows me where to find the towels.

"Some clothes and bathrobes are hanging in the closet. There's a hairdryer in the cupboard," he adds.

"Thanks," I reply, and before he walks out, I grab his wrist and say, "I don't want you to think you can't talk to me about what's bothering you. We keep getting distracted from talking about your problems. I don't mean for that to happen."

"It's okay. I never talk about this stuff outside of my family." Ash looks back at me with an apprehensive smile. "In all honesty, I'm jealous of your family."

"Really?"

"Yep. You're all so close. It's clear that your parents love you."

"Your parents love you too."

"But your parents adore you. They treasure you and trust you."

"Yours trust you to take over a company."

"Not yet." Ash lets out a frustrated sigh. "I can't think about the future. The present is too infuriating. Vanessa doesn't understand that traveling to the other side of the world means she's playing our parents' games."

"Ash, you're shivering," I say with a gasp. I nudge him toward the shower. "Get in. The water will be roasting."

Ash slides behind the stone wall, tossing his towel and underwear to the floor.

Before I leave the room, I ask, "Does Vanessa side with your mom?"

"No, she doesn't take either side," Ash calls as steam fills the room. "She spends her days with a tutor, waiting to see if Mom will change her mind on her own. She doesn't say how she feels. She lives with Mom but never talks to her."

"So you call Vanessa to convince her to talk to your mom?"

"Yeah. She doesn't listen to me, and I just end up the bad guy. Now,

I'm always fighting with Dad. I look like the brat, while Vanessa looks like a saint."

"Your dad's not mad at Vanessa for leaving?"

"He just says Vanessa is doing what she feels is right," Ash calls over the running water. "Dad always deflects. That's why I was so mad the first morning I saw you. We'd been fighting nonstop for a week, and then he brought in a buffer. He said I can't talk about Mom when your family is around."

"Ash, that's terrible," I say, stepping closer so he can hear me over the running water. "I want you to know I'm fine with you voicing your opinions with me in the room. If it's the only chance you get with your father, take it."

"Thanks, but it's more complicated than that."

I frown, not knowing what to say, and the water turns off.

I hold my robe closer, squeezing the wet towel and nightshirt against my skin. My mouth hangs open as I'm stuck, twisting toward the door and unable to move.

"Christie," Ash calls. "Are you still there?"

"Uh, umm, ah... oh..."

Ash laughs. "It's okay. I just wanted to ask you to hand me a towel."

My body turns tomato red. I grasp a towel and hold it past the stone wall. I turn my head so I don't see anything.

He takes hold of the towel. "Thanks."

I turn to the doorway, and footsteps follow me.

"I'll leave you to it," he says from behind me, which makes me stop in place.

He slides by me, towel wrapped around his middle, and I dash to the shower so I don't take in any more of his naked torso.

I enter the shower and turn on the water. I throw my layers to the ground, feeling free.

After a perfect temperature shower, I towel off and find something to wear. A white kaftan hangs in the closet, but it seems see-through. I rummage a little further and find the thickest, fluffiest robe I've ever felt. I pull on the kaftan and layer it with the robe.

Oh my gosh. Yes. Heaven.

I towel off my hair and consider reaching for the hair dryer, but then I yawn, and my eyes grow heavy. I have zero energy to worry about my hair. I scrunch the towel through it one more time and then leave the bathroom.

Ash is in the main room. His fingers glide through his blow-dried hair, and he's also in a plush robe.

"Hey," he says with a grin. "Did you find everything okay?"

I nod. "Yes. I'm just not in the mood to pick up the hair dryer. Is that okay?"

"Sure. Your hair looks good wet, anyway."

"I hope it wasn't weird I was in the bathroom when you were in the shower," I ramble and wish I'd stop talking. "It's just, I wanted you to feel you could talk if you wanted to."

"I'm glad I got it off my chest," Ash says, sitting on a lounge. "Don't panic, Christie. If I wanted you out, you'd know."

"I believe you," I say, moving closer to the lounge. "Do you feel better?"

Ash rubs his forehead. "Better than before. But my messed-up family is always on my brain."

I sit beside him and gently touch his shoulder. He releases his forehead and gazes at my hand.

"Talk to me," I whisper. "I'm here for you."

"The video chat at dinner," he murmurs. "It was unbearable."

I remove my hand as he hunches forward. "How so?"

"My parents are complete fakes. Do you remember when my mom made a crack about having to stay up late to speak to Dad?" Ash shifts in place. "Mom makes excuses during her daytime hours not to talk to Dad. She plays games more than he does."

"Ash, I'm sorry you're caught up in the middle of this. Families shouldn't be this difficult."

"Dad only got Mom involved in the video call at dinner so she could convince your parents to send you to the academy." He sits up and turns toward me. "Mom arranges all our school stuff. She agreed to help Dad because it was good for business, and the money Dad makes benefits her."

I look down and furrow my brow. "So sending me to Ashworth Academy was an advantage to your dad? I knew it." I look up at Ash with determination. "Why is your dad so intent on keeping my dad around?"

He shakes his head. "No idea. But maybe I can find out."

I nod. "I need to know what's going on."

"Is this the first time your parents haven't kept you in the loop?"

"Yes, and it's killing me."

Ash slides a hand over my hair and eyes me with concern. "Do they know about your nightmares?"

His question takes me off guard. I wanted to focus on him and leave my issues for the next time I go to sleep.

I clear my throat and say with a mild squeak, "They know I haven't been sleeping well."

"Can't you talk to them about it?"

"I don't want them to worry. I can't tell them I'm awake at night because I'm too afraid to go to sleep."

Ash plays with a wet curl beside my face. A hint of a smile brightens his face. "But you can tell me?"

I rub my lips together. "Is that okay?"

He nods. "Of course it is. Do you want help sleeping? I have sleeping pills in my bathroom."

I shake my head, wincing. "I don't want to take sleeping pills."

"They help. There's no shame in taking them."

"What if I still have the nightmares and I can't wake up?"

Ash bites into his bottom lip as he contemplates that. "That would be messed up. Maybe you should see a doctor?"

I shake my head. "The dreams have to pass. I need to tell my brain I'm out of the house and that I'm safe."

Ash's hand slides over mine as he whispers, "It's okay to get help."

"I'll think about it," I say in a small voice. "The dreams just feel so real. Tonight, I dreamed my bedroom here was on fire."

Ash winces and rubs my arm. "That's awful. Does it feel real when you wake up?"

"Yeah. I wake up in a cold sweat. It takes a while to realize it was a dream."

"You can't go through this every night."

"I get out of bed to take my mind off it. But that doesn't always help. The hallway lights have an orange tinge. It reminds me of the fire in the darkness."

"I'll tell Murphy to change the bulbs or the shades," Ash is quick to reply. "Whichever causes the orange."

"No, don't," I say, shyly pulling away from his embrace. "I don't want to create work for anyone."

"Christie, you need to stop thinking you're trouble. Murphy will organize maintenance to change them out. It's his job."

My stomach flips, and words are rambling out of my mouth before I can stop them. "I don't want to seem like a charity case or like I need handouts."

Ash sucks in a breath, and his face falls. "I never should have said that stuff. I was just mad that Dad brought in a new distraction. I just wanted you and your family out of the house. Despite how mesmerizingly pretty I found you."

I suck in a fast breath and almost choke. "What?" I croak.

His hand presses against my cheek, and his thumb swipes under my eye. "I don't want you to feel scared. I hate knowing you're having trouble sleeping, and there's nothing I can do."

"I don't want you feeling alone," I say, and our closeness gives me goose bumps. "Can I do anything to help with your family?"

"Tell my mom to come home?" he says with a hint of a laugh.

"I can try."

Ash smiles, and his hand combs into my damp hair. "So if you've always been invisible," he whispers, "does that mean no one's ever kissed you?"

A shiver runs down my spine. The light dances in his spectacular eyes, and my lips rub together.

Without answering, I lean into him. Crinkles form around his eyes the way they do when he's smiling, and then they close. I close mine too, and then a warm and gentle sensation pushes against my lips.

Ash's lips press against mine. Our first kiss. My first kiss ever. Electric tingles spread across my pouty lips. Never would I dream a kiss would feel so good, especially from a guy like this. He is not the guy I pictured for this moment. This isn't my ideal situation, but I wouldn't give him up for the world. He's been so raw and vulnerable with me tonight. I have my missing puzzle pieces, and now this mysterious guy makes sense. All his bored, sullen, and agitated moments now have a purpose. Ash has so much sadness, and I want to help take it away.

Our lips pull apart, and I rub mine together as if tasting his kiss all over again.

"Wow," he whispers.

"Really?" I ask bashfully. "It was my first time."

"Best kiss ever," he says and leans in to kiss my nose.

It sends me into giggles, and Ash takes my hand.

"You really are special, Christie Klein. I want to make sure you always feel that way."

"I'm so happy for the fresh start here," I whisper. "I now wish I had been braver at my old school and made friends. Although, I'm glad there's no one left behind who misses me."

"I bet people miss you," Ash says, and our fingers interlace. "I bet you were more liked than you realize."

122

I cuddle into him, resting my head on his shoulder. "I don't want you feeling sad anymore. I don't want you feeling like you have no options but anger. You have me to talk to. I'll always be here for you."

"Thank you," he replies and leans his face in close.

Instinctively, I close my eyes. His lips press onto mine with an extra layer of passion. The electricity runs down to my toes, making them curl. My hands move from his shoulders and into his hair. His lips move to my cheek, and my eyes open from the pleasure of his touch.

"Wow," I whisper.

Ash laughs under his breath. "Better this time?"

I link my hands behind his neck. "Yes. I didn't think that was possible."

He grins. "We have to make sure every kiss keeps getting better."

Settling into the comfort of his warmth, heartbeat, and plush robe, I sigh with happiness. "I can deal with that."

Thirteen

I wake to a rocking sensation. As I squint my eyes open, daylight filters in around me.

"Huh?" I mumble.

I rub my eyes and realize Ash is moving beside me.

Oh geez. Did I fall asleep beside him?

Ash leans over me with a beautiful smile. "Hey," he whispers.

I smile, heart thudding. "Hi."

"Did you sleep okay?"

I nod. "Yes. I wouldn't have slept a wink if I'd gone back to my room."

Ash leans in and kisses my cheek. "Good. I'm glad."

Butterflies flutter in my stomach. What a way to wake up!

Ash flicks his smartwatch in front of his face, and his eyes widen.

"Oh crap."

"What?"

He lowers his arms, and his teeth grit, although the corners of his mouth are curling.

"Umm," he begins. "We are super late."

"What?" I gasp, shooting up to sitting, and clunk my forehead against Ash's.

"Ow!" he yelps, clutching his forehead and falling backward by my feet.

"Ash," I squeak, grasping for his arm. "I'm sorry. Are you okay?"

Ash splutters a laugh, rubbing his forehead. He sits up and nods. "Yeah, I'm okay. I wasn't ready for such brutality in the morning."

My shoulders bunch to my ears, and I sit back. "I'm sorry."

"I'm kidding," he teases, clutching my hands. "I'm okay."

My eyes fall on his watch. "So what time is it?"

"Nine thirty."

"Double crap." I gasp, squeezing his hands.

"Ouch," he says with a laugh. "Christie, it's okay. We both needed sleep. School's already begun, so we'll just take the day off."

"But it's my first week."

"You wanted a day off before starting your first day."

My hands go limp in his. "True. But my mom..."

"Don't panic," he says and swoops in to kiss my cheek. Oh boy. "I'll do damage control. You'll be fine. Trust me, I'm good at this part."

"I... I don't... like... getting into trouble," I stammer, bottom lip trembling. "I... I never... never get in trouble."

"Hey," Ash whispers, running his hands up my arms to the sides of my face. Warmth ripples under my skin and replenishes my energy to pump blood through my veins. "It'll be okay. You won't get into trouble. I'll make sure of it. If there's any heat, I'll take care of it."

"I don't want you to get into trouble either."

His lips press onto mine, causing every thought to jump out of my

125

head.

"I told you," Ash says, "I don't want you feeling afraid. I'll take care of you."

I nod in his hands. "And I don't want you to be alone."

Ash slides off the lounge and gives my hand a final squeeze. "I got this."

He moves to the rear wall toward a phone similar to the one that hangs in the kitchen. He looks at his watch again and mutters to himself, "I wonder where Murphy will be right now."

He then shakes his head and smiles as if a light bulb flashed above his head.

Ash hits a single button on the phone and holds it by his ear as he leans against the wall.

"Yeah, hi, Claudia," Ash says into the phone.

This beat, my heart jumps a little less into my throat. Claudia is my guardian angel. I'm so glad Ash called her first.

I brush a hand over my hair and swipe beads of sweat in my hairline. Geez, Mom must be frantic. I didn't arrive at breakfast, and I wasn't in my room. My gut twists in on itself. I feel awful!

"No, she's with me," Ash says into the phone. He twists the cord of the phone around his fingers as he smiles at me. "Yep, she's okay. Where's her mom?"

Ash listens to the other end of the phone line and then replies, "Ah, okay. Can you tell her Christie is okay? And where's Murphy? Uh-huh... Okay. I'll meet him there. Can you ask him to bring Christie's mom with him?"

My heart palpitates. My mom? With Murphy? Meeting Ash? Like an ambush?

"Thanks, Claudia," Ash says and hangs up the phone. He tilts his head at me. "There goes the panic again."

My hands tremble in my lap, and I stammer, "How can I not?"

He walks toward the lounge with a serious expression. "Do you

126

trust me?"

I look up into his beautiful brown eyes. I sigh and repeat, "How can I not?"

A grin fills half his face. "Wait here," he says. "I promise it'll all work out."

"Okay," I murmur and watch him hurry out of the pool house.

Oh boy. What have I gotten myself into? Last night flashes through my mind. The pool, the shower, the kiss... The kiss. My toes curl just thinking about his lips on mine.

I rub my lips together and fall back against the lounge.

Oh, Ash.

Will the first brave thing I do be the best thing to ever happen to me? Or is it wrong to get mixed up with Ash?

Time might have rushed past, but for me, it stood still. My mind stayed on Ash and his strong arms that held me all night.

"Christie?" My mother's voice breaks through my daydream.

I shoot up to sit and turn toward her voice. She rushes into the room and scoops me into a hug.

"Oh, honey," she gasps. "Are you okay?"

I latch on to her, heart racing. "Yes, I'm fine."

"Ash told me to find you in here," Mom says, stroking my hair. "He said we need to talk. There's something I should know."

Mortified, I suck in a sharp breath.

"Sweetheart," Mom says softly, cupping my face and staring into my eyes. "Why didn't you tell me? I thought we didn't have secrets?"

"What?"

"Why didn't I know about the extent of your nightmares?" Mom says, eyes welling. "You should have let me know you couldn't sleep."

I exhale and slouch. "He told you about that?"

"Honey, you should know you can talk to me."

I flop my head against her shoulder. "I do. I just didn't want to worry you."

"It worries me more if you are keeping this all to yourself," she says, rubbing a circle on my back. "But I'm glad you opened up to Ash."

I sigh, a smile creeping across my lips. "Me too."

"Christie?" Mom asks, intrigue dripping off the syllables. "Your voice has an interesting tone."

I lift my head and blush as I meet Mom's eyes. "I was wrong about him. Ash is wonderful."

"You look happier than you've been in days," Mom says. "I'm glad you had someone with you last night. But I wish you had revealed the full extent sooner. You're having nightmares about the fire?"

Despair wells in my gut as I try not to let the images form in my mind. "Yep."

"Honey, it makes me sick to my stomach that your dreams are scaring you. I'm so sorry. You could have opened up yesterday when I said I was struggling."

My frown sinks in hard. "I know. I'm sorry."

Mom pushes back one of my curls as tears sparkle in her eyes. "Don't apologize, honey. It's a hard thing to talk about. But I'm here for you, and so is your dad."

At that, a tear pricks my eye. I fold my arms and grumble, "Yeah, right. I never see Dad."

"I know. He's trying. It'll be different once he's settled into his new position."

"Why don't I know what his new position is?" I question.

"It's no big secret," Mom replies. "He'll tell you his new title. It's just the project that is confidential. Besides, you know me with computer stuff. It goes in one ear and out the other. Too boring to listen to everything he says."

I wipe my eyes dry. "Okay. I'll ask him about it once I get some one-on-one time with him."

Mom smiles. "He'll love that."

"Sorry for not talking to you about this sooner," I say. "But I'm glad it's off my chest now."

"Me too. Do you remember the group Mrs. Ashworth was putting me in touch with?"

I nod in reply.

"They are coming here this afternoon for a meeting and to include me in their latest fundraiser."

"A snooty women's fundraiser?" I tease. "Sounds like a ball."

"All jokes aside, I think we should do it together," Mom says, wrapping an arm around me. "Many of the women bring their daughters along. It'll be good for us."

"Okay," I reply and surprise changes Mom's expression. She was waiting for me to say no, like usual. "I told Ash last night, I wish I'd been braver. You know, at my old school... I wish I'd push myself to make friends."

"I think it's wonderful you and Ash have become friends."

I bite into my lip and shy away.

"What is it?" Mom asks, with concern coloring her face.

I giggle, and it eases Mom's tension. "Umm," I begin. "I was just wondering if you'd be okay with how friendly Ash and I've become."

Mom's brow furrows. "Wait. You and Ash were in this room together all night?"

I inhale sharply. "*Mom.* It wasn't anything sinister. We just both couldn't sleep."

I cup a hand over my mouth as my cheeks flame red.

Mom's forehead crinkles as a smirk appears. "Christie?"

I lower my hand and blurt, "We kissed."

Mom gasps. "What? How did this happen?"

I shrug and joke, "I dunno, our lips touched."

Mom shakes her head, grinning. "No, I know that. You hated him last weekend... and now you've kissed him?"

I raise my palm. "I don't know what to say. We got to know each other at school. Last night, we opened up. He's more than he appears on the surface."

"I'm shocked and happy," she says and kisses my forehead. "My little girl is growing up."

"*Mooom*," I whine. Ugh. Mortifying.

"I'm just delighted for you. But no more alone time in the middle of the night."

"Yes, Mom." Does it count if it's the early hours of the morning? "And, I promise, I'll try to be friendly at your meeting this afternoon."

"I know you will. And I'll try to ensure time for you and your dad."

"At least we are living with Dad," I say and then lower my voice. "Did you know Mr. Ashworth and his wife have split up?"

Mom nods. "Tom opened up about it at lunch on Sunday. It's so sad. He says the tension between him and Ash has never been so hostile."

"Ash said he stayed behind to save his family. He wanted his mom and sister to stay with him."

Mom frowns, hugging her middle. "Poor guy. It's terrible for a family to go through it. They all must be deeply hurting."

Mom and I leave the pool house and enter the mansion. Inside, Mom asks if I want to get breakfast, but I decline and choose to go upstairs to change into fresh clothes. Oops. I left my soaking pajamas in the pool house bathroom. Hopefully, someone who works here finds them, and they magically appear in Vanessa's bathroom, cleaned with no questions asked.

"Everything work out okay?" Ash says as I turn into the hall of the kids' wing.

Resting against his bathroom doorframe, he has his arms crossed at his middle and his leg tucked behind him. He's in a light blue button-down shirt, dark gray trousers, and brown suede shoes. And, of course, his hair is impeccably styled.

I clasp my hands in front and glide toward him. "Yes, thanks to you."

"See," he says, pushing off the wall and stepping toward me.

130

"Never helps to panic." He winks. "It always helps to trust Ash."

I giggle and meet him in a hug.

"Thanks, Ash," I whisper into his chest.

His chin rests against my head. "No problem."

"Miss Klein," Claudia's voice calls through the hall.

Ash and I pull out of the hug, and I turn around to find her bouncing frame hurtling toward us.

"Miss Klein, I was so worried when I could not find you this morning," Claudia says, panting. "I thought I would wake you for breakfast, but your bed was empty. I didn't know what to think."

"I'm okay. I'm sorry I worried you."

"You needed some fresh air, Master Ashworth said," Claudia says, forcing her breathing to slow.

"My bad," Ash says. "It's my fault you got startled, Claudia."

Claudia smiles at Ash. "With you, I know not to worry. I didn't think Miss Klein was sneaky like you."

Claudia giggles as her eyes fixate on Ash. I'm smiling as I pivot between the two.

"You wrap everyone around your finger," I say to Ash.

He replies with a wink.

"Miss Klein, can I help you get ready this morning?" Claudia offers.

"I'm fine on my own. If that's okay," I reply. "And you can just call me Christie."

Claudia's smile expands. She pinches my cheek and then turns and walks away.

"Huh?" I puff out.

"She can't call you that," Ash remarks.

I turn to him quizzically.

"Murphy is head of the household, and he'd never allow it," Ash elaborates.

"At least she knows how I feel," I reply. "You know I'm not a fan

131

of formality."

Ash swoops in and kisses my cheek. "You're gonna have to get used to it," he whispers. "I'm never letting you go."

I giggle and shy away as I blush.

"I'll let you get ready," Ash says and leaves to walk down the hall.

"Bye," I whisper, mid-giggle.

He looks over his shoulder as he walks. His smile is gorgeous, and he blows me a kiss.

He is heaven.

I float into my bedroom and flop backward on my bed. My mind forms an artwork, and my veins enliven with enthusiasm. Once I'm dressed, I dart to the third floor and work on new artwork to give to Ash.

My fingers twitch with excitement. I can't wait to see his face once it's completed.

Fourteen

The smile won't leave my face after working on the new artwork for the past few hours. I took inspiration from the bench Ash and I sat on outside school when I was too chicken to play hooky. It was the day I saw a lighter side to Ash. He was no longer the mean boy, eyeing me like an enemy invader. The bench helped break down walls between us. It brought us to a place that made tender moments like last night possible.

I painted the bench surrounded by a beautiful floral garden. The seat is empty. I'm not sure what to depict about my relationship with Ash. It's hard to say if this relationship will grow deeper or not.

I took a break from painting to have lunch with my mom. We enjoyed the sun on the back lawns, and I got a thrill when Ash joined us. Now I wash the paint from my hands, ready for the society meeting.

"Wow, you look exquisite," Ash says as I step into the hall.

My pink dress balloons out at the waist with a top layer of tulle. A pink ribbon holds my ponytail in place, and I bashfully pull at the sleeves of my yellow cardigan.

"Thanks," I mumble as my cheeks strain in my happy smile.

"Did you have fun painting?"

I rub the space over my heart. The interest ignited in his eyes sends me floating.

"Yes. Thank you for the supplies."

"Again, you're more than welcome. Are you ready for afternoon tea with a gaggle of snobs?" Ash jokes, clasping my hands.

"I'll try to get through it."

His thumbs rub against the top of my hands in a delightfully soothing way. "You'll be fine. They're not scary. They're just boring."

I laugh. "Thanks, that helps."

"I'm going to the theater," Ash says. "You should come down afterward."

My heart swells. "I will."

"And, please, don't tell anyone I'm here," Ash says, exhaustion oozing from him. "I'm forced to make an appearance when my mother is here, and it's always unbearable. If anyone asks about me, tell them I went into town."

"Okay, I will. You're not filling me with confidence to get through this."

Ash pecks my cheek with a light kiss. "You'll be fine. I'm just avoiding the swarm of nosy women."

I giggle and lean into him for a cuddle. "I can't wait for it to be over. I want more time with you."

"Hopefully, they won't drone on forever. You can always excuse yourself for the bathroom and then escape to the theater."

I pull out of the hug. "No, I have to show Mom I'm ready to make an effort."

Smiling, Ash caresses my face, and his eyes sparkle. "Good luck with being brave."

"Thank you."

Ash walks me to the staircase that lands by the parlor. He doesn't walk down with me. Instead, he turns back to take a less conspicuous route to the theater. His deep wish to avoid this bunch makes me laugh.

"Miss Klein," Murphy says, greeting me by the parlor door. "Refreshments are on the table inside. Guests are mingling before the meeting commences."

I thank Murphy and make my way inside the room. Chatter bounces off the walls as I take in the new faces. I pivot, attempting to spot Mom, but embarrassment grabs me first. I move toward the punch station and busy myself with filling a glass. Hopefully, Mom will find me, and I can avoid taking the lost sheep role.

"You look like you don't want to be here as much as me," a girl says. She stands beside me with marvelous ginger hair and a smattering of freckles.

I chuckle as I put the ladle down. "It's just a little out of my comfort zone," I admit.

"Mom has pulled me to plenty of these things," she says, "and they are never comfortable."

Her kind smile welcomes me, and I choose to be brave.

I hold out my hand. "Hi, I'm Christie."

She takes my hand. "I'm Meghan. I don't think I've seen you around before."

"We just moved here," I reply. "My mom spoke with Mrs. Ashworth, and she put this together."

She grins. "Oh, so your mom is who I have to blame for this."

I laugh and appreciate the way Meghan jokes

"Do you go to Ashworth Academy?" I ask, hoping she says yes because she seems like a cool person to befriend.

"No," she says, smile shrinking. "I used to, but I'm homeschooled now."

"You're kidding," I say with a smirk. "I was just talking with someone about wanting to be homeschooled. Why did you leave the academy? Is there something wrong with the school?"

Other than nasty girls and belligerent teachers?

Meghan sucks in a hasty breath and twists her lips before answering. "No, I had to stop going to school because I kept fainting."

I set the glass on the table before I drop it. "Oh my gosh. I'm so sorry. Are you okay now?"

Meghan shrugs. "Okay, in relative terms. I have a disease that gives me chronic fatigue." She gestures to the crowd of ladies. "The benefit they're planning is a fundraiser for my condition. There's no cure, so they're raising money for research."

I cup a trembling hand over my mouth. "I feel so bad. I had no idea."

Meghan grins warmly. "Don't sweat it. It's no big secret. That's why we're here. Plus, you're new. It must be hard getting to know everyone."

"To be honest, I haven't met many people. This is one of the first real conversations I've had."

"Have you met Ash?" Meghan blurts, curiosity seeping across her face.

Don't blush. Don't blush. Don't blush.

I nod. "Yes, I have."

Meghan lifts on her tippy-toes and cranes her neck toward the open doorway. "Do you know if he's here? I'd love to see him again."

A small jab penetrates my gut. "Ah, no. He's out at the moment. Are you and he friends?"

Meghan giggles and plays with her long, soft red hair. "We were never super close when I was at school, but I hope to change that."

A clamminess hits me behind the neck, runs up the sides of my face, and camps on my forehead. I pivot my gaze so Meghan doesn't see the stress overwhelming my body. My eyes wander through the crowd, and

136

then I freeze. My body is moments from shutting down as a figure moves through the crowd.

Hope Fisher.

"Oh my gosh." The words whoosh out of me.

"What is it?" Meghan asks, searching the crowd.

I turn away and cup a hand around my eyes. "Just someone I don't want to make eye contact with."

Meghan smirks. "It looks like you were staring at my sister."

I lower my trembling hand, and my lip quivers as I stutter, "Who... Who... is your sister?"

"Hope. Do you know her?"

My heart plummets to the pit of my stomach. Despair swirls around my internal organs, and I'm about to keel over from the heavy information.

A sour frown pulls at Meghan's mouth. "Are you not a fan of Hope?"

I force myself upright and fan my chest. "No, it's not that. I just didn't know you two are related."

"We are more alike than it appears on the surface," Meghan says with a laugh, playing with her hair.

When I wished there weren't other girls like Hope Fisher in this town, I wasn't fearing a sister.

Meghan taps a finger to her lips, which grows into a bashful smile. She bites her nail, and then whispers, "Hope is the reason I want to see Ash again."

My insides contort harder.

Hope's words growl in my mind. *"Ash is spoken for."*

"See, there was this party," Meghan continues, leaning in to reveal juicy gossip. "And she and Ash kissed."

Blood drains from my head and rushes to my feet.

"Hope said it was the best kiss of her life," Meghan gushes. "You know, an out-of-this-world kiss."

137

I asked Ash if he and Hope were an item... Ash lied to me. How could he do that?

Meghan's eyes enlarge as she shifts to daydream mode, her lips rubbing together. "I couldn't get Hope's story out of my head. Ash is all I think about."

Ash's words from this morning play in my mind. *"Best kiss ever."* Does he say this to every girl?

Meghan squeals as she fills a glass with punch. "I just can't wait to see him. I'm always hoping for a chance with him."

"Hope and Ash?" I murmur.

Meghan bats a hand, laughing. "Oh my gosh. Do you think she tested him out for me?"

As Meghan continues to giggle behind a cupped hand, Hope emerges from the crowd and lands by her sister.

Hope latches onto Meghan's shoulder, saying, "We're about to begin. Come and sit with Mommy and me."

Acid escapes my stomach and leaps upward. I gulp and push it down.

"Oh, hi," Hope says, glaring at me. "Trying to get into high society, are we?"

"I should find my seat," I squeak timidly.

I slink past Hope and hurry toward the vacant seat by Mom.

"You were talking with Meghan," Mom says with a sympathetic smile. "Lovely girl. It's so unfair she's battling such a debilitating disease."

I nod and settle into the seat. "Agreed. It's unfair."

The meeting begins, and Mrs. Fisher takes the lead. She formally introduces Mom as the newest member of their group, which is followed by a warm round of applause. Mrs. Fisher runs through the tasks and makes room for something Mom can undertake. I hear the event is two weeks away, but nothing more.

I can't think of anything besides what Meghan said.

Hope and Ash kissed. A Shakespeare-level kiss that can make the world stop spinning.

I asked Ash if anything happened between him and Hope, and he said no. Who am I supposed to believe? Why would Meghan lie to a complete stranger? Why would Hope lie to her sister? Why would Ash lie to me, especially when he's been so blunt in the past?

Maybe Ash thought I wouldn't find out about his fling with Hope. From meeting Hope, I can tell she can't keep her mouth shut.

My skin crawls, and I jolt in my seat. Eww. That mouth has been on Ash's. Gross!

And it was a fantastic kiss? It was enjoyable!

I retch and fidget in my seat, causing Mom to elbow me in the ribs.

"What's up?" Mom mutters out the side of her mouth.

I shake my head, ridding the images of Hope and Ash from my mind. "Nothing," I mumble. "Sorry."

"We need a few more items for the silent auction," Mrs. Fisher says, reading from her clipboard. "Any suggestions?"

"I don't know if this is appropriate," Mom pipes up. She squeezes my shoulder and announces, "My daughter, Christie, is a fantastic artist. Perhaps she could create a piece and enter it in the auction."

I squirm under the view of every eye.

"We are looking for more than amateur pieces," Mrs. Fisher says flatly. "No offense, dear."

I want to utter, "None taken," but Mom is off her seat, thrusting her phone at Mrs. Fisher.

"She is beyond amateur status," Mom says and scrolls through the gallery of my prior work. "I uploaded everything she's ever done to the cloud. Take a look."

Mrs. Fisher and two other ladies view the images. The other two ladies *ooh* and *aah* at the images, and Mrs. Fisher nods.

"Unfortunately, the fire destroyed all this hard work," Mom says, which is followed by a round of awes.

Mrs. Fisher looks at Mom and then at me. With pinched cheeks, she says, "We'd love you to submit a piece to the auction."

Meghan steals a glance my way, eagerly grinning and lightly clapping.

"Excellent," Mom says, giddy as she takes her seat.

"*Mom*," I grizzle under my breath. "I've never had my work on display before."

"You've never lived in a mansion and made friends before, either," Mom says with a giggle.

I huff and sit back in my chair.

The rest of the meeting hums along, and Mom volunteers to oversee the flower arrangements. Again, she praises me to the group for my flair for color and eye for detail. Seriously, Mom, stop saying things that make everyone look at me.

When the meeting ends, I tell Mom I'm meeting Ash. The bonus is avoiding the Fishers. I can't even look at Hope. The thought of her lips on Ash's will put me off food for a month.

I walk into the theater, and Ash pauses the game. He sits up in his reclined seat and beams a smile at me.

"How'd it go?" he asks. "Did they bore you to tears?"

"It was fine," I say, taking the steps to his row. "I met Meghan Fisher."

"Oh, yeah," Ash says. "The benefit they're planning is for her disease, right?"

"Yeah," I reply, moving between the seats toward him.

I sit next to him, and he clutches my hand. He lifts it to his lips with a kiss, and my heart pitter-patters.

Why must he look so irresistible right now?

"Guess what?" he whispers.

I try to rid the images of him and Hope materializing in my mind. "What?"

"I'm going to work with our dads tomorrow."

140

"Whoa. Seriously?"

He nods. "Yeah. Dad wants me to witness something they're working on. It's good news, right? Because then I can find out what ground-breaking thing your dad is doing."

My heart thuds. I should be over the moon, but my mind won't leave the last earth-shattering news.

"Christie?" he asks, lowering his posture and finding my eyes. "Are you okay?"

My eyes prick with tears, and I blurt, "Did you lie to me?"

His face falls with an off guard frown. "What?"

"I asked if you and Hope were an item. You said no."

"Because we weren't," he says, pulling away from me.

"Meghan told me you kissed Hope."

Ash's brow furrows like I made it up.

He rubs a thumb between his eyebrows and lets go when he says, "Wait. Is she talking about that stupid party?"

I bite into my lip, too scared to reply.

"It happened a few months after Vanessa left," Ash explains. "None of the girls bothered me when she was here. When Ness left, it was like my bodyguard had disappeared." Ash sighs, fidgeting in his seat. "I was stupid enough to be talked into playing spin the bottle. I leaned in for a quick peck, and Hope basically sucked my lips off. It wasn't pleasant."

I frown as I grumble the words, "According to Hope, it made the world stop spinning."

"She's lying."

"Well, Meghan thinks it's real, and she wants you."

"It'll never happen," Ash says rigidly. "I'm not interested in Meghan."

I stare into his mesmerizing brown eyes as his hand brushes my cheek and combs into my hair.

"I thought you'd know I'm not interested in any other girl," Ash whispers.

A shiver runs down my spine, and I want to melt into him. But I'm locked in place.

"So... Nothing... Nothing happened between you and Meghan?" I stammer.

"No way. I'd never be with Meghan."

Something sour leaps into my throat, and I grimace as I swallow it.

"Is it because of her disease?"

A horrified look seeps into Ash's expression. He pushes back in the chair and says, "No. No way. I'm not that shallow."

"Then what is it?"

"I've known Meghan all my life," Ash says. "She might seem sweet and innocent, but she's far from it. Her actions might be slower now, but she'll always be the same cruel girl."

I hunch in the seat, feeling gut-punched. "Oh, she seemed nice to me."

"Hope has been pushing me toward her sister for months. I haven't outright stopped it because of Meghan's condition. I didn't want to seem like a jerk." He huffs and then runs his hands along my shoulders. "But I like you, Christie. I'll make it clear so no one gets between us."

My heart leaps against my ribs. "Do you really like me more?"

Ash smiles and slides a hand behind my neck. "Of course, you beautiful girl."

I smile and lean into his kiss. My toes curl in my shoes, and something pulls me out of enjoying it. The gnawing feeling of another girl feeling this way with him.

He holds my face in his hands as his lips pull from mine. He whispers, "Want to be my date for the benefit?"

My heart accelerates as his breath tickles my skin. "Your date?"

He pushes his lips against mine, and my arms swoop around his neck. I press my body against his and am addicted to his warmth. I massage my palms between his shoulder blades and end the kiss with a nibble on his cheek.

Ash moans by my ear. "How could you think I'd have feelings for any other girl?"

At that, I grow limp against him. I kiss him by the ear, and whisper, "I'd love to be your date."

If there's one thing I need to do, it's believe Ash. If he said the kiss with Hope was bad, so be it.

Because why on earth should I believe Hope?

Fifteen

"What are you doing here?" I yell at Hope. "Why are you in my bedroom?"

I squint at her, and it's not Hope. They have the same hazel eyes, but it's Meghan with Hope's chestnut hair.

What is she playing at? She's disguising herself? She's picked a despicable person to become.

Hope's villainous laughter echoes through my bedroom. Something seals Meghan's mouth shut, and she stands frozen like a prisoner.

Hope appears from behind Meghan and saunters forward. In her hand, Hope shakes a box of matches.

Slick sweat coats my back, and my palms grow wet.

Hope lights a match, and the air grows thick. She holds the lit match to the end of her sister's hair.

"Wait! Don't!" I yell.

From the touch of the flame, Meghan's hair turns her normal ginger.

"Ash! Quick!" Hope yells. "Come and save her!"

Meghan's hair is on fire as my bedroom door bursts open. Ash barrels into my bedroom, fueled by adrenaline. His eyes never land on me. He goes directly to Meghan, who is now a ball of fire.

"Ash! No!" I scream.

Flames engulf Ash as his arms wrap around Meghan.

"Ash!" I scream. "Ash!"

Hope holds on to her belly with a wicked cackle. She drops to her knees, hyperventilating with laughter.

"No!" I wail. "Ash! Ash!"

I scream so loud, I shoot up in bed. I'm drenched in sweat, and the room is pitch black. The shock of waking hits me hard. I fall forward as tears flood my eyes.

My door opens, and Ash's voice calls my name. He races to the bed, and his arms wrap around me.

I hunch onto his chest, wetting his T-shirt with tears. His strong hands hold me. One presses into my back, and the other runs through my hair.

He kisses my forehead and whispers in a strained voice, "Another nightmare?"

I sob against him, unable to give more of an answer.

"Miss Klein? Christie?" Claudia yelps, racing into my room. "What's the matter? I heard screaming."

"She's okay," Ash says. "Can you get her a cold washcloth or something?"

"Of course," Claudia says and darts out of the room.

I hold on to the fabric of Ash's T-shirt, hoping to calm down and stop the tears. My breathing is heavy, and it's impossible to lift my head.

Not that it matters. Ash holds me against him, not wanting me to budge an inch.

Claudia returns with a cold cloth, and Ash holds it against my forehead. I feel so loved and comforted. Yet the fear still tugs at me.

"She'll be okay," Ash says to Claudia

"I can't do anything else?" she asks.

I want to thank her, but I have no energy to speak.

"I'll stay with her," Ash says.

"Okay," Claudia says. I feel her touch on my shoulder. "I hope you are better soon."

Claudia's footsteps exit the room, and my tears dry up. The coldness from the cloth is a welcomed relief.

"I'm so sorry," Ash whispers. "I hate that you're so scared."

"It was you…" I say in a garbled voice.

"It was me what?" he asks, stroking my hair.

I sniff hard, pressing my hands into his back. "In flames."

"Oh, Christie. I'm sorry. I'm okay," he soothes. "I'm okay, and I've got you."

I wrap my arms tighter around his midsection and sigh a heavy breath.

"Do you want to lie down?" he asks.

"No," I blurt, rocking my head against his shoulder.

"Okay," he whispers and holds me securely. "I'll stay here as long as you need."

My lip tremors as I ask, "Did I wake you up?"

"No. I was already awake."

"Talking to your sister again?"

"No, I've given up on her."

"Oh, I'm sorry."

"Don't be," he says, cuddling into me. "I had something more interesting to fill my time."

"What were you doing?" I ask.

"I can show you."

146

I unlatch myself from him, sit up, and gaze into his eyes.

"Where?" I murmur. "In your bedroom?"

He smiles in the most gorgeous way. "Yeah. Do you want to see?"

I nod, and Ash slides off the bed. He holds out his hand. I clasp it and follow him out of the room. The light in the hall is now a cozy cream color. It fills me with calm, and I give Ash's hand a snug squeeze.

We go into his bedroom, which is twice the size of mine. His king bed sits against one wall and opposes a large walk-in closet. His workspace is at the rear of the room. He has a large desk covered with papers, a laptop, and a wide monitor, plus thick textbooks. On the walls around his desk are large movie poster-sized frames. The frames hold images of galaxies, planets, and other incredible celestial images.

"Wow," I breathe out.

"It's out here," Ash says.

I follow his pointed finger to the balcony. Once outside, he shows me to a telescope.

"You're a stargazer?" I ask, intrigued.

Ash puffs a laugh as he touches the telescope. "That'd be putting it mildly." He beckons me closer. "Take a look."

I can't help smiling. Another mystery about Ash is revealed. How many more layers does this boy have?

I dip my knees and look into the eyepiece. A bright, creamy-white circle illuminates the pitch-black sky.

"Is that the moon?" I ask, glued to the telescope. As I focus on the shape, I notice two thick lines running across it.

"It's Jupiter," Ash says. "It's a perfect night to get a view."

"What?" I splutter. With my mouth ajar, I look at Ash for confirmation.

He smiles in the most delicious way. He nods, patting the telescope. "Yeah, it's Jupiter. Isn't it awesome that we can see it from here?"

"It's unbelievable," I whisper and move back to the eyepiece. As I focus on the planet, one word draws out of me. "Wow."

"I'm sorry that you woke up, but I'm so glad you're here," Ash whispers, lingering beside me. "I've always wanted to share this with someone."

"Oh, Ash." I sigh as I look up at him. I've never sounded sappier, but how could I avoid it? I'm standing on a moonlit balcony, planet gazing, with a sensitive and drop-dead-gorgeous boy.

Ash steps in close and gives me a soft kiss.

My knees knock, and I hold on to the telescope for support. I lean against it, and the tube falls. I stumble, lifting my weight, and slam my hands over my mouth.

"Oops," I mumble.

Ash laughs, tilting the tube upright. "Don't worry about it. No harm done."

"So," I say, fanning my face and stepping away from the telescope, "how long have you been into astronomy?"

Ash grins at the night sky. "Forever."

"That's so cool." A thought jumps into my head, making me ask, "But you told me you didn't have a passion."

"I said I didn't have a creative outlet," Ash corrects. "I didn't know what I'd take with me in a fire. I can't take the stars with me. They are always in place."

I clasp my hands under my chin. "Why haven't I heard you talk like this before?"

Ash rubs behind his neck, wincing. "Because it's always been private. I haven't included anyone in this stuff before because the guys I hang out with would think it's lame."

"So you keep it to yourself?"

"I have a mentor. He's a teacher, just not at the academy."

"Huh? What do you mean?"

Ash smirks and looks away as if embarrassed. "I unofficially take college classes."

I try to speak, but only a puff of air comes out. Too many thoughts

148

collide in my head, leaving only one word to say. "What?"

Ash grins and takes my hand. "Come inside and sit down. I'll explain."

Ash leads me inside the bedroom, and we sit on the edge of his bed.

"Remember your first morning at school?" Ash asks, massaging my hand in his. "When I ditched you... I met with my professor. It was a video chat, but he didn't have any other time available. I wasn't willing to give it up."

"Wait," I say, pausing for my brain to catch up. "You ditched me for academic reasons?"

"Yeah, I guess."

I shake my head and intertwine my fingers with his. "I can't believe you're studious. I assumed you were lazy."

Ash laughs. "Maybe I am. I get bored, or I've already passed my grade level. I have an eidetic memory. That's why I remember useless crap, like other people's class schedules."

"Oh, so you're super smart... Why do you still go to high school? It doesn't make sense."

"Because the longer I waste time at school, the longer it is until I'm forced to work for my dad."

"Oh," I say, frowning. "That sucks."

"Yeah, I'm just trying to avoid the ticking clock at this point."

"But you're smart," I say, rubbing his knee. "You deserve more than being bored and wasting your time."

"If I take an acumen test and get sent to college early," Ash says, sighing with exhaustion, "it'll only encourage Dad to put me on his path sooner. Right now, he's fine with me partying and being lazy. But all that goes away if someone points out I'm capable of more."

"I'm sorry, Ash. It's not fair."

"I don't want to run a commercial company," Ash says, pulling me into his embrace. "I want to live off my inheritance and build a home somewhere perfect for viewing space. I'd build an observatory bigger

149

than my house and spend my time documenting and researching."

"Do you want to do it alone?" I ask. "Instead of working for a research facility?"

"I've thought about it," Ash says, chewing his lip. "I've considered NASA and the possibility of becoming an aerospace engineer."

"Wow, Ash," I gush as his chin nestles against my forehead. "That's incredible."

"I like studying astrophysics," he replies. "That's my mentor's field. But I don't think I'm smart enough to work toward a doctorate."

"Don't say that," I say, cuddling him. "I hear in your voice how passionate you are about this stuff. You can do anything you set your mind to. I believe in you."

He blows out a breath and then kisses my forehead. "Thanks, Christie. I'm just scared about not measuring up. That's why building my own sounds like a better option. I can do whatever I want without a school telling me I'm not good enough."

"I get that. Fear is something I'm too familiar with," I say. "But aren't you always telling me to be brave? I didn't think Thomas Ashworth the third would ever be too chicken to go after what he wants."

Ash laughs, pulling out of the hug to find my eyes. "Did you just call me chicken, Klein?"

I raise an eyebrow and shrug with a veil of confidence. "If the shoe fits."

Ash slides his hands to the sides of my face and lays an affectionate and tender kiss on my lips. I kiss him back, gaining real confidence. My back straightens, and I sit taller.

As our lips part, another layer of mystery sheds from him. He is truly beautiful. His dark, soulful eyes penetrate mine, and the slow beat of my heart is perfect music.

"I've needed you around long before we met," Ash whispers.

I have no words to answer him. I'm not tongue-tied, or squeaky, or embarrassed.

I am strong, brave, and falling in love.

I sweep my arms around his neck and press my body against his. His hands cradle my lower back, and his face nestles into my hair and shoulder. Our hug is all the conversation we need, and moments turn into minutes.

When we both yawn, Ash suggests getting under the covers.

"I can go back to my room," I say, hoping he says no.

"No way," Ash replies. "I like waking up next to you."

We crawl into his oversized bed, and it's like falling into dreamland. I whisper, "Hmm. How is your bed even softer than mine?"

Ash snuggles behind me, pulling the down comforter over my shoulder. "Only the best in this room." He kisses the side of my head and says with a yawn, "Good night, Christie."

I fold my arms over his and melt into his embrace. With a happy smile and heavy eyelids, I reply, "Good night, Ash."

Sixteen

The beeping of a bedside alarm stirs me awake. Ash leans over me, turning off the annoying sound.

His lips press against my forehead with the most pleasing pleasure, and I smile in a daze.

"Good morning," he whispers with a groggy voice. "I've gotta get ready for work."

I squint my eyes open and turn my head toward the curtains covering the balcony doors. Not a sliver of light passes around the edges.

"But it's dark out," I mumble, reaching to cuddle him.

Ash laughs under his breath. He hugs me close but then pulls away.

"Sorry," he whispers. "I've gotta go."

"Boo." I yawn, stretching my arms over my head.

As I starfish on the bed, a genius idea sparks in my mind. I jolt up and throw off the covers. At the door, Ash does a double take.

"What are you doing?" he asks. "I thought you were still sleepy."

"If you're leaving with my dad," I say, moving toward the door, "it means he hasn't left yet, and there's a chance for me to talk with him uninterrupted."

Ash slides out of the doorway. "Go for it," he says with a happy grin. "Good luck."

I lift on tippy-toes and kiss his cheek. "Thanks. Have fun at work."

Ash rolls his eyes with a sarcastic reply. "I'm sure it'll be an absolute riot."

I move into the hall and hurry to the next wing. If I spend another second in Ash's presence, I will never let him leave. I haven't had a real conversation with Dad since we arrived at Ashworth Estate. Just five minutes with him, without Mr. Ashworth buzzing around us, will be amazing!

I hurry out of the kids' wing and toward my parents' suite. I almost trip over my feet in my haphazard jog. When I get to their door, I overzealously bang on it. I bounce in place as I listen for footsteps, and the door opens to Dad, straightening his tie.

"Hey, kiddo," Dad says as I leap into his arms. "You're up early."

"I took a chance," I say. "I need to see you and actually chat."

"Well, this is a nice surprise," he replies. "I apologize about us not having more time together since we've been here."

"I get that you're busy with your new job and all. I'm not mad. I just miss you."

"I miss you too," Dad says, stroking my hair. "This weekend. No excuses. It'll be our time."

"I'd love that," I say, moving out of the hug. "Even though we're in someone else's house, that doesn't mean we can't have family time. I'd love it if you, me, and Mom could watch a movie, or play a board game, or just have lunch together."

"I wholeheartedly agree," he says. "It's locked in for this weekend."

153

"Yay!" I squeal.

"What's all the noise about?" Mom asks, walking down the hall in her bathrobe.

Dad grins. "Just booking in some family time for this weekend."

"It's definitely in order," Mom says. She stops beside me and pats my shoulder. "How are you feeling today? Did you sleep better?"

I suck in a breath and remind myself I don't keep secrets from my parents. "To be honest," I begin, "I did have another nightmare."

"This is getting serious," Dad says, the lines on his face creasing with concern.

"I got back to sleep," I say, trying to make them feel better. "I do think I'm getting better."

"What about school?" Mom asks. "Are you able to go in?"

Dread slithers through me, and my stomach flips upside down.

"It won't hurt to have the rest of the week off," Dad says. "Start fresh next week. How does that sound?"

My body slouches with relief. "Amazing."

"This isn't an invitation for you to homeschool," Mom adds.

"I know, I know," I reply. "But the extra rest will help."

"I'll contact Ms. Thornesmith," Mom says, "and have her arrange homework to be sent here."

"Yay," I groan. "Anyway, it'll feel weird to go to school without Ash."

"That's right," Dad says with a snap of his fingers. "Ash is coming into the office with us. This will be interesting."

"He's eager to find out about your new role," I say to Dad, wiggling my eyebrows. "Unless you want to clue me in."

Dad laughs as he checks his collar and tie in the mirror. "I'd tell you, but you'd just glaze over. You've never taken an interest in computer science before."

"You weren't a billionaire's right-hand man before."

"I wouldn't classify myself as Tom's right-hand man."

"You're on a first-name basis with him."

"Because I live and work with him," Dad replies. He turns to me with a goofy grin and tousles my hair. "Just like you and your new friend Ash."

"Okay, whatever," I say, dodging Dad's hand. "I'm looking forward to this weekend."

Dad kisses my cheek. "Me too, kiddo."

He kisses Mom goodbye and continues down the hall.

"Do you want to come in?" Mom asks. "Or continue standing in the doorway?"

I drag myself into the room and flop onto their bed.

"What's with the attitude?" Mom asks.

"It's nothing. I just feel disconnected from Dad."

"I know. We're all still adjusting. You understand it's just as hard for him to be away from us?"

I nod, forcing myself to smile. "Yeah. I do."

"What will you do with yourself today?"

"I'd love to spend all day in the studio. I want to finish the painting for Ash."

"Come with me to the florist?"

My lips turn up. "The florist? Why?"

"My task for the benefit is picking out the flower arrangements," Mom explains. "I need your eye for color to back me up."

"Yeah, okay. That could be fun."

"Perfect. We will head out midmorning, and you can paint once we come home."

"I'll get dressed and meet you downstairs for breakfast."

Sam drove us to Victoria Falls this morning for our appointment at the florist. Mom and I window-shopped on the way and picked up vanilla lattes from a cute, rustic-style café.

The florist is a warehouse yet styled with chic French sophistication. We peruse the selections, and my mind pairs different

155

varieties by shape and color.

"Look," Mom says, nudging me. "It's Mrs. Fisher and her daughter."

The name Fisher submerges me in dread. The threat of Hope's presence has me on high alert.

"Hi, Christie," Meghan says, pulling me in for a hug. "How are you?"

I awkwardly hug her back, stammering, "I'm good. You?"

Sweet relief. It's the less scary Fisher.

"Yeah, I'm good, thanks," she says, releasing me. "My mom is a control freak. She wanted to check on your mom."

"Oh gosh, I hope Mom doesn't see it like that, or her feelings will get hurt." I nod at our moms and smile. "But look at her. She loves having a friend."

Meghan giggles. "Well, my mom loves being everyone's friend, so I'm sure they'll be fine."

We walk around a row of flowers, and I keep my eye out for something truly striking.

"So how is school?" Meghan asks, following. "Gotta be tough as the new girl in town."

"Well, I spent two days at school, and now I'm taking the rest of the week off. So I guess I'm glad to be out."

"Did Hope give you a hard time?"

I swallow hard. "No. Why do you ask?"

Meghan tosses her ginger hair over her shoulder with a knowing smile. "Because I know she can be a bit much sometimes. If she's given you trouble, I can tell her to lay off."

"Oh no, it's fine. I mean, Hope and I did have a misunderstanding, but Ash helped sort it out."

"Oh, that's so sweet of him," Meghan gushes. "I knew he was a great guy."

I swipe a hand against the back of my clammy neck. Sheesh. Can

156

this get any more awkward?

"I guess it's easy for him to defuse the situation when he and Hope are already such good friends."

I fidget with the hair sticking to my face, and reply, "They are?"

"Yeah, I mean, Ash and Luke are really good friends, and Luke is Hope's boyfriend. I think that's why Hope wants Ash and me to date, so we can double. That would be so freaking cute. Especially because I'm stuck at home all the time. I need my sister's help to coordinate a dating life."

I busy myself with examining flowers and mutter, "Mmm, that'd be tough."

"You have no idea," Meghan continues. "My life is dang boring. But at least you're out of school, too. We can pretend this is an after-school hang. It's a better alternative than a dull benefit thing."

"You hate being home all the time?"

"It's like I stopped existing," Meghan says, the intensity growing in her eyes. "All my friends stopped reaching out. I can't go to parties, so they stopped caring."

My eyes water, and my frown hangs low. "That's awful."

"It totally sucks. But I can pretend the benefit is a real party. Not just a fundraiser for poor little incurable Meghan."

My guard lowers as the thought of Meghan wanting Ash grows further from my mind.

"Maybe it will be a fun party," I suggest.

Meghan smirks, draping an arm over my shoulders. "You've never been to one of these society benefits before, have you?"

I giggle and shake my head.

"So you've actually been looking at the flowers?" Meghan says. "You know you don't have to. The moms love busying themselves with this stuff."

"Oh no, it's fine. I like being creative."

Meghan smiles. "Oh really? Like, you're artsy?"

I nod. "Yeah, you could call me artsy."

"You know how colors come together and make something look beautiful?"

"I like to try."

"Then let's blow this florist and go to the boutique two shops down," Meghan says, tugging on my arm.

"What? Why?"

"A photographer is coming to my house tomorrow to take my portrait," Meghan explains. "They're blowing it up huge for the benefit. Totally embarrassing, but I'm like the mascot for this soiree. Anyway, my mom had a designer bring over a heap of options, but they were all hideous. I need a second opinion. Come on, come with me."

"Okay, but are we allowed to leave before they select the flowers?" I ask, hating the idea of ditching Mom.

"Oh, please." Meghan chuckles. "My mother will have the final say, no matter what. She'll be happy for us to check out early."

"Okay, lead the way."

We say farewell to the moms. My mom opens her mouth to speak, but Mrs. Fisher waves us off while turning Mom to a new arrangement option.

Meghan and I giggle our way out and skip onto the sidewalk.

"So do you know what you're gonna wear for the benefit?" Meghan asks, bouncing her way into the boutique.

"No, but I never know what I'll wear. The Ashworths supplied me with a new wardrobe. Claudia slips a few choices into the bathroom for me to decide between."

"Vanessa has great taste, so I'm sure it's always hard to pick."

"Are you friends with Vanessa?"

"She's my sister's age. Sometimes they would hang out, and I'd hang out by proxy. But Ness is kinda strange. She's a lone wolf."

"Apparently, she spends most of her days with a tutor and not doing much else."

"Sounds like Vanessa."

I look around the magnificently merchandised boutique and fall into a happy smile. "So what style do you want for your outfit?"

"I want sophisticated yet playful and young. My mother keeps dressing me like a mature-aged lady."

"Hasn't Hope stepped in to help you?"

Meghan snorts a laugh as she moves toward a rack. "As if. Hope is too busy sucking face with Luke."

"Yeah, they do seem inseparable."

Meghan smirks. "It would make me jealous if they weren't so gross."

"Hello, Miss Fisher, how are you today?" an impeccably dressed salesperson asks, walking toward us with a tray of drinks. "Care for a strawberry-peach iced tea?"

"Sure," Meghan says, taking two champagne flutes. "And we are fine. I have Christie's help today."

The salesperson gives me a curt smile, then nods at Meghan. "As you wish, Miss Fisher. I'll be here if you need me."

Meghan hands me an iced tea, and I reply with, "Thanks. She seemed a bit put off."

Meghan shrugs, taking a sip. "She just wants to use me for a bigger commission. Everyone has an angle."

"Well, I'm happy to help you if I can."

"You always look so cute. It might be a wardrobe based on Vanessa, but you have your own style. I could tell you were creative."

I smile as my heart swells. "Thank you. My art is the most important thing to me. It was what I'd be working on today if Mom hadn't dragged me out." I tap my glass against Meghan's. "To be honest, I'm glad I'm out of the house. I'm happy we can hang out."

Meghan thrusts an arm around my neck and forces me into a hug. She squeals and says, "Oh my gosh, me too! You are so cool, Christie. I'm so glad we can be friends."

I giggle in her hug. "I wouldn't call myself cool."

Meghan clicks her tongue, letting me go. "You are. You have an air of confidence I really admire."

"Confidence? Okay, now you're confusing me with someone else."

Meghan takes another sip of her iced tea. "No. You don't play games. You're not fake and looking for attention. You're the real deal."

I blush and stare into her sweet, wholesome eyes. "Thank you. That's one of the nicest compliments I've ever gotten. I hear that stuff from teachers, but never from someone my own age."

"I wish we could have gone to school together."

I rub Meghan's arm. "We don't need school to be friends."

Meghan grins. "Yay. Okay. I want something glitzy and fun. Something far away from feeling sick."

"Well, with your gorgeous hair color, striking eyes, and fair skin, I'd suggest green shades. Emerald screams class and wealth. Or you could be more subdued with a teal outfit." I move toward a mannequin and feel the thick yet soft material. "This dark green would look magical on you. And this detail work with the gold thread and beading elevates the outfit."

"It is a stunning dress, but it still feels old to me."

"Well, you could go super playful with purple."

"Purple?" Meghan questions, twisting her lips. "With my hair color?"

"Sure," I say, excited to open her eyes to the possibility. "A plum outfit will bring out the pink in your cheeks. A dark lipstick would look so sophisticated. Eggplant might be too old for you. This violet in the shimmery fabric would be so fun."

Meghan dashes to a rack, picking out a shiny, vibrant purple number. "Like this one?"

"I love it," I gasp as Meghan pulls out the hanger and drapes the dress in front of her. "You would look gorgeous in your portrait."

Meghan claps her hands together, squealing with excitement. "Oh, yay! What about a hairpiece? Am I crazy for wanting a tiara?"

I giggle. "You're not crazy. But is your mom okay with this turning into your sweet sixteen instead of a charity dinner?"

"Forget my mother," Meghan says, moving to the glass cabinets that house the accessories. "She's using me as a mascot. I should get something out of it."

"What about this one?" I say, tapping on the glass. "The bronze piece with the flower rosettes. It's not overwhelming but still makes a statement."

"I would never have picked these things out," Meghan says, looping her arm around mine. "Pick out my bracelets and earrings too."

"Are you sure? Don't you want a say?"

"I want to look good," Meghan says with a laugh. "You have a good eye for this stuff."

I giggle. "Okay, I'll pick them out."

Meghan tries on the outfit I selected, including jewels and shoes. The salesperson hovers around the changing room, asking Meghan if she needs any extra help. She huffs at me when Meghan tells her to take a hike.

It's a blast to hang out with Meghan. She's delightful and kind. I can't understand why Ash would call her cruel. Or is he lying? Is he covering for not being truthful about his past with Hope? Does he have secret feelings for one of the Fisher sisters?

Ugh. My head will explode if I keep going in circles like this.

I have to bite the bullet. I need to know what went down between Ash and Meghan when she attended Ashworth Academy.

Meghan exits the changing room and is an absolute knockout.

I clasp my hands over my mouth and gush, "Meg, you look stunning."

"Thanks, babe," Meghan says with a giggle. She smooths down the sides of her dress and sighs happily. "I feel like a princess. I think this might be my outfit for the benefit."

"You look radiant, Miss Fisher," the salesperson butts in.

"Thanks," Meghan says. "Where's my next iced tea?"

"Right away," she says and scuttles to the back room.

Meghan cups a hand over her mouth, laughing. "She just can't take a hint."

I move over to the full-length mirror with Meghan. "This dress is a winner."

Meghan flicks her hair off her shoulders, saying, "Now I just need the right guy on my arm."

"Umm, Meghan," I say, stumbling over the syllables.

Her eyelashes bat innocently. "Yes?"

"Umm…" My voice wavers. My cheeks grow rosy, and an ache pings between my eyebrows.

"Hun, what's wrong?" Meghan asks. "You look like you're about to fall over. And, believe me, I should know."

"No," I say with a nervous laugh. "No, I'm fine. I was just wondering… What was it like for you at Ashworth Academy?"

"What do you mean? Did I like it?"

"Yeah."

"I loved the social aspect," Meghan says, eyeing her reflection. "But not the studying part. I mean, who is?"

"Right," I say, in the most light-hearted voice I can muster. "Did you have any classes with Ash?"

"Sure," she says, eyes lighting up and voice growing higher in pitch. "You know Ash, he always skipped classes. But if you're in the ones he likes, you can spend the whole time staring at him."

"So you've always had a crush on him?"

Meghan shakes her head and moves to a rack of sequined outfits. "No, I was like the other girls. Everyone tries to get Ash to notice them. You've seen it at school, right? Everyone is nice to him and gets out of his way. He's absolutely gorgeous, so you have to stare, right?"

I nod. "Right. The first thing I noticed about him was his

attractiveness. But then he opened his mouth and was rude."

"Oh gosh, he's such a hard nut to crack, isn't he?"

"You really like him, don't you?"

"I don't have many options," Meghan says coyly. "I have plenty of crushes on movie stars. Ash is the guy I wanna be with in reality."

"And you never dated when you were in school?"

"No, I dated this guy named Cody." Meghan scowls. "Such a lowlife. I thought he loved me, but he treated me like I didn't exist once I got sick."

"Oh, I'm so sorry. That's awful."

"It's okay. I just feel sorry for his new girlfriend." Meghan tousles her hair and pushes a smile on her face. "Ash never dates. I want to believe he's waiting for the right girl. Like, he wants to treat a girl like a princess. I want to be his princess."

My heart splinters. Poor Meghan. She's built a fantasy around Ash. I know the truth. Ash has found the girl he's looking for, and she's standing in my shoes. How can I tell Meghan? I can't break her heart, especially when she considers me a friend. Everyone erased her from memory when she got sick, and she's depending on me.

I can't keep it from her. How will she feel when I walk into the benefit as Ash's date? Her only friend betrays her with the only boy she likes. I should tell her the truth. Ash and I became close before I met Meghan. It wasn't a betrayal. It was bad timing.

"I heard you and Ash didn't get along at school," I say, more bluntly than I meant.

"What?" Meghan gasps. "Who told you that?"

"It was just an impression I got."

Meghan's eyes are round and water. "From Ash?"

"I don't know any details," I say more delicately. "But I was just wondering, how would he get the wrong impression of you?"

Meghan sucks in her bottom lip and wipes under her eye. She turns away from me and mutters, "I don't know."

163

Her change in demeanor tells me otherwise. Something went down. She's aware of it, but I'm guessing she didn't know Ash had picked up on it.

Perhaps I've shattered her illusion, and she'll back off from wanting my guy.

This is my moment. Say it, Christie. Ash asked another girl to be his date for the benefit. I'm his date. We've been kissing. We are growing closer every night.

"Miss Fisher," the boutique salesperson calls.

Meghan turns to her, replying, "Yes."

The salesperson places her phone on the cradle. "That was Janine from the florist. Your mother has finished and wants you and Miss Klein to head back."

"Okay," Meghan says, pointing at her outfit. "Ring all this up and have it shipped to my house."

"Of course, Miss Fisher."

Meghan turns to me with a bright smile, like nothing unpleasant was said. "I'd better get changed before Momzilla takes over the shopping precinct."

I felt sick to my stomach as Meghan went back into the changing rooms. Our mothers met us outside the boutique, and after some rushed goodbyes, our driver took us back to Ashworth Estate.

Mom said Mrs. Fisher is intense but a good woman to know. She will help Mom build connections in the town.

"So does that mean you want to buy a home in Victoria Falls instead of returning to Thornton?" I asked.

"There's so much community here. It feels good to be here. Plus, darling, I've never seen you make friends as easily as you have here."

Those words stay in my head as I paint in the art studio. The afternoon sun bathes the space in light. I work on the details in the artwork until my brushstrokes grow sloppy.

I'm so confused.

Ash and I are becoming so close. He's divulged secrets, and I'm unwilling to give him up. Yet other peoples' opinions about him leave me disoriented.

Meghan is nothing but lovely to me, and Ash called her cruel. I get it. She's Hope's sister. However, today she was sensitive, bubbly, and wanted to be my friend. But maybe Meghan is the one thing to tear Ash and me apart. He might have feelings for her. This upcoming benefit could bring them together, and they'll kick me to the curb.

I'll be back to my default. The invisible girl with no friends.

The girl I no longer want to be.

Seventeen

Ash, his father, and my dad weren't home for dinner. I waited for Ash in the theater, hoping to hear about his day. As the hours grew later into the evening, I admitted defeat and headed upstairs.

I lie awake, staring at the ceiling and listening for footsteps in the hall. As my eyes draw weary, I take comfort in the dreaded nightmares. The one perk is waking up and rushing into Ash's arms.

Imagine my shock as I wake up. My phone says 7:00 a.m. I didn't wake in the middle of the night, and I didn't have a single nightmare. I hug the comforter around my shoulders and smile in my dreamy state. I'm happy now. I no longer hold on to my fear. Ash is my cure.

I fling back the covers and throw on a robe. I'm sure I've missed Ash already, but I have to try. I knock on his bedroom door, and there's no answer. I place my hand on the doorknob and want to check inside.

Pressing my hand on his door, I exhale slowly. I'd love to soak up the scent of his cologne, melt into his bed, and gaze at his astronomy posters. But I can't do it. I can't go into his room without an invitation. It's too weird.

I trudge back to my bedroom and spy something on my door. It's a handwritten note stuck with tape. The bottom is signed, *From Ash*. With glee, I rip the note from the door and curl my fingers around the edges.

Christie,

When you didn't scream, or come to my door, or crawl in my bed last night, I hope it means you had a good night's sleep. From the bottom of my heart, I hope you didn't have any nightmares. It kills me you go to sleep scared and wake up scared. I don't want that to happen to you anymore. I care about you too much.

I hope you had a pleasant night's sleep. It would suck if you were just avoiding me.

It sucked not seeing you last night. I hated getting back home so late, but things are definitely interesting at work. And I have to admit, your dad is pretty cool.

I can't wait to see you soon. Fingers crossed it's tonight. Either way, we'll make up for it over the weekend.

From Ash.

Oh my gosh. He is just the freaking cutest!

He really likes me. Every line reassures me. Ash is my lifeline. My missing piece. I hug the note to my chest and can't wait for tonight. If he thought our kisses were good before, he has no idea what I'm ready to lay on him.

I make my way back to my bed, focusing on Ash's penmanship. I sit on the edge and analyze every pen stroke. Every word flows evenly, with a satisfying space between each letter. The letters have a consistent height, yet the words aren't overly big. His pen doesn't lift until the word is complete, leaving no errors in his writing. It oozes confidence and conciseness. I love the way his cursive writing connects, and his pen pressure is even and not heavy. He's measured and thoughtful. His handwriting is an artwork I want to frame.

I give the letter a gentle kiss and set it on my bedside table.

Oh, Ash. I can't wait to kiss you for real.

Once I get dressed, I skip breakfast and move to the third floor and into the art studio. My feelings for Ash are off the charts. My heart pounds in my ears, my eyes are wide, and my smile is gargantuan. My face hurts from the pressure happiness brings. I'm willing to get used to this pain because, without it, my life is nothingness.

My increasing desire for this boy splashes across the artwork. My hands can't paint fast enough. I strain my neck from leaning in, and my eyes grow dry from lack of blinking.

I only leave the art studio because my stomach rumbles one too many times.

Ash and our dads aren't home for dinner again. Mom and I watch a tear-jerker in one of the family rooms, and my ears stay prick for any movement.

When Mom and I say good night, I stay vigilant. I can't stand going this long without seeing Ash. I need my fix!

I pace the halls with alibis ready in case I'm caught by Mom or Murphy. I'm going with headache, hunger, or nightmare, depending on the situation.

As I wander the second-floor landing, I hear voices below. I jump and squeal in delight.

Descending the staircase, my excitement has me tripping over my feet. I look around for my dad, but I've come down a different set of stairs than usual. I land by Mr. Ashworth's home office.

The office door is ajar, and lights are on inside.

"All you think about is yourself!" Ash's voice yells in the room.

I stand rigid and am mortified I've walked in on an argument. I want to flee, but the intensity and aggression in Ash's voice have me frozen.

168

"Ash, you know that's not true," his dad fires back. "Everything I do is for this family."

"Bull!" Ash retorts. "You mold us into the versions you want. No wonder Mom and Vanessa left. Why don't you do everything you can to get them back? Why do you keep pushing them away?"

"That's not fair," Mr. Ashworth says firmly. "You have no right to talk to me this way."

Ash storms out of the room, and his fiery stare meets my eyes. He stands in a form-fitting black suit. The top three buttons of his white shirt are undone, and his black tie hangs loosely from his collar.

Upon seeing me, Ash's expression somewhat softens. His features twitch, and then a scowl appears. Anger coats his face. First from the heated argument with his dad, and now laser focused in my direction. At the eavesdropper in his way.

I want to say I'm sorry. Or just mouth it. But I'm stuck in time.

"Ash!" Mr. Ashworth yells, marching out of his office. His stride halts when he spies Ash and me, standing motionless in the open space.

Ash races toward the staircase without a word spoken to either of us. His father moves toward the stairs, calling out to him a few more times to no avail. Ash has left the scene, yet his tension remains, filling the air to the point of choking.

Mr. Ashworth doesn't return in my direction. I stand alone in the silence as my mind stays on Ash's face. His aggression was in full swing. It's been days since I've seen that side of him. It's scary to think it's lying under the surface. Is it safe to be around someone who can snap?

"No," I say, calm and collected.

No. This is crazy. Ash is a good person, and he cares about me. He's been upfront about his chaotic relationship with his dad. They've been in close quarters for two days, allowing tensions to rise. It is a case of being in the wrong place.

But then why didn't he hug me? Why didn't he ask me to follow him and talk it out? His disgust wasn't just at his dad. It was in his eyes when he looked at me.

He still sees me as an inconvenience.

Another project to keep his dad busy while the Ashworth family falls apart.

A tear drops from my eye as my fingernails dig deeper into my palms. I can't let Ash see me this way. He can't push me away from him again. I care too much about him now.

I force myself up the staircase for my least favorite activity. Confrontation. The stance outside his dad's office was beyond awkward. He looked ready to take his frustration out on me. It was too much when we didn't know one another. Now it'd be agony.

When I make it to the kids' wing, Ash is nowhere in sight. I linger in the hall, wondering if he's in his bedroom or his bathroom. I pivot toward his door and then turn to my bedroom. Fidgeting in place, my insides are squeamish and my limbs tremble. I don't want him to blast me for hanging around his door if he's in a bad mood. But I want him to know I'm here. He's angry, hurting, and deserves better than to feel this way.

Ash's door opens, and I hug the wall. He steps into the hall, and we exchange awkward stares. His hostility has been minimized, but his guard remains.

I don't know what to say. Does sorry mean anything?

Ash breaks the silence with, "I don't want to talk about it."

I step toward him. "That's okay. We don't have to talk about it."

He frowns and folds his arms across his middle. "I'm sorry you had to hear me yell like that."

"I didn't mean to interrupt," I say, leaning against the wall. "I was excited to see you. I didn't want to miss you again."

Ash drops his arms, and his lips curl upward. "You missed me?"

I sigh effortlessly. "Like crazy."

Ash steps forward and caresses my face. "I missed you too."

"Thank you for my note."

He blushes. "You liked it?"

"It was so sweet. I've looked at it all day."

"Nice. So you're happy to hang out this weekend?"

I reach for his hand on my cheek and pull it away. "Yes, but I've made plans to hang out with my parents."

"Oh."

"I've had zero time with my dad, and I need time with my parents." I clutch his hand. "You understand?"

"Of course," he says, squeezing my hand back. "I also want to steal time with you. Can you make time for your parents and for me?"

He bats his lashes and gives me a charisma-filled smile.

I giggle and kiss his cheek. "There's always time for you."

He pulls me in close and kisses my lips with weighted pressure. His hands press into my back, and the hunger in his kiss and the flex of his arms show me he needs me.

I'm not an inconvenience.

I wrap my arms around him and lay more pressure on the kiss.

I am wanted.

Ash bites my bottom lip, and a moan sizzles out of me as he pulls away. The electricity buzzing at my lips has my desire surging. I don't let him go, running my hands higher on his back. He rests his forehead against mine, and his heavy breathing has me smiling.

"I'm kinda hungry," he whispers mid-pant. "Wanna come to the kitchen with me?"

I nod against his shoulder and unwrap myself from him. He takes my hand and leads me out of the wing. I soak up our connection as we hold hands on our way to the kitchen. I don't want to say anything that might change his now happier mood. Under the surface, the aggression could linger.

"I know you don't like when I call Murphy," Ash says in the kitchen, picking up the phone from the cradle. "But it's not that late, and I need him."

"It's okay," I reassure. "You look beat."

Ash rubs a hand over his face and sighs. "I am."

He presses a button on the phone, and Murphy answers.

"Hey, Murphy, can you meet me in the kitchen?" Ash says tiredly.

"Right away, sir," Murphy replies through the speaker.

Ash hangs up the phone and sits on a stool by one of the stainless steel benches.

I move over to him, rub his tense shoulders, and then sit beside him.

"I know you don't want to talk about it," I say softly. "But I'm here for you."

Ash smiles and takes my hand, rubbing a circle on it with his thumb. "I know," he replies. "And thanks. But I don't want to talk about what happened in the office."

"It's fine with me."

"It's just... My dad..."

"You don't have to say anything. It's okay."

Ash finds my eyes, and sadness encircles his pupils. "He's trying to buy me off."

I tense at his words. "What does that mean?"

"When I was at work with him... What he and your dad were working on... It's like... Uh, he was so fake... He's trying to suck me in."

"Why do you feel that way?"

"Because he's never taken an interest in me before," Ash says flatly. "And I know it's another ploy to stop me from bringing up our family issues."

"Oh, Ash. I hope that's not true."

Ash sighs and whispers, "It's what it feels like."

I rub his back, unable to find comforting words.

"How do you feel about a party?" Ash asks, changing the subject.

I tilt my head. "A party?"

"Tomorrow night," Ash replies. "Do you want to go with me?"

My voice quivers with a squeak as inadequacy weighs me down. "I don't know if I'll fit in."

"You will. School was easier than you predicted, wasn't it?"

"I guess so. Why do you want to go to the party?"

He shrugs. "It's what's expected."

"Do you enjoy being predictable?"

His eyebrow arches. "Do you?"

I stammer a string of sounds, heat spreading across my face.

He lifts my chin with his index finger and whispers, "You're predictable, Christie Klein. How could I guess you'd hate the idea of a party?"

My eyes well as I stare up at him. What am I supposed to say? Does he hate me now?

His hand moves from my chin and into my hair with a gentle touch. "I thought you wanted to be brave."

I breathe out slowly, and the heat dissipates from my face. Staring into his big brown eyes calms me. I can be brave. With him, I am brave.

"Don't you want to make other friends? Not that I want to share you with anyone else."

"Well..." I drag out the word. "I kinda have."

"What do you mean?"

"Mom and I went to a florist to pick out arrangements for the benefit. Meghan Fisher and her mom met us there." I pause to gauge his reaction. "Meghan and I got along really well."

Ash's eyebrows lift. "You and Meghan?"

"Yeah. Is that a problem?"

Ash is quick to shake his head. "No. Be friends with whoever you want."

"You told me there was some rocky history between you and Meghan. If there's a reason I shouldn't be friends with her, let me know."

Murphy walks into the room. "Master Ashworth, Miss Klein, how may I help you?"

"Can you make the mac and cheese with the bacon and chili and all that good stuff?" Ash asks, in dire need of comfort food.

Murphy smiles, walking deeper into the kitchen. "Of course, sir."

"You want in?" Ash asks me with the cutest grin.

"Mac and cheese?" I ask like it's a dumb question. "Sounds amazing."

"Murphy's mac and cheese for two, coming up," Murphy says, igniting the burners on the gas stove.

"I didn't know rich kids ate things like mac and cheese," I tease.

"I'll bet you've tasted nothing as good as Murphy's mac and cheese," Ash says, salivating.

"I can already tell it'll be delicious."

"I promise you won't be disappointed."

"So are you okay about me hanging out with Meghan?" I ask timidly. "Something happened between you two, and both of you are reluctant to tell me."

"Why? What did Meghan say?"

"She said nothing, but her eyes welled with tears."

Ash sits back on his stool, his body stubbornly rigid. "I don't know Meghan's deal. We were never friends, and I have never really liked her. You know when you get a gut instinct about people?"

"Gut instincts can be wrong. I never thought I'd grow to like you."

Ash splutters a laugh. "Brutal, Klein."

"Okay, my first impression was you were crazy hot. My second was that you were a brat with no empathy. But now I know you were taking your family frustrations out on me."

Ash's face falls flat. "I promise I'll tell you about the stuff that went down with Dad. I need time to think it over."

"I wasn't trying to pressure you."

He pats my hand. "I know. I just don't want you to think I'm closing off."

I smile in response and cup my hand around his.

"So what happened with you and Meghan? You went from hanging with your moms to becoming friends?"

"We ditched our moms, and Meghan took me to a boutique."

"Which one?" Ash asks.

I bite into my lip as I try to recall a street sign or logo. "Mmm, I don't know. The one near the florist."

Ash smirks. "Which florist?"

I hide my face and shrug.

Ash laughs and turns in his chair. "Murphy, do you know where Christie and her mom went today?"

"Yes, sir," Murphy says by the stove. "Mrs. and Miss Klein were taken to Greenhouse Floral Designs. One of the closest fashion boutiques is Magnolia's Closet. It is also a favorite of Miss Ashworth."

"If Ness likes them, that's a seal of approval. Can you call them tomorrow and have them bring over a few dresses for Christie to try?"

I nudge him and blurt, "Ash, no."

Ash turns to me, saying, "For the benefit. You'll need formal wear. And they can bring over some less formal outfits for the party tomorrow."

I suck in a breath and slowly let it out. "You really want me to go to a party with you?"

Ash takes both my hands and pecks my lips. "I really do."

My shoulders ease, and I can't look away from those alluring brown eyes.

"Okay," I whisper.

Ash grins and turns back to Murphy. "Got that? Formal dresses for the benefit and dresses for a casual party. She'll need them tomorrow morning."

Murphy nods. "I'll see to it right away."

"Thanks," Ash says, turning back in my direction. "Hey, I almost forgot. How have you been sleeping?"

My hands leap under my chin as I squeal. "No nightmares."

175

Ash grasps my shoulders, surprise and delight taking over his face. "Are you serious?"

"I went to sleep last night thinking about you. The good vibes carried me through. I didn't wake up once throughout the night."

Ash kisses my cheek, and says in an elated voice, "I'm so happy for you, Christie. I mean, I'm bummed about not cuddling with you, but selfishness aside, I'm so glad you had a pleasant night's sleep."

"It's all because of you."

"No way," he says bashfully.

"Yes way. You make me feel better than I ever have before."

The shy modesty doesn't leave his demeanor. "Right back at you, Christie Klein."

"Bon appétit," Murphy says, making his way to us with two steaming bowls of his famous mac and cheese.

"Yum," I moan. "That smells so freaking good."

We take our few mouthfuls in silence. After Murphy checks if we need anything else, he leaves, reminding us he's only a phone call away.

"What do you have planned with your parents?" Ash asks between mouthfuls.

"Nothing really," I reply, digging my fork into the bowl. "I just want to recreate our usual weekends. Easy stuff, like chatting about our week, or watching a movie, playing a board game or finishing a puzzle."

"We need a board game rematch," Ash suggests. "It was fun that time."

"See, board games aren't that bad, are they?" I tease.

"It was opening up to you I remember the most," Ash says, his eyes growing delicate as he reminisces. "I like that you helped me slow down and be more thoughtful."

"Aw, that's nice to say."

"I mean it, Christie. It's been so good having you in my life."

"I never thought I'd be so happy to start my life over," I say, swirling my fork in the cheesy pasta. "Being with you is a change I never

176

saw coming. I'd never believe it could feel so good."

"I have to say, your dad was a welcomed change at the office," Ash says. "He made being around my dad bearable."

I grin. "It must be that Klein charm."

He nudges me with a cute smile. "Must be."

"So what does my dad do all day?"

"He designs computer codes and works on programs for the robotics lab," Ash replies.

"Excuse me? My dad is working on robots?"

"Okay, get this," Ash says, sitting back on his stool. "When my great-grandfather started his business, it was a metal fabrication factory. My grandfather expanded part of the business into manufacturing vehicle parts. He then went into chemicals and plastics, which grew his wealth. When my dad came onboard, he convinced my grandfather to buy manufacturing companies in computers and technology."

"That's the section my dad works in."

"Right. Now my father wants to combine every asset he has into his latest big idea." Ash rubs his forehead and softly says, "He wants to build autonomous self-driving cars. And his end goal is to engineer a flying version."

I laugh because I don't know how else to react.

"Your dad was working on a program that sped up my father's plans," Ash says. "That's why my dad is all over him. Your dad is his golden goose."

My eyes narrow. "My dad is working on a flying car?"

"Not yet. Everything is in early development. But yeah, one day, they hope. This is how my dad plans to keep me under his wing."

"Aerospace engineering fascinates you. Therefore, you must be into flying cars," I conclude.

"He's never cared about my interests before," Ash says, picking up his fork and dragging it through his food. "My grandfather did. He was the one who always supported and encouraged me. But Dad... for the

177

past few days, he's been fake."

"Maybe your dad is eager. Maybe it's just the shock clouding your perspective."

Ash frowns, staring at his pasta. "No. It's just another act to distract me."

Sensing the tension building inside Ash, I take the scrumptious food as a much-needed mood lifter.

"Speaking of distractions, just the smell of this food makes my mouth water. Do you get to eat when you're away with your dad?" I ask. "Or does he leave you starving until midnight?"

Ash laughs and then answers, "No, we eat. Today was this fancy stuff one of Dad's clients brought. I wasn't in the mood for it, so I waited to get home."

"Did my dad eat?"

Ash smirks. "Out of politeness."

I giggle. "Dad isn't one for fancy dinners. He would love *this* placed in front of him."

"You should ask Murphy to make it when you're having your family time."

"That's a good idea," I reply. "You're cool with me spending time alone with my parents?"

"I don't own you," Ash says mockingly. "Sure, I'll be jealous, but I'll survive."

"*Ha.* Don't pine for me too hard."

"You joke, but the pining is for real," Ash replies. "Is it a yes to the party?"

"If my parents are okay with it," I reply, "then yes."

"Awesome." Ash smiles and kisses my cheek. "Where do you want to sleep tonight?"

I bite into my lip and feel the heat spike in my face. "I can't sleep in your bed again."

He nudges me and whispers, "Why not?"

"I appreciated being so close to you," I reply nervously. "It really helped me, but we can't. My parents would totally freak out."

"Okay, we won't start the night in bed together," Ash says with a naughty wink.

"Don't," I whine with a giddy smile. "Don't be bad."

"I forgot," Ash says with a laugh. "You're a Goody Two-shoes."

I flick back my hair and grin. "And proud of it."

Ash rests an elbow on the counter and slides his cheek into his palm. "You are so beautiful."

My mouth falls open. "What?"

"Beautiful," Ash whispers, staring at me with dreamy eyes. "Sweet, gorgeous, and beautiful."

"Stop making it hard for me to go to my room."

"Don't worry, I'm not letting you share my bed," Ash replies.

My heart drops. "Why?"

"Because I like you too much, and I want your parents to approve of me."

My heart bounces again, and I clasp my hands in front. "You care about what my parents think?"

"Of course. You've always told me how important they are to you."

I kiss him, soft and slow.

"You're the best, Ash."

"I bet we will both have sweet dreams tonight."

His eyes fall shut, and he leans into me. As my eyes close, his sumptuous lips envelop mine. His kiss is magic and lights me up inside.

How am I supposed to resist cuddling with him all night?

Eighteen

"So tell me everything I've missed," Dad says, slinging his arm around me the next day. "Highlights and lowlights."

We are sitting in the living room on the third floor, where Ash and I played a board game. Knowing this usually vacant area has fun games made it the perfect place to take my parents. Although the two couches face each other, I sit nestled between Mom and Dad. I've never needed to be closer to them.

"I have to admit that every day I'm more comfortable in the manor," I reply.

"I love that you are finding your way around," Mom says. "I didn't know this room existed. It's quite cozy and serene."

"Ash brought me here," I explain and point at the stuffed bookshelves and board games section. "We played a board game and had a chill time."

"Look at our little girl, Peter," Mom says, beaming with pride. "Since moving here, she's come out of her shell."

"I'm proud of you, kiddo," Dad says, squeezing his arm around me. "Especially after the hell that brought us here. I wouldn't have blamed you for retreating."

"It wasn't up to me," I reply. "Ash and other kids at school have approached me. I'll admit, it's not in a positive light all the time, but it's like I'm actually seen here."

Mom pats my knee. "Speaking with Meghan was positive, wasn't it?"

I smile. "I really like Meghan. I'm glad I got to hang out with her."

"She and her mother will be visiting on Monday," Mom says. "We are having another society meeting since the benefit is only a week away."

"Meghan says the meetings are always boring," I reply. "It'd be cool if she and I can sneak away while her mother controls the meeting."

Mom purses her lips. "You'll be polite and listen to Mrs. Fisher. We want to make a good impression."

I nod, careful not to let my eyes roll. "Okay. You're right."

"So you two are happy here in Victoria Falls?" Dad asks, his eyes narrowing with intrigue, and his smile lifts.

"Now that I have a purpose," Mom says, nodding, "I feel comfortable here."

"I'm still nervous about going back to school," I admit, "but Ash made sure I was comfortable while we were together. I'm sure it'll be easier at Ashworth Academy than at my old school. *Ha*. Despite the annoying uniform."

Dad chuckles and sits taller. "Would you two be open to making this town our permanent home?"

"Can we afford it?" Mom asks. "The friends I've made are not short on money."

"With my new contract," Dad says, nodding, "we can afford to live here. I suggest we find a modest house in town. What do you think, Christie?"

"No one is missing me at home," I say quietly. "And I'm not missing home. Well, I'm not missing anything that wasn't turned into ash. I'd be happy to move here. I don't want to lose the friends I've made."

Mom grins and kisses my forehead.

"You said some interactions with kids at school weren't positive," Dad says with concern. "Anything you want to chat about?"

"I don't fully understand what happened," I say softly. "I was in the middle of a drama that started before we moved here. This snooty girl didn't want me hanging around Ash, and it was this weird misunderstanding. Anyway, I told Ash about it, and he set it all straight. I'm hoping I'm not dragged in the middle again."

Am I kidding myself? Hope wants me gone because she wants to matchmake Meghan and Ash. I looped myself in this mess further by becoming friends with Meghan. And there is some unspoken past between Meghan and Ash, which leads Ash to believe Meghan is cruel.

Yeah, this mess isn't going away soon. Everyone ignoring the problem isn't an option. Ash is happy to forget Meghan exists. I'm just not sure Hope will let it go. Her eyes are too intense to give up easily.

"So you and Ash," Dad says, giving me the protective father routine. "Do I have to be concerned?"

His façade shatters, and he reverts to a goof.

I laugh. "He's really nice to me. I really like him."

"I am glad you two are getting along," Dad says. "He is a good kid."

"Did you have time to talk to him when he was with you?" I ask, curiosity to the max.

"Yes, but it revolved around work," Dad replies. "Tom was very eager to get Ash's feedback on our projects."

"I still can't get over the fact you didn't spill the beans on your project," I say. "A freaking flying car!"

"That's a very broad way to describe my work," Dad says. "I doubt I'll have anything to do with an actual flying car. Right now, I'm having fun working with my little robots and getting them to hover in coordination."

"Unreal. Ash didn't go into detail about it," I reply. "It seems like he and his dad didn't get along very well. I accidentally walked in on them arguing last night."

Dad shakes his head. "I know nothing about that. I know there's tension concerning Mrs. Ashworth and their daughter being overseas."

I nod. "Ash misses them."

"Tom does too," Dad says. "His work responsibilities are immense, but he does his darnedest to be a family man. It was easy to get home for dinner when Ash wasn't with us. It was an excuse to break Tom away from his desk. He loves that kid."

My brow furrows as I replay what Dad says. "What do you mean? Mr. Ashworth would come home for Ash but stay longer at the office when Ash was with him?"

"Yeah. I couldn't bear to break up the moments they were sharing." Dad leans across me and pats Mom's knee. "Sorry again for missing dinner two nights in a row. Tom is my ride home, and I didn't want to appear impatient."

"It's fine," Mom says. "You need a better work-life balance once we're settled."

"I promise," Dad replies. "We will work on the house, and car, and our new routine."

"Did Ash seem happy when he was working with you?" I ask, piecing information together.

Dad nods, his eyes lighting up. "That kid has some head on him. His ideas were revolutionary. I can see why Tom wanted to fast-track this project."

"For Ash?" I clarify.

Dad grins. "I can see that boy running this division."

This makes no sense. If Mr. Ashworth dedicated time to his son, then why did Ash become upset? He called his dad fake. Is it Ash's spoiled upbringing rearing its ugly head?

"Are you okay, Christie?" Mom asks, rubbing my shoulder.

I blink hard and relax against the couch, forcing a smile. "Yeah, I'm good."

"It's curious how interested you are in what Ash was up to," Dad says, his mouth fighting to hold back a laugh.

I blush hard and blurt, "Why?"

"Because he was asking about you while at the office," Dad says, still fighting his laugh.

The blush intensifies. "Really?"

"Oh, that's so cute," Mom gushes.

"*Mom*," I moan.

"Aw, I think it's adorable you two like each other so much," Mom says, clasping her hands over her heart. "Have you upgraded this relationship from friendship?"

"*Mom*," I yelp. "You're so embarrassing."

"What?" Mom says with a giggle. "It's a fair question."

"I don't know," I squeak. "We are friends, but he asked me to be his date for the benefit."

Mom shrieks and claps in approval.

I have to roll my eyes, and Dad unleashes the laughter he was holding on to.

"And…" I drag out the word, feeling cloaked in embarrassment. "He's asked me to go to a party with him tonight. I want to spend a night with you guys. You know, popcorn, a movie, and a puzzle."

"We've done that a million times," Mom replies, grinning from ear to ear. "Never, ever, have you gone to a party."

"Well, not *never* ever," Dad says, rubbing my arm. "There were those kindergarten parties."

"Christie has wiped those from her memory," Mom counters.

It was true. I don't remember going to any parties.

"I don't know if I'll fit in," I say, hoping they push for our original plan of a movie night. "Maybe I should stay home."

"You should go," Mom and Dad say in unison.

"Christie, you told us you don't want to lose the friends you've made," Mom says, cuddling me close. "Go out and have some fun. The more you do it, the easier and more natural it'll feel."

I gulp an answer.

"I know it's scary," Dad whispers. "But you've got a boy who's smitten with you. I'm sure you'll have a great time. If you don't, that boy will have to answer to me."

The three of us collapse in laughter. My chest eases, and I float in happiness. They are right. I should give it a go. Ash made sure no one messed with me at school. He wouldn't take me to a party where I'd be in social danger.

I have to trust Ash. And he was too ridiculously cute when he asked me to go with him. I get why other kids treat him like a god. How can anyone say no to him?

Nineteen

When I return to my bedroom, two racks of expensive and unique dresses take up the floor.

"Whoa," I utter at the glitzy display.

"Too much?" Ash asks, leaning against my doorway.

I turn to him and grin. "Just a little."

Ash pushes off the doorframe and walks toward me. "We will send back whatever you don't like, and Mom's tailor will be here tomorrow to make sure everything fits."

"Thanks for organizing all this stuff," I say, finding a stack of high heels and clutch purses. "But you don't need to go to any trouble for me."

Ash takes my hand and lifts it to his lips. He kisses it and whispers, "Who else am I gonna go to trouble for?"

I bite into my lip, and my insides turn to goo. Oh gosh, this boy.

Ash lowers my hand and asks, "Any favorites?"

I turn back to the racks and reply, "It's a little overwhelming."

Ash runs his finger along the tops of the hangers. "What if I randomly choose two dresses and you have to pick one?"

I shrug. "That'll work."

Ash points at the rack to his right. "This is the casual one?"

"I guess. They are both glamorous, but yes, it looks the least formal of the two."

Ash moves to the casual rack. "We should pick for the party." He swoops his hands in and plucks an outfit from each end. "Okay, first impressions. Which one do you pick?"

"Should we match?" I ask, feeling like a total goof. "Is this what you're wearing?"

Ash looks down and makes a face. "Are you kidding? I wore this all day."

My shoulders bunch high, and I squeak, "Sorry. It looks nice. You're always dressed like you're going to an event."

"These are my casual clothes."

"I don't think you know what casual means."

Ash laughs. "You'll have to teach me the joys of T-shirts and jeans."

"The joy is the comfort level."

"If you insist," Ash says and raises the hangers higher. "Come on, gun to your head. Which do you choose?"

"I hate that expression," I mutter. "What is with this obsession with guns?"

"*Christie*," Ash whines. "Is it really this hard for you to make a decision?"

"Sorry," I say, taking the dark-brown silk cocktail dress. "They are gorgeous dresses. I just don't see myself in either of them."

"You will look great in whatever you wear."

I drape the dress against my body. "I don't think it suits me."

187

Ash swaps hangers with me. "This would be pretty."

I hold the velvet plum dress against me and move toward the mirror. "I've never worn anything like this. I'd have to wear dark makeup. No, it'd be too weird."

"You like pastel colors," Ash says, digging in the rack.

He retrieves a baby-blue dress that sways below the hanger. It hangs from spaghetti straps to a neckline that won't make me feel on display. It falls into a ruffled skirt that swishes playfully. I smile at the thought of dancing in it.

"That smile looks like a yes," Ash says, swapping hangers with me.

I drape it against me and nod. "I really like it."

"You must be ready for a party then," Ash says, stepping beside me in the mirrored reflection.

"I can't believe you picked my outfit."

"I guess I must know you pretty well."

I smile at his reflection. "What are you going to wear?"

Ash looks down at the dress. "I can have Claudia look through my wardrobe for something that matches."

"You can ask Claudia nicely."

Ash smirks. "What's that supposed to mean?"

"You tell everyone what to do. Last night you said thank you to Murphy, and I almost fainted in shock."

Ash laughs. "You make me sound like a brat."

I lean into him and giggle. "Sometimes you are a brat."

Ash kisses my cheek and then backtracks out of the room. "I'll let you get ready and see you in an hour?"

I nod. "Sounds good."

For the party, I'm happy to have Claudia's help getting ready. Everyone says Vanessa Ashworth has incredible style. Claudia had to help create that reputation.

I might not have experience with parties, but I have plenty of expertise in applying colors with brushes. Applying my makeup was a

188

breeze, despite the tremor in my hand. Hope and other mean girls will be there.

When I meet up with Ash, he's wearing slate-gray trousers and a navy button-down shirt with a minimalist dot design in baby blue.

He shrugs. "I kinda match."

"You look handsome," I say, leaning in and kissing his lips.

"Thank you. I needed my A game to look good next to you. You look irresistible, Christie."

"Irresistible?" I question. "Wow. I would never imagine someone calling me that."

Ash kisses me soft and slow. He whispers in my ear, "I don't understand how you can't see yourself as beautiful."

At that, I shiver. His presence is reassuring and makes me feel desired. The compliments still sound foreign. A part of me truly wonders if he's just saying it to be polite. *Say she's beautiful so things aren't awkward because we live in the same mansion and share a bedroom wall.*

Hand in hand, we leave the manor. Sam, our driver, waits by the limousine.

"Are you excited about the party?" I ask on the drive into Victoria Falls.

"Yeah. It's been a few days since I've listened in on the latest gossip."

I look at him with skepticism. "You like to gossip?"

Ash smirks. "No. I like to keep an eye on everyone and gather intel." Before he continues, he sends me a wink. "You never know when it'll come in handy."

I run a hand into his silky brown hair. "Your brain is too special to fill with silly nonsense. Imagine the incredibly important stuff that could take that space."

"High school politics are important," Ash replies. "A lot of these kids' parents work for my dad. One day, they'll all work for me. This

189

knowledge will be valuable."

"That is, if they all follow in their parents' footsteps."

Ash muffles a laugh and then replies, "They will."

I shake my head as I smile in a silent laugh. "Whatever. Don't expect me to get involved in these games."

"If it involved a board, you'd be eager to play," Ash teases, tickling my ribs.

I giggle and squirm away from him. I bat his hand away, squealing, "Stop it."

Ash laughs, pulling his hands away.

I compose myself and rest against him. "So whose party is this? Have I met them?"

"It's this guy named Cody?"

"Cody?" I question as the name rings alarm bells in my head. "As in Meghan Fisher's ex-boyfriend?"

"Yeah. How did you know that?"

"Meghan told me about him when we were at the boutique," I reply. "She told me he dumped her when she got sick."

Ash scoffs. "Is that the story she is telling?"

I raise an eyebrow. "Are you saying she's lying?"

Ash fidgets against me and then fastens his arms around my middle. "I don't want to talk about Meghan."

"You want the gossip but won't share it."

"*Ha*. You just told me you didn't want to be involved in gossip."

I snort a laugh. "Oops. Yeah, I did."

"See, sometimes curiosity gets the better of us."

The limousine slows to a stop at an impressive two-story house.

"My first party," I mutter, clutching Ash's hand as my nerves frazzle inside me. "Wish me luck."

Sam opens the door, and Ash holds my hand as we exit the car.

"This can't be your first party," Ash says.

"Just because you don't think I'm invisible doesn't mean other people acknowledge me," I reply. "Most people ignore my existence."

"Most people are idiots," Ash says with a smirk.

At this, I smile and lean into him. Ash kisses me softly and sensually. His hands smooth over my hair, letting the moment linger.

"Yeah, Ashworth!" a voice cheers from the house.

Our lips break apart, and we turn toward the house. Ash's friend Luke ambles his way toward us with a bottle in his hand.

"About time I saw you locking lips with someone," Luke jokes, lifting the bottle into the air.

Ash's eyes roll at the comment, yet the corners of his lips curl.

Luke shoves the bottle at Ash and continues to mock, "Well, someone other than *my* girlfriend, that is."

"Shut up," Ash says with a fizzled-out laugh. He takes the bottle from Luke but doesn't lift it to his lips. The smell of the contents makes my lips pucker.

Luke looks me up and down. "Looking good. Ready for your first Victoria Falls party?"

"I guess," I mutter. I look at Ash for reassurance and then turn back to Luke. "Same as any party, right?"

Luke laughs and lassos his arm around me. "Girl, you ain't seen nothing yet."

"He's kidding, Christie," Ash says as Luke forces me toward the house with him. "There's nothing special about the parties in this town."

"Don't downplay it, man," Luke says. "You know how crazy things get."

My eyes swoop in Ash's direction. What does that mean?

Ash shakes his head, giving Luke another eye roll.

As we walk into the house, Ash steals me away from Luke. Without a glance our way, Luke wanders off. My back stiffens, and I suck in a tight breath. Luke runs his hands around Hope, who looks ready for a *Vogue* cover shoot.

I swiftly look away and let Ash lead me into the party.

"You want something to drink?" Ash asks, abandoning the bottle Luke gave him on a side table. "Or let me guess," he begins with an adorable smile, "you're hungry?"

I giggle, playfully elbowing him in the ribs. "You make it sound like I eat all the time."

"I always find you snacking," Ash says as his hand slides down my back and nestles on my hip.

"Well, I'm good at the moment," I respond. "So tell me, what makes these parties so crazy?"

"Don't listen to Luke. He's just blowing smoke."

"But apparently, you're the one who knows how crazy things get."

"Because everyone assumes my boredom means I want an adrenaline high."

"Don't you prefer not being bored?"

"Sure, but a crappy party won't do it for me."

"Then why are we here?"

Seriously, I could be in pj's and watching a sappy movie with my parents.

"What else are we going to do?" he asks, fidgeting with his collar. "Last party, I choppered in a DJ. There was one where I turned a pool into a Jell-O pit. Another, I rented a hotel."

"And it didn't excite you?"

Ash scratches the back of his neck as his eyes wander the party. "I just made calls, and it happened."

I don't want to spend the evening with bored, fidgety Ash. It's the side of him I dislike. When he acts like that, he says blunt and hurtful comments. I want fun and cute Ash.

"What makes a party fun in your eyes?" I ask.

Ash's jaw rocks as he thinks about it. "Fewer people," he begins. "Outside, starry night, chill music…" He looks into my eyes and smiles. "And you by my side."

I smile and loop my arms around his middle. "There's one checked off your list."

Ash silently laughs and kisses my nose.

"Your idea of a party sounds way better than this," I say. "Why don't you organize a party like that?"

"Because I've never had anyone who didn't think it was lame." He nudges back in Luke's direction. "Luke's my best friend, and he would hate it. I'd have to invite Hope, who would hate it. Beyond that, I don't know who else I have."

"The whole school is infatuated with you. Maybe you need to widen your circle of friends."

"I've never looked for friends. Hope's and Luke's families are entangled with mine. They've just always been around. If everyone is using me for connections or money, I may as well have people my family trusts."

"Hope and Luke are older than you. What about kids from your classes?"

He shrugs, eyes wandering away in boredom. "I'm never in my classes."

I frown. "I don't like hearing you this way."

Ash flicks his eyes back in my direction, and they are doubtful. "Are you saying I don't try hard enough? At least I know everyone's names. You told me you didn't know a soul at your last school."

I unravel my hands from his and lower my gaze to my shoes. "I'm sorry... I..."

Ash lifts my chin, and his expression is soft. "I don't care if you don't make friends. Don't make it a big deal if I want to blend in."

"Okay," I whisper, even though I'd rather ask him why he feels he has to be fake. He doesn't care about anyone here. He doesn't care about the party. It's all for show. So everyone can say Thomas Ashworth III was at the party.

Ash sighs. "What?"

"Nothing."

193

"You're giving me those judgmental eyes again. I hate that. Just tell me what you're thinking instead of assuming the worst."

My face falls. My mouth hangs open, and my eyes well. An ache grows in my heart, and I sniff back a tear.

"I'm sorry, Ash," I whisper. "I was spiraling in my head. I was judging you again. Seriously, I'm sorry."

"It's okay. Just tell me what's wrong."

I shake my head. I can't say it. I don't want to say anything negative to him. I don't want to be hurtful.

"There's nothing wrong," I insist. "I'm happy to be here with you. Even if it's not the ideal place for either of us."

"Just because I don't think parties are fun doesn't mean this one won't be," Ash says. "I've never been to a party with you before."

"I don't see how I can make it more fun."

"Well, I like your company," Ash says, caressing my face. "That has to make things more fun."

I giggle and once again turn to goo.

"Hey, Ash," a couple of girls say, passing us by and waving at him.

Ash flicks his hand in a mediocre wave "Hey.".

"That's one thing I like about you," I say. "Even though the big crowds annoy you, you always say hello to individual people. I need to work on that. I feel so tiny when people talk to me, and I just babble nonsense."

"Because you need practice," Ash says. "You'll only get better by regularly interacting with people. Without confidence, you appear rude."

"I assumed people knew I was shy."

Ash turns away, muttering, "I didn't."

How could he not know?

"Ashworth, what did you do with the bottle?" Luke asks, making his way toward us. "You didn't chug it already, did you?"

Ash hangs a thumb over his shoulder. "I ditched it."

"*Man*," Luke whines, and in one swift move, he spins Ash around

194

and pulls him away from me.

"Umm," I stammer, turning on my heels and wondering if I should follow.

"Hi, Christie," Hope says, sliding beside me and looking me up and down. "You look super cute tonight."

"Thanks," I say through a clenched jaw.

"I see you came with Ash."

My composure crumbles. Despite the kissing, and Ash calling me his date, I falter at making this clear to Hope. "Yeah, we live in the same house."

"You two are sticking close together," Hope says, scrutinizing my face for clues. "Couldn't help but notice you both had days off from school."

I hold my hips, trying for something resembling confidence. "What about it?"

"I thought I made myself clear. Ash is taken."

"Meghan and Ash have spent no time together."

Sarcasm lays thick over Hope's words. "And you think you're something special to him?"

I swallow hard as the threat of tears builds behind my eyes. "I know I am."

"Has he even made it official?" Hope asks in a harsh whisper. "Huh? Does he call you his girlfriend?"

I cower under her looming frame and stumble over my words. "Ah, well, uh… No, not… Umm."

Hope plants a hand on her hip and stares at me with a wry smile. "*Ha*. I didn't think so."

Should our relationship have an elevated label? Mom asked if we were more than friends. Would it be more normal if we were officially boyfriend and girlfriend? Doesn't being his date mean we are dating?

Ugh. This is so confusing.

"I thought you and Meghan were friends," Hope says in a softer

195

tone.

It takes me by surprise, and my words come out clearly. "We are."

"Then why are you hogging the boy she likes? Nothing in life goes her way. Every day, she is more miserable. Ash's love life was never complicated. He could make my sister happy without outside interference. Why are you coming into town and ruining everything for her?"

"I didn't come to town with a plan to mess up Meghan's love life," I say, quivering in my shoes. "Ash and I got to know each other before I met Meghan."

"You're at Ashworth Academy now," Hope says, standing over me. "You have your pick of boys. Everyone at school has distanced themselves from my sister. Can't you imagine how it must feel to be invisible?"

My heart drops to my gut.

Yes.

"Look around at this party," Hope says, gesturing to the boys in the room. "Any of them would happily be your date for the benefit. Call it off with Ash."

I blink hard and take a step back from Hope. "Even if I did, it doesn't mean Ash would want to date Meghan. You don't have mind control powers over him."

"I had this plan long before you showed up," Hope says. "I have a history with Ash. Don't worry about how I'll fix them up."

"Ash and I have a relationship," I say, standing taller and with a slight fear I'll puke on her shoes. "We don't have to have an official label to care about each other. Back off, Hope. You can't control Ash, and you can't control me."

Hope's stern expression doesn't falter. "Don't test me, Christie."

"Excuse me," I mutter and slip past her.

I can't let Hope in my head. I know Meghan is infatuated with Ash, but that's all Hope's doing. Hope told her stories about him to lift her

196

spirits and get her out of her depression. I commend her for being a loving sister. But tormenting and manipulating people isn't the way to make Meghan happy.

Tomorrow at the manor, I'll talk this out with Meghan. Meghan is excited about the benefit, like it's her big sweet sixteen party. Everyone will give her attention. With the right encouragement, I'm sure she can find a nice boy. Someone who will be happy to visit her and create fun and romantic dates.

Ash isn't the guy for Meghan.

I walk toward him, and he greets me with a stunning and affectionate smile.

He's not hers because he's my guy.

Twenty

"Hey, where'd you go?" Ash asks, holding his arms out.

I step into him and melt into his hug. "Nowhere important," I say into his ear.

"Well, you realize there's no way I'm letting you go now."

I giggle. "Fine with me."

Ash tilts his head. "Come on. Let's get out of this noise and find a spot outside."

"I like the sound of that."

"I hope I wasn't too blunt with you before," Ash says as we make our way outside. He waves to people who call out to him and returns his focus to me. "I didn't mean to make you feel bad. I'm sorry if anything I said offended you."

"Ash, it's okay. We are still figuring each other out."

"I just don't want to say anything hurtful to you," Ash says, cupping my hand as we walk through the moonlit garden. "I know I have in the past. I don't want to repeat it."

"I'll work on my communication, too. You've pointed out that my face says things that my mouth is too chicken to spit out."

Ash smiles. "We'll work on this stuff together."

"Deal."

The garden is like a piece of living artwork. The hillside slope is landscaped into stepped garden beds of yellow and pink flowers. Each flower bed surrounds a staircase waterfall. It's magical under the garden lights. I'd love to see the flowers in their glorious colors during the daytime.

The garden path winds in curved shapes, and we find a timber deck with plush patio furniture. A few kids spread out on the outdoor sofas call out for Ash to join them.

Ash waves and turns away. His hand presses on my back, guiding me to the edge of the decking. It is a good distance from the group, where we can talk without disruption.

Before I sit, I force myself to smile and wave to the group. The kids take the bait, smiling and waving back. I sit, hoping not to do anything awkward and ruin my small victory.

"Nice work, Klein," Ash says, sitting beside me.

"I promise, I will try to be more outgoing."

"Do it for yourself, not for me."

I breathe out slowly.

He tilts his head to find my eyes. "What?"

"I have to convince myself I want to do it."

"You do. Your friends with me after my horrible first impression. Somehow, you found something to like about Meghan Fisher."

"Seriously, what's the deal with you two? She's got a crush on you despite spending no time with you. Plus, you think she's evil when all I've seen is a bubbly and sweet girl."

Ash looks at the stars and tugs his arms around a bent knee. "No way. You're a sweet girl. Meghan is your opposite."

"Tell me what happened. Is there an important reason I shouldn't be friends with her?"

Ash releases his knee and turns in my direction. "My bad for bringing her up. We have better topics to discuss than Meghan."

"Ash, please. You don't want me to judge, so tell me the truth. I need to know what happened to decide whether I want to be friends with her."

Ash's beautiful brown eyes are bigger tonight. They gaze into mine without blinking, yet they keep the delicate detail I love so much.

I place my hands on the sides of his face and whisper, "Did she hurt you?"

"I'm not talking about it," Ash mutters and slides off the deck.

Ash flops back on the grass and stares at the sky, ignoring my questions.

After fumbling with the straps of my high heels, I yank the shoes off my feet. I collapse on the pillow-soft grass and lay my hand on his. I watch him in silence as his chest rises and falls. His eyes remain steady.

Ash's face tenses, and then he turns my way. His nostrils flare but not in anger. His downcast eyes and gloomy frown make my heart hurt.

I roll onto my side and wrap his hand in mine.

"She broke up my family," he whispers in a broken tone.

I lie still, unable to take my focus off his eyes. "What?"

"There were posters all over the school," Ash says, his eyes growing glassy. "They showed pictures of my mother and a teacher, telling everyone they had an affair."

My mouth forms an o, and my hands want to slam over it. I keep them clutched to Ash's hands, showing all the support I can give him.

"It wasn't true," Ash says, his voice fracturing. "It was a lie… but it didn't matter. It was already planted in everyone's minds."

"And Meghan did this?" I ask, anger boiling inside me. "Why

would she do this?"

"I told you," he whispers roughly. "She's a cruel girl."

"It's just not the impression I got," I reply. "I'm sorry, Ash. If I had known…"

"Can you believe Hope would do that?"

I nod in response.

"Meghan always copied her big sister," Ash says, blinking his eyes clear. "Don't you ever wonder why she never gets visitors? Hope works hard to make people visit her sister and pretend to be her friend."

"How did you find out it was Meghan?"

Ash shrugs and turns his gaze back to the stars. Whenever he focuses on the twinkling display, a calm washes over him.

"I was on everyone's case," Ash says. "I was questioning everyone and demanded they find out who did it. Before I'd gotten too far into the search, Meghan confessed."

"What was her excuse? Her reasoning?"

Ash shakes his head. "I had no desire to listen. I walked out on her."

"Were you two close at the time?"

He turns to face me. "No. She spent time with Hope and Vanessa. I'd see her around the manor, but no, we weren't friends."

"I don't get it," I mutter. I look at the stars and sigh. "Not that I expect to get it. Bullies make no sense."

"Meghan ruined that teacher's reputation. He had to move to another state and now works at a crappy underfunded school. My parents lost trust in one another. Other factors led to their breakup, but Meghan helped speed it up."

Why would she make these posters? What did she have to gain? Was it to attack the Ashworth family matriarch? Are the Fishers fighting for the Ashworths' stature in the community?

"Don't overanalyze this," Ash whispers, turning on his side and resting his head on my shoulder. "I didn't want you to know. I don't like thinking about it."

I smooth my hand over his hair and kiss the top of his head. "Okay, I won't. It's from before my time. It's none of my business."

Ash lifts his head and pastes a small, brave smile over his lips. He gives me a peck and whispers, "Thanks."

"Is there anything interesting up there?" I ask, pointing at the sky. Ash lies on his back, and I continue, "Any cool constellations you can teach me?"

Ash points upward, saying, "Well, you know the Big Dipper, right?"

"Nope."

"What?" Ash blurts, flabbergasted.

I giggle at his response.

"How?" he blurts. "How is that possible?"

"Because not everyone is a big old star nerd like you," I tease.

"Then I guess we're going back to basics," Ash says.

As Ash points out each star in the constellation, commenting that it looks like a wonky frying pan, I try to pay attention. I make a joke about how a rich kid couldn't know what a frying pan looks like. I love that it makes him laugh, but I can't get Meghan out of my head.

She publicly humiliated Ash, and she ruined her relationship with Vanessa. Vanessa went overseas with her mother, so the fallout didn't leave her as Team Meghan.

Meghan wanting a romantic relationship with Ash doesn't make sense. Unless her illness gave her memory loss or she suffered a severe bump to the head. Why would she think she'd ever have a chance with him?

"Christie?" Ash says in a tone like it's taken several attempts to gain my attention.

"Sorry," I say, blinking at the sky. "Just taking it all in."

"Everyone at this party knows that story," Ash says softly. "Everyone saw the pictures and heard the rumors. You didn't, and it was nice not having that hanging over me."

My eyes water. "I'm sorry I made you tell me."

"You're the only one on the grass looking at stars with me." Ash grins. "You're the only one making this party bearable. Thank you for being with me."

I wipe under my eyes and smile. "I wouldn't be anywhere else."

"It was photos of them leaving a parent-teacher conference."

"What?"

"On the posters. My mom and the teacher were in the parking lot talking. It was photoshopped to appear suspicious. No one cared that they were fake. The lie grew bigger."

"It's horrible your family had to deal with this."

"Dealing with rumors about our family money or business is fair enough. But stories about my parents' infidelity..." Ash pauses as a scowl twists his lips. "I hated it. Online trolling would be one thing, but sticking posters on lockers was a personal attack."

I brush a hand across his cheek and swallow hard.

"It's terrible that Meghan has this illness, and I hope she gets a cure or better medication," Ash says. "I feel sorry for her, but I don't forgive her."

"I understand. I don't even want to talk to her now."

"She is alone, and you two get along. I don't want to be the reason she gets more depressed."

"You would really be fine with me hanging out with Meghan?"

"I never told you that you couldn't. I don't own you."

"I don't know if I could be that open-minded."

"What am I supposed to do? If I publicly hold a grudge against her, it'll look so bad."

"You're saving face?"

Ash sits up and brushes the grass off his shirt. "That's what you do when people constantly watch you."

I sit up and notice the kids on the couches who whisper in our direction. I peer over my shoulder at the house, and the few kids in the backyard are also gossiping in our direction.

"You truly are Mr. Popular," I remark. "It's like you're this town's celebrity."

"They all just want a story."

"And you play along and act like you blend in to never give them something to talk about."

Ash leans in and kisses me with the perfect pressure.

He pulls away. "Do you feel like you get me now?"

Whistling fills the open space after our kiss receives an audience. I blush and nod. I could never get used to this amount of attention.

"I'm more timid than a wallflower," I whisper. "I don't have any experience that will help me understand your past."

"I can handle having eyes on me. I want people I can depend on. Since my family's divided, I've had nothing that comes close. I know how to handle the clowns circling us at this party. None of them care what's going on between us. But I do. I want to know you, Christie."

"You do," I whisper. I pull at the skirt of my baby-blue dress. "You knew I'd love this dress."

"I just don't want us to misread the signs."

"Isn't honesty a good first step?"

"True."

I gesture to the ogling crowd. "I don't want to join all these onlookers."

"If you run, they'll think there's a story. If we go inside, act casual, and get a drink, they'll leave us alone and move onto a better target."

"That's all there is to it?"

Ash grins and stands up. He holds out his hand to help me up. He grabs my shoes and holds my hand as we take the path back to the house.

"Hey, Ash," a girl says, bouncing on the balls of her feet. "Who's your friend?"

"This is Christie Klein," Ash replies. "The most beautiful girl in school."

"*Ash*," I gasp.

Ash laughs and continues to drag me along.

The girl squeals and dashes off to her friends to gossip about me.

I squeeze Ash's hand as a thought bubbles in my mind. Is this his way of telling the school we're official?

My heart pounds, and goose bumps cover my limbs. A smile creeps on my face as we pass more people wanting to know my name. Shockingly, I want them to know it. I want them to know Christie Klein is the girl Ash wants to spend all his time with.

We make our way into the party, and just like at school, kids move out of Ash's way like he's Moses parting the Red Sea. I loop my arm with his, proud and confident to have every eye on us as a couple.

I avoid scrutinizing the observing faces. I only have eyes for Ash. He grabs two lemonades, and we snag a couch in a corner. Just like he predicted, we become old news. The party is lively with dancing and macho drinking games. Ash and I snuggle together, and in our little space, everything else turns into white noise.

It's easy to ignore everything else when you have such a beautiful boy next to you. Ash looks at me like I'm the only girl in the world. My heart swells, and my cheeks hurt from smiling. I'm relieved my first party has a monumentally positive ending.

As the party winds down, Ash calls Sam, and we make our way toward the front door.

"Ashworth, can we hitch a ride home?" Luke calls out, his arm slung around Hope.

Ash beckons them over. "Yeah. Come on."

Okay, so maybe not the positive ending I was hoping for. Best-case scenario, Hope and Luke live extremely close to Cody, and they get their butts out of the limo ASAP.

It doesn't take long for Sam to arrive, and I instantly feel bad. He's been sitting in this neighborhood, waiting for Ash's call. His job would suck.

Ash and I take one seat and face Hope and Luke, who practically wrestle to sit on top of one another.

"You two look awfully close," Hope says, staring at Ash and me. The back of our hands touching between us.

Ash smirks. "You haven't noticed the fact we're dating."

I involuntarily gulp as Hope's eye twitches.

"I'd call that close," Luke jokes. He nudges Hope. "You should see these two, babe. They were sucking faces."

"Shut up." Ash laughs. "That's you and Hope all over."

"So just dating?" Hope clarifies with a mocking undertone. Her eyebrow rises as she intently stares at Ash. "Just some fun. Is that all she is, Ash?"

"*Babe*," Luke whines. "Give the guy a break."

"What?" Hope retorts. "I just want the facts. I care about him."

"Since when do you care about facts?" Ash hits back.

Hope scoffs, and Luke laughs, cuddling into his girlfriend.

It's not long until the car stops at a house, and Luke's arms unwillingly release Hope.

"See you tomorrow, Ashworth," Luke says and then smooches Hope before leaping off the seat.

He slaps Ash's thigh as he exits the limousine.

Ash waves him off. "See ya round."

Hope blows a kiss out the tinted window. "Bye, baby," she says in a high pitch.

Ash's fingers play with mine in the space between us. I rub my lips as my smile grows. I don't latch onto his hand because Hope's laser focus is on us.

"What do you and Luke have planned for tomorrow?" Hope asks Ash.

"Nothing much," Ash says, laying his hand on the leather seat beside mine. "He's coming over while you ladies have your meeting. It's the only time he's allowed out of your sight."

Hope giggles. "I have him well trained."

Ash smirks. "That's one way to put it."

"I'm glad you'll be at the estate when we visit," Hope continues. "Meghan will be in bed by now, but she'll be so sad she didn't have the chance to say hi. You'll say hello tomorrow, won't you, Ash?"

"You will all be in the manor," Ash says, fidgeting in his seat. "Luke and I will be on the grounds."

Hope clicks her tongue in annoyance. "It takes no effort to say hi."

Ash looks at the floor as he replies, "You know I'll say hi if I see her."

Hope smiles, flicking her shiny brunette hair off her shoulder. "It would mean so much to her." Her eyes move from Ash to me. "She'll be delighted to see you again, Christie."

I nod as the blood drains from my head. "I can't wait to see her too."

The limousine slows, and we pull up at another grand two-story house with a manicured front lawn.

"Here's my stop," Hope chirps. She bounces toward us and kisses Ash's cheek as she says goodbye. She then tugs me into a non-consensual hug, squishing me in her grip. "Thanks for being Meghan's friend," she whispers harshly. "You know what to do to make her happy, and it's greatly appreciated."

I tap her back. "Bye, Hope. See you tomorrow."

Hope leaves the car. I've never been so relieved and tense at the same moment.

"Don't let her pressure you," Ash says as the car drives away.

"She's just so overbearing," I say, staring out the blackened window. "Her eyes are so intense, and her words are so controlling."

"It's just a game to her," Ash says, lacing his fingers with mine. I draw my eyes from the window and find peace in his gaze. "Don't let her use you as a plaything. You deserve better than that."

"She wants me out of the way because Meghan has a crush on you."

"I'm sorry she's giving you trouble because we are friends. If she didn't see us together, maybe she'd never talk to you."

"It will take a lot more than Hope's pettiness to keep me away from you."

Ash's shoulders relax, and an easy smile curves his lips. He leans in and kisses me gently.

The next fifteen minutes back to Ashworth Estate are spent in silence. Ash's arms are secure around me, and my head rests on his shoulder. When my eyes grow heavy, my head slides onto his chest. His heart races by my ear, and I briskly rub his arm. The situation with me, Hope, and Meghan is stressing him out.

I pull my head up and kiss his cheek. Our noses touch, and I keep my eyes closed. I want him to feel safe with me. He has enough to deal with regarding his family. I want things with me to feel easy.

Our lips press together again, but this time, the suction is feverish. I slide my hands into his hair, my blood pumping in overdrive, and my lips are hungry to devour him. Ash's arms link behind my back and draw me closer. Not in my wildest dreams could I imagine being so close to someone, both physically and emotionally. Never did I imagine meeting someone like Ash and falling so hard.

Ash's lips nibble against my neck, and a soft moan pours out of me. His warm breath tickles my skin, and I bite into my lip.

My fingertips dance behind his neck, and his kisses stop when he laughs.

When Ash's face pulls out of my hair and away from my neck, I ask, "What?"

His goofy smile makes him even cuter than before. "You were tickling me."

I giggle, collapsing forward. "Whoops. Sorry."

Ash laughs. "It was cute but totally killed my momentum."

The limousine pulls to a stop at the tall gates of Ashworth Estate.

"Looks like we ran out of time anyway," I comment.

Ash caresses my jawline and then plays with one of my curls. He whispers, "I don't know about that."

The car winds toward the manor, and we thank Sam when he opens the door for us.

Ash leads me inside by the hand. Murphy greets us in the foyer, but Ash tells him we're going upstairs. I want to get my midnight snack container before we go, but the tender way Ash holds my hand leaves me no option but to go wherever he leads. Seriously, I cannot get enough of this boy.

Upstairs, we are hands, elbows, and lips. My back presses against the wall between our bedroom doors as passion flames our kisses. I loop my arms around his neck, and with strength and comfort, he holds my hips.

One of his hands slides along my dress. He plants the other on the wall by my shoulder. I tease his bottom lip. I should let go. Take a breath. I can't. My desire levels are off the charts. We pressed into each other as his hands sneak around my back.

I pull my face away, taking an influx of air. Ash pants in front of me. A playful grin spreads as his face grows red with heat.

"Wow," I whisper, my chest rising and falling.

"Yeah," he says, composing himself. "I've been avoiding something, but maybe I should ask."

Dread falls into the pit of my stomach. I hate that my mind always catapults to the worst-case scenario.

"We're dating, right?" Ash says, keeping his body close to mine. "We kiss, we talk, we're great together. Should we be more than friends?"

I suck in a breath and splutter a cough. I slap my chest, and blurt, "Are you asking me to be your girlfriend?"

Ash muffles a nervous laugh and looks away bashfully as he nods.

"Yes!" I exclaim. "I want that so bad."

Ash turns back to me, grinning. "Whoa."

"I'm crazy about you, Ash. I want this to be official."

Ash replies with another monumental kiss.

"What a great night," he whispers and then kisses the spot below my earlobe.

I giggle and admit, "I need a cold shower now."

Ash laughs. "Me too. So you're my girlfriend, Christie Klein?"

I bite into my lips but can't hide the smile. My whole face hurts. "Yes, boyfriend."

Twenty-One

Thomas Ashworth III is my boyfriend. Who could have foreseen a bratty rich kid becoming my favorite person? I was wrong about him. He's generous, protective, and a fabulous kisser. All the feels sent me to dreamland with no bad thoughts. No more nightmares for this girl!

On my way to breakfast, I visit my parents' suite. Inside, I find Dad at the desk, hurriedly typing on his laptop.

"Don't you ever stop working," I joke, stepping through the doorway.

Dad sends me a smile. "Just checking a few things off the list. Good morning, Christie. How was last night?"

"Better than expected," I reply, giving Dad a hug.

"Great. I'm proud of you, kiddo."

"Are you coming to breakfast?"

Dad nods at his laptop. "I have a few things to wrap up. I'll see you down there."

"Okay. Don't work too hard," I say, leaving the suite.

Downstairs, I walk into the dining room and find Mom scrolling on her iPad.

Mom sets it on the table and grins as I take my seat. "Good morning, sweetie. Did you sleep well?"

"Very," I say as Murphy pushes my chair in behind me.

Mom taps the iPad screen. "I was just getting my daily news fix while I waited for someone to join me. Your dad is upstairs replying to emails."

"I know. I just tried to pry him away."

"Did you have fun at the party?"

"It was fine. I stuck with Ash. I could have done that here."

"You can't rely on Ash for your social life. You need to make more friends."

"I'm trying," I reply. "I made an effort to say hello to some kids. Some of them learned my name. I dunno, maybe school will be easier this week."

"That's great," Mom beams. "Maybe you can try talking to other girls at the society meeting tomorrow instead of limiting yourself to the Fisher girls?"

"Believe me, I'm ready to widen my circle. Those girls are trouble."

"Meghan can't be a troublemaker."

"Pancakes, Miss Klein?" Murphy asks, pouring orange juice into my glass.

I pat my stomach. "I'd better not if I need to wear an evening gown next weekend. Can I have muesli and yogurt, please?"

"As you wish," Murphy replies. "Would you like it accompanied by seasonal fruits?"

I grin. "That sounds amazing. Ah, Murphy, has Ash already eaten breakfast?"

"Master Ashworth hasn't left his suite yet," Murphy replies. "Can I get you anything else?"

"Oh. Ah, umm, no. I'm good, thanks."

"Did you get in late last night?" Mom asks.

"No later than I usually go to sleep. A little after midnight."

"You need a better routine on school nights."

I nod. "I know. I will. It's just been hectic adjusting to everything."

"I agree. That's why I haven't been on your case." Mom picks up her coffee cup. "What are you going to do today?"

"I want to finish the artwork for Ash. I have new ideas I need to get onto the canvas."

"It's good to see you excited again."

"Last night at the party, Ash and I spent time stargazing. It gave me epic inspiration."

Mom leans forward. "Does Ash like stargazing?"

"He loves it. He has a telescope set up on his balcony and used it to show me Venus."

"Wow. That's exciting."

"Ugh." I hit my forehead. "No, it was Jupiter. Mom, it was so cool."

"You're so smitten," Mom says giddily.

I lean forward and stage whisper, "He asked me to be his girlfriend."

Mom leaps from her seat, cheering and punching the air.

"*Mom*! You're so embarrassing."

"I am elated for you. You are radiating happiness."

"Geez. Please, just sit down."

Mom laughs and plonks in her seat. "What else is a mother to do than embarrass her child? So you two are officially a couple?"

I fan my face and nod in confirmation.

"You must be dying to see him," Mom says, bouncing in place.

"I can't wait. But if he sleeps in, I'll have more time to paint. I want the artwork to be a surprise."

"Aw, he'll love that. And what about the silent auction piece?"

I clear my throat and sit back as Murphy arrives with my breakfast. "It's coming along," I lie.

"Mrs. Fisher is counting on it."

"I know. I know. I'll have it done in time."

"Of course you will, sweetie."

I zip through breakfast and bound up the stairs as Dad ambles his way down. I tell him I'll catch up with him later, and continue to the art studio.

The bench seat is the focal point of the artwork. Today, I want to focus on the sky. Instead of continuing with my intended daytime setting, I want to paint a romantic evening. I mix a dark-navy color and study the saved images on my phone. My goal is to reimagine the constellations Ash had pointed out. Perhaps I'll paint a wonky frying pan in the midnight sky.

My hands tingle as I work on the delicate stars. My heart swells with the desire to show Ash the interest I take in his passions. I see things in a different light because of him. It's crazy that we haven't known each other our whole lives.

When I'm in the zone, hours feel like minutes. I do not know how many have passed when I hear footsteps.

"Hey, can I see?" Ash asks, entering the studio.

I leap off my stool and hurry toward the door. "No, don't come in," I blurt.

Ash's eyes widen, and he takes a step backward. His shoulders tense as he mutters, "Huh?"

"It's a surprise," I say, panting.

His eyebrow lifts. "Isn't it for the benefit?"

I look over my shoulder and point at an easel further back, showcasing a blank canvas. "I haven't started working on the auction piece yet."

"But I thought you were Miss Goody Two-shoes," Ash jokes.

"I had something else I needed to paint first."

It intrigues Ash. "And it's a surprise for me?"

I fan my face and nod my head.

"Aw, now I wanna see."

"No, I need more time," I say with a giggle. "You slept in today?"

"It was a long night," Ash says, followed by an exhausted huff.

"What happened?" I ask, worried.

Last night ended in such a thrilling and delightful way, yet he seems drained. Will he take back his commitment to me?

"Don't worry about it," Ash says, waving it off.

"Ash," I say, reaching out for his arm. "Talk to me."

Ash blinks, and his eyes turn irritated, and then soften into sadness.

I caress his cheek and wait for him to find his words.

"I was talking to my mother," he says, taking my hand. "Well, I tried to talk. Ugh, it was just so frustrating."

"You were arguing?"

"I wanted to tell her about you."

My heart balloons in my chest, and I can't help but smile.

"She didn't equal my enthusiasm," Ash says, frowning.

My smile disappears. "What did she say?"

Ash holds my hand. "She said nothing bad about you. She just changed the subject."

Ash fidgets in place, huffs, and rolls his eyes.

Sweat builds in my palms. "If you don't want to, you don't have to discuss it."

"She kept talking about the benefit," Ash blurts, dropping my hand. "She's controlling all the society stuff without physically being here." He groans with frustration and steps away from me. "She's just like my dad, using any excuse not to deal with family issues. Why don't either of them care about reuniting our family?"

My bottom lip quivers, but I steady myself to be strong for him.

In a low tone, Ash says, "Mom didn't want to dwell on you because she was talking with Mrs. Fisher. Mom wants me to take Meghan to the benefit."

Instantly, I'm dizzy. My ankles grow weak, and I'm one false move from falling over.

"I won't be her pawn," Ash says, moving toward me and wrapping his arms around me.

My heart pounds as my face plants against his shoulder and his head buries beside mine.

He stood up for me.

He stood up for us. Our relationship.

Relief spreads through my body, and I hug him.

He sighs against me. "My sister still won't answer my calls."

"Still?" I question. "You said you'd given up talking to her. I didn't know that meant she was giving you radio silence."

Ash nods as he pulls away. "Ness became difficult, and now she's shutting me out. It must be the Ashworth curse." He holds my waist. "I just need you."

I kiss his cheek. "I'm not going anywhere."

"In that case, girlfriend," Ash says, "can I take you out on a date tonight?"

My eyes alight. "A date? Absolutely."

"We spent the entire party together," Ash says, blinking his eyes dry. "We may as well do something intimate."

I bite my lip. "Intimate?"

"As in alone," Ash replies. "Just you and me."

"Sounds perfect."

"I have something planned. Do you trust me?"

I grin and run my hands along his back. "You haven't let me down yet."

He kisses my nose, and whispers, "Well… I need your trust because we need to take the chopper."

I choke on air. "Excuse me?"

"It'll be worth it. I promise."

"Do you remember how I feel about helicopters?"

Ash jokes, "I believe the words were 'death trap.'"

I huff. "Exactly."

"It won't be as bad as you're imagining."

"It'd better not because I have a very vivid imagination."

Ash smiles, replying, "You should wear something from the formal rack."

"Really? Intriguing."

Ash pecks my lips. "Do you think you can take a break from painting?"

"Hmm. Stand in a cute boy's arms, or go back to painting? That's a tough one."

Ash laughs and lifts me into the air. I'm a squealing mess as he spins me in a circle.

It wasn't a hard choice to leave the art studio.

When it's time to get ready for our date, I rope in Claudia for hair duty. She helped me choose a dress from the rack. It's lilac and glistens with rhinestones. I work on makeup to match.

With my hair in a high bun and diamante high heels on my feet, I feel like a princess. Ash meets in the hall in a dapper suit. His jacket is crushed velvet, his hair is slicked back, and he smells irresistible.

"My gosh, I didn't think you could get more handsome," I gush.

"I'd give you a compliment," Ash replies, "but I'm speechless."

I playfully hit his arm in response. We link arms, and Ash escorts me from the manor to the helipad.

My gut flips like it's trying out for Olympic gymnastics.

Ash holds me close, saying, "You'll be okay. I've got you."

The pilot helps me into the cockpit, and Ash nestles in beside me. He gives us headsets so we can talk during the journey. When the propeller starts, I'm close to vomiting.

"The view of the mountains from above is worth it," Ash says. "I'm

217

sure you'll have great inspiration for your next masterpiece."

I take comfort in Ash's words and squeeze the life out of his hand as we ascend.

"Leave some blood flow," he jokes.

I relieve the pressure with a quick apology.

"It's all good," he says with a laugh.

"I can handle planes," I say. "This thing feels low to the ground."

"Our dads take this to work," Ash replies. "If it wasn't safe, your dad wouldn't have let you come with me."

I exhale loudly, and it reverberates through my headset. Sinking into the seat, I say, "You're right. Thanks."

The helicopter glides over mountains and valleys in unique shades of green. The land below is lush with trees, and the blue water slithers throughout.

"This place is magical," I say, eyeing the view.

"There's Victoria Falls," Ash points out. "Cody's house is somewhere in that corner. Logan's Point is over that hill. It's a small town, more working class."

"Oh, so it's not all glitz and glamour in the mountains?"

"Not at all. There is a lot of adventure. Like hiking, rock climbing, and canoeing. Are you into any of that stuff?"

"I've already told you that I'm a homebody."

Ash cuddles me close as the helicopter pans over the majestic mountains. The shades of green darken as the sky succumbs to the night. As the land clears, the helicopter turns in a wide half-circle. As we descend, we circle a large domed building surrounded by vacant land.

"This is our stop," Ash says.

"What is this place?"

"It's an observatory."

I gasp and pivot my gaze between the building and him. "Your dream place."

"I love this place," Ash says. "The dream is to build my own. But for now, I visit here."

When the helicopter lands, my stomach jumps up and down at will. Ash helps me out, and we make our way into the observatory.

"Mr. Ashworth," a friendly man with graying hair and dressed in a navy suit says at the entrance. "Welcome."

"Thanks, Gerald," Ash says. "Everything ready?"

"Just as you requested," Gerald responds. He nods at me. "Good evening, Miss Klein."

It's a surprise he already knows my name. I smile in reply.

Ash holds my hand as we move through the foyer. We enter a hall decorated with large photographs of constellations and planets hanging in thin black frames.

"I've rented this place for the night," Ash says as we approach the gigantic telescope. "We can point this thing to anywhere in the universe."

"Wow," I whisper, wrapping my head around the fact my boyfriend rented out an observatory.

Ash continues, "And there's a balcony upstairs where our dinner will be served."

"Excuse me," I say, dumbfounded. "We are having dinner here?"

"I arranged for a top chef to prepare his signature dishes."

I struggle to gasp against my widening smile. Eventually, I spit out, "We're eating a gourmet meal above a telescope?"

Ash swoops in and kisses my cheek. "Pretty cool, right?"

"Extraordinary, more like it."

Ash tugs me toward the telescope. "Come on. What do you want to see first?"

"I wouldn't know where to start."

"How about Venus?" Ash suggests, wiggling his eyebrows. "You know, the goddess of *lurve*."

I giggle. "You goof."

Ash punches in coordinates, and I'm impressed by how capable he is with massive technical equipment.

"How often do you come here?"

"Every few weeks, if I can. Maybe every couple of months when life stuff gets too busy."

"Do they always let you monkey around the equipment?"

"My grandfather made a hefty donation," Ash says. "They have a soft spot for me."

"That's cool that your grandfather took an interest in your passion."

"My grandfather is a cool guy," Ash says, peering into the eyepiece. "I don't get to see him much since he retired and moved to the Bahamas with wife number four."

"Oh, whoa."

"I know. She's younger than my mom." Ash smirks. He pulls away from the eyepiece. "Do you want to look?"

"Is it Venus?" I ask, trading places with Ash.

"No. The coordinates for Saturn came to mind."

"Whoa," I gasp, looking at the planet. "I can see the rings! Wow, this is so cool."

"I love that you get as excited as me."

I pull away from the eyepiece and turn to Ash. "I love that you want to share this stuff with me. I know what it's like to keep everything to yourself. It's so cool we have each other now."

He takes my hand and looks deeply into my eyes. "I agree. You're so special, Christie."

I lean into him. He is as incredible as his kiss.

Ash shows me a few of his favorite constellations. His genius-level mind knows how every gadget works. When our stomachs rumble, Ash takes me up the elevator to our private dining balcony. A quaint round table with a white tablecloth and a single pink rose sits in the middle of the balcony.

"How romantic," I gush.

"Did I do all right?" Ash asks with a lop-sided grin.

"It's so elegant and refined," I say, approaching the table.

220

Ash pulls out my chair, and I fan out the skirt of my dress as I sit.

"Would you like my jacket?" Ash offers.

"I'm okay right now. Maybe later."

Ash sits across from me and says, "Just ask."

"Thank you."

A man in a white dinner jacket, pressed white shirt, and black trousers enters the balcony, pushing a cart. He fills our glasses with sparkling mineral water and serves our entrées. Melt in your mouth lemon-butter scallops presented on their shells. When I clear my plate, I instantly want more.

The main course follows. Until now, I didn't know what made beef Wellington special. The tenderloin is thick yet juicy, wrapped in exquisite prosciutto and perfectly flakey pastry.

Oh my gosh. I've died and gone to food heaven.

When our main plates are cleared, Ash asks, "Have you got room for dessert?"

I grin. "It's always a yes to dessert. I just need a minute."

"Good call," Ash says, sliding his chair back. "Do you want to dance?"

"Uh, umm," I stammer. "No, I don't dance."

"Sure you do."

"No, I don't."

"You're going to a benefit next weekend," Ash says, rounding the table and extending his hand. "You'll have to dance."

"Is it a requirement?" I ask skeptically.

"You can't be my date and leave me hanging," he says with a downright irresistible smile.

I admit defeat and stand, tossing my linen napkin over my plate.

"I'll dance," I reply, taking his hand, "because we're alone. I'll only embarrass myself in front of you."

"There's nothing to it," Ash says, holding my hand high as his other hand nestles on my back. "Just place your hand on my shoulder and follow my lead."

"But where do I step?"

"In an easy circle, like this."

"But this dress is too long."

"No, it's not. Seriously, Klein, is there a scenario where step one isn't panic?"

I stop the comeback from flying out of my mouth. Instead, I pay attention to my feet. Ash holds me with grace. Our closeness takes me out of my head. I stop focusing on my clumsy steps and stare into his eyes. They sparkle like the night sky, and I give in to the dreamy fairytale moment.

Ash finishes the dance by lifting my arm high, and instinctively, I twirl. I giggle as he pulls me back. He pecks my lips and thanks me for the dance.

"Thank you for getting me out of my comfort zone," I reply.

"No sweat," he says and gestures to the railing by the balcony's edge.

We walk across and lean against the railing.

"I'm so glad you're here with me," Ash says.

"I can see why this is your favorite place," I admit. "It's magical."

"I can crash a party," Ash begins. "I can throw money at people. None of it registers. I like the quiet, looking above, and finally having someone to share it with."

Resting my head against his shoulder, I wrap my arm around him. "I'm so glad you shared this with me. It makes me feel so close to you."

"Good, that was the idea."

We settle into the silence, gazing above at the glitzy sky. No one ever said dating could feel this good. We end the night by sharing a sinfully decadent chocolate layer cake, and I take home the pink rose to sit by my bed. It'll be the perfect accompaniment as I drift off to dreamland.

Or, hopefully, my mind drifts back to this evening.

Twenty-Two

From breakfast to the ride to school, Ash and I are a lovesick mess. At the dining table, we slide our chairs impossibly close together, and in the limo, I practically sit on top of him. I only restrained myself out of fear of crushing our blazers and starting crude rumors at school. Kids at school would say we were making out. It'd be true, but I don't want a spotlight on me.

Ash walks me to my locker, and my pace is a dawdle at best. When we reach the locker, he is leaving me. He has his Monday morning meeting with his physics professor. I need him by my side. I don't want to brave the school hallways without his protection.

"Are you sure I can't sit in on your meeting?" I ask in a whiny voice.

Ash laughs. "You'll be bored out of your mind."

"I have experience from the observatory."

He smirks and squeezes my hand as my locker nears. "It won't help you with what we're discussing."

I huff in a joking way. "Fine."

He gives me a peck on my cheek. "You'll be fine on your own. You survived your first party, so school will be a piece of cake."

I reach for my locker and sigh. "Whatever."

Ash's hand curves around my lower back, and he pulls me against him. His lips press onto mine, and I melt into the kiss. Cheers and whistles erupt around us. My skin crawls as Ash pulls away.

He strokes my hair, kisses my cheek, and whispers goodbye.

I wave him off, and my face heats with embarrassment. The moving crowd goes back to their conversations.

"Hi, Ash," a tall girl with bright-blond hair and slender blue eyes says.

"Hey," Ash says with a wave and continues along the corridor.

The girl steps closer to me and waves. "Christie, isn't it?"

I nod. "That's right."

"I saw you at the party with Ash. I'm Wendy," she says with a wave. "I was at the last society meeting at the Ashworth Estate, but Mrs. Fisher blocked me from mingling."

I relax into a smile. "She is a tad intense."

"I saw you were talking to her daughter Meghan."

"Ah, yeah," I say, scratching behind my ear. "We've hung out a few times, but I didn't know her history at this school."

Wendy fidgets with her footing, and asks, "Did she say anything about me?"

"We haven't talked about anyone she went to school with," I reply. "Only that she had a boyfriend who dumped her after she got sick. I didn't realize I was at a party Cody was hosting until I got there."

Wendy chews on her lip, and then confesses, "I ask because I'm Cody's new girlfriend."

I hug my arms around my middle. "You want to know if she's trash-talking you?"

Wendy's eyes droop as she whispers, "I just miss her."

The surprise response leaves me speechless.

"Meghan and I were friends," Wendy explains. "She always preferred to hang out with her sister and the older crowd. I was used to her pushing me away, but I never expected her to shut me out after she left school."

"Maybe she feels hurt because you're dating her ex?"

Wendy shakes her head. "No, she didn't let me visit before she and Cody broke up."

"Really?"

I raise my hands to my face and press them over my mouth. I feel like a fool. I thought Meghan was cool. Since learning how she humiliated Ash and now finding out she lied about her friends not wanting to visit, I must be a horrible judge of character.

"Meghan leaving school brought Cody and me together," Wendy continues. "It was like we were in mourning... but she's not dead. It's messed up."

"What is Meghan really like?" I ask. "She seems so bubbly and sweet. Is it all a façade?"

"She acts bubbly with you?"

"Yeah."

Wendy smiles. "That's great. Maybe she's coming back."

"So... Meghan was always nice?"

"Always nice?" Wendy says with a chuckle. "You've met her older sister, right? Her mentor?"

Ugh.

The bell rings, and Wendy pats my shoulder. "Just be careful around Meghan."

As Wendy walks away, my mind wars with the two versions of Meghan inside my head. Talking to Wendy made things more confusing.

Above that, Meghan hurt Ash, and it's inexcusable.

I wander to my first class. Bummer. No Ash all morning. I hate my classes away from him. It's unreal that I used to want to be away from him. It now feels so foreign. It hurts to be without him. I need him like oxygen.

I spend my classes filling my margins with doodles. When lunch rolls around, I toss up my options. Roam the halls in search of Ash, or cut my losses and hide in the library.

Luke appears from my left and asks, "Are you looking for Ash?"

I sigh happily. "Yes. Have you seen him?"

He nudges ahead. "He'll be in the cafeteria."

"Okay."

I walk alongside Luke and follow him into the cafeteria. The noise hits me before my vision focuses on all the people. It's like someone has unlatched the wild monkey cages.

Absolute mania.

On Ashworth Academy's website, the images showed orderly students. A non-disruptive environment filled with calm and obedience. Inside the cafeteria is another story. Students stand on chairs, calling across the room. One table hosts arm wrestling matches. There's a corner dedicated to make-out sessions. Big groups rearrange tables and chairs, marooning ostracized kids to small tables by the wall.

Luke's pace hastens toward a table. Hope sits on the tabletop, legs crossed and back arched. Most chairs are filled, but none by Ash.

Great.

I pan around the room, hoping he's at another table.

"Uh, hello," Hope calls in a mocking tone. "Earth to Christie. You coming, or what?"

Geez, she wants me to join their table? Why? She can't stand me.

I obey and move toward the table. When I sit, no one introduces themselves. As they continue with their conversations, an invisibility shield forms around me.

Finally, something familiar.

I pan around the room, looking for faces I recognize from the party or my classes. Wendy enters the cafeteria. She waves to me as she moves to a table two over.

Should I sit next to Wendy? She doesn't seem hostile like Hope.

I stand from my seat, and Hope snaps her neck my way.

"What's up, Christie?" Hope snaps.

"Umm," I say in a wavering voice. "I was going to say hi to someone."

Hope clicks her tongue, rolls her eyes, and flips her hair. All the sudden movements make me dizzy.

"I thought you liked Ash," Hope says, sounding somewhat wounded.

It takes me aback. "Huh? I do like Ash."

"Then why won't you wait for him?" Hope asks, and all the heads at the table turn in my direction.

Hello, giant unwanted spotlight.

"I'm not sure he's coming," I say with an embarrassing squeakiness.

"You admit you're ditching him?" Hope accuses.

How does she get away with manipulating words?

"I'm not ditching him," I reply. My posture droops as every eye watches me.

Do they all agree with Hope? Is there some unwritten rule that girls must sit around, waiting for their boyfriends? They have to know it's common for Ash to leave school early. Or are they staring because they're jealous I'm dating Ash?

Something courageous stirs inside me, and I take a seat. A grin stretches across my face as I eye every female face at the table. That's right, ladies, he's mine.

I turn to Hope. She scowls, wanting me to be uncomfortable and alone. I sit tall with my hands resting in front of me. Hope's eyes twitch, and it spurs me on.

Sorry, Hope, sometimes you don't get to win.

Thankfully, there was only one more class after lunch before I saw Ash again. After the last bell, I wait for him by my locker.

"I missed you today," Ash says, clasping my hand at my locker.

"Right back at you," I reply as he kisses my cheek. "But I wasn't hiding. I was in the cafeteria at lunch, and you know my timetable."

"I know," he says as we move toward the front doors. "I just couldn't get away today."

"I contemplated walking into a physics classroom to find you," I joke, which makes Ash smile. "But I couldn't have lasted five minutes."

"I'll have to prep you with one-liners to help you sail through your first class."

"Classic phrases every physics nerd knows?"

Ash laughs. "Yeah, something like that."

We move down the parted steps onto the front lawns and make our way into the limousine.

"I'm so ready to go home and chill," I say once inside the limousine.

Ash smirks, checking his watch. "You won't have a chance. By the time we get home, your society meeting will have started."

"Dang." I grizzle, tilting my head back as I sink into the seat.

"I know. I have to scram before anyone sees me."

"And I need to change into something *appropriate*," I say with sarcasm. "I just want to be comfy."

"You should rock up in your T-shirt and jeans," Ash jokes. "I'd love to see Mrs. Fisher's reaction."

"Yeah, right," I say mockingly. "And give Hope more ammunition against me? I think not."

"Hope is cool with you," Ash says, slinging his arm around me. "She knows her place."

"She's cool with you," I correct. "She tolerates me."

"Don't keep your guard up with Hope," Ash replies. "She'll manipulate your actions. You'll get frazzled, and Hope will call you rude."

I nod as my jaw clenches. Toying with Hope at lunch was a fluke. Next time, she will be prepared for my fake bravery.

At the manor, I changed into a floral maxi dress in record time. I hurry to the first floor to find Meghan before the meeting begins. Hope has been a thorn in my side since we met. But with everything I'm now learning, Meghan seems like the bigger baddie. First, kindness drove me to suggest Meghan should find a new crush. Now, I'm ordering her to back off from Ash. He's my boyfriend, and she hurts everyone she comes in contact with. I need her away from Ash and away from me.

As I descend the stairs, I find Meghan alone. I raise a hand and call her name, but I'm a moment too late.

Meghan's face brightens, and she lifts on her tippy-toes. She waves and calls out, "Ash! Ash, come over here."

I step off the stairs, and my eyes well. My gaze follows Meghan as she skips to the rear of the manor. She meets Ash, who enters from the rear balcony. He's motionless, like a criminal caught by the police.

"Sorry, I…" Ash mumbles, throwing a thumb behind him. His eyes lift upward, searching for the rest of his excuse.

"Can I just talk to you for a minute?" Meghan asks in a rush. She grabs Ash's arms and steps in close to him. "It's important. I promise."

Ash frowns, huffs, and then nods. "Yeah, okay."

My gut spasms as Meghan leads Ash onto the balcony.

"Coming, Christie?" Hope's voice calls out to me.

How could I guess she'd have a role in this?

I don't answer her. My eyes remain peeled on the pair. Meghan's hand glues to Ash's bicep. Intensity fuels their gazes. Ash is attentive to her every word.

This is murder. What are they talking about? I've gotta get out there.

As soon as I take a step forward, Hope's hand is on my shoulder.

"What's up, Christie?" Hope asks in a teasing tone. "Don't you trust them?"

I bump Hope's hand off me, sending her into laughter. My teeth grind as my lips press hard into a frown. Why did Meghan take Ash outside? She couldn't have anything important to say.

The rampaging thoughts in my head slow to a sedated speed. As if in slow motion, my mouth falls open as Meghan's body sways. Her head droops, and her body slumps. In a quick move, Ash takes hold of Meghan. He spins her, and her back collapses against him.

"Meghan!" Hope screams, pushing me out of the way and hurrying toward her sister.

I race behind and reach the balcony as Ash sits on the ground with Meghan's head in his lap. He puffs, wiping his brow, and looks at Meghan with relief.

Meghan blinks her eyes open and mumbles that she's okay.

Hope pushes me away with a shrill scream, "Get help! Get my mother!"

I glance at Meghan, who blinks and wriggles on the floor.

"Go!" Hope orders.

I turn around and rush inside the manor.

"Murphy!" I yell, racing toward the parlor. "Meghan's had a fall. Where's Mrs. Fisher?"

"What happened to Meghan?" Mrs. Fisher calls out in a boom, speeding out of the parlor. Her glaring eyes demand information.

Panting, I point behind me. "On the balcony."

Mrs. Fisher clutches her handbag and strides toward me. "I have her pills. Murphy, she'll need a glass of water and a damp cloth."

"Right away, madam," Murphy replies hastily.

I follow Mrs. Fisher's long strides toward the balcony.

"Mommy," Hope says fretfully.

"Hey, Ashworth, what gives?" Luke's voice sounds toward us.

Luke emerges from the staircase that leads to the grounds. As he joins the scene, his smug expression vanishes and is replaced with concern.

"Help him, Luke," Hope blurts. "Help Ash pick up Meghan."

"Of course," Luke says, growing pale from his inappropriate outburst.

The boys carry Meghan into the living room, resting her on a chaise lounge. Mrs. Fisher knocks two pills out of a small canister and takes a tall glass of water from Murphy.

"Here, darling," Mrs. Fisher says, helping Meghan to take a sip.

Ash kneels beside the lounge, his eyes never leaving Meghan's face. It must have freaked him out to witness her fall. I want to hug him. I wish he would throw a glance my way. I feel so awkward, standing around gawking.

Murphy holds a damp washcloth out on a tray, and Ash leans forward to collect it. As Mrs. Fisher helps Meghan lie back on the lounge, Ash gently presses the cloth against Meghan's forehead. A caring gesture that is unsettlingly familiar.

"You gave us quite a scare," Ash says to Meghan.

A shy smile twinges Meghan's lips, and she whispers, "Sorry about that."

Ash brushes Meghan's hair back, and replies, "As long as you're okay."

"Meghan, honey," her mother says, fawning over her daughter. "Are you sure you're feeling okay?"

A look of embarrassment falls over Meghan's face. "Yes, Mom. I've dealt with worse than feeling a little dizzy."

"Okay," Mrs. Fisher says, grasping Hope's hand. "We must conduct the meeting, but I don't want you feeling miserable on your own."

Before Meghan replies, Ash responds with, "I'll stay with her."

Meghan and Ash share a glance and smile in unison.

My stomach quivers. Why is Ash caring for Meghan when he hates her?

"Come on, ladies," Mrs. Fisher says, holding hands with Hope and nodding at me to follow.

I fidget in place, jutting my mouth open to at least say, "I hope you feel better, Meghan."

But it won't come out. Some garbled nonsense comes out, which only infuriates Mrs. Fisher. She glares at me with ferocious intensity.

It's easy to see where Hope's temperament comes from. I move like my life depends on it.

"How is Meghan?" Mom asks when I sit beside her in the parlor.

"She's okay," I murmur.

Mom pats my knee. "That's good to hear."

With a tyrannical mother and sister, it isn't hard to believe Meghan is as cruel as everyone says. My mind wanders back to Ash, holding the washcloth over Meghan's forehead.

Meghan humiliated Ash in school. He's being kind to her even though she doesn't deserve it. Okay, she's sick. She's incurable. I wish that wasn't the case. But like Ash said, she's cruel. What changed to make him volunteer to stay with her?

Did Ash feel guilty for her fall?

Yes, that has to be it. They had to be arguing. Ash must have told Meghan that he wasn't interested in dating her, and she collapsed.

My stomach flips, and my heart aches. My memory doesn't lie. They weren't arguing. Their conversation was civil.

Ash held a washcloth over Meghan's forehead, and it made me want to scream. The sympathy and care he showed Meghan were too close to what he'd shown me. If he can flip a switch like that, maybe his concern for me doesn't mean much. When we met, he acted like he hated me.

Is that his deal? Step one, treat a girl like he hates her. Step two, when she's in need, act considerate. Step three, move on when things get

232

serious.

Wait. Am I really thinking he's moving on?

Stop it, Christie. Stop freaking out. You know Ash better than this.

Isn't it good that he's kind to others?

But Meghan…

She's fallen for him, so it will give her the wrong impression. It'll only be harder when she finds out I'm Ash's girlfriend. This is awful. Why didn't I tell her about Ash and me at the boutique?

Now they are alone, in an intimate position, and Ash wasn't put off.

Ugh. This is driving me crazy. I need to know what's happening.

With a jolt of energy, I spring to standing.

"Yes, Christie?" Mrs. Fisher says, staring down her nose at me.

"Excuse me," I say with an insufferable squeak.

"This is important information," Mrs. Fisher replies. "We all need to be on the same page. You can have a bathroom break after the meeting."

Mom clutches my wrist and tugs.

Weighed down by embarrassment, I sit.

"I know Meghan is your friend," Mom whispers, "but you can see her after the meeting. Mrs. Fisher wouldn't have left her side if she was in any danger."

No. The only thing in danger is my relationship.

Twenty-Three

The meeting was forty-five minutes of torture. The entire time, my mind conjured the most hideous images. The worst was a Snow White–worthy kiss between Ash and Meghan.

After the meeting, I make a break for the door. I need to see them. I need to witness Ash and Meghan sitting far apart. Better yet, finding out Ash already ditched Meghan to play video games with Luke.

"Christie," Mom calls out as she exits the parlor.

"Mom, can it wait?" I ask, edging my way to the living room.

"I wish it could. It's about the house."

Images of the fire, smoke, and blackened house frames flash through my mind. I stop by the staircase and lean against the banister.

Mom strokes my arm. "It's being torn down. Tomorrow is the last chance to see it."

My eyes well, and I roughly swipe at them. "They are tearing it down?"

Mom nods. "The investigation and insurance claims are complete. Some items were recovered from the wreckage, and your father and I will collect them tomorrow. You don't have to join us. I just wanted to give you the option."

I blow out a defeated breath, slumping against the banister.

"I didn't want to tell you before the meeting," Mom says softly. "I knew it would be hard to hear."

I throw my arms around her and nestle my head on her shoulder. "Of course I want to join you."

"Are you sure, sweetie?"

I nod against her. "It's our family home."

Mom rubs my back and suggests, "You should take some time to relax. Perhaps a rejuvenating bath? The tubs here are incredibly deep. They've gotten me out of a few rough headspaces."

I massage my temple and whisper, "Yeah, that could be exactly what I need. My head is throbbing."

"Let me walk you upstairs."

When Mom and I reach the kids' wing, Claudia greets us in the hall. In no time, she insists on drawing the bath. Essential oils and thick suds fill the deep stone tub. Like the ultimate spa treatment, lit candles and flower petals frame the bath. I thank Claudia and let the subtle ambient music transport me into a safe cocoon.

To keep me relaxed, the sights, smells, and sounds need to work overtime. With a mixture of house fire memories and the new twist in the Ash and Meghan story, my brain is about to short circuit.

Mom told me to skip dinner, and she'd have Murphy send up food. I thought the cafeteria experience and not seeing Ash would be the hardest things to deal with today. Now I have to fight off nightmarish memories while trying not to imagine my boyfriend's lips on another girl. A girl who has done nothing wrong to me, but I can't act deaf. Ash

235

and Wendy both knew Meghan, pre-illness. I need to take their warnings to heart. Meghan could have been playing me from the start.

A knock on the door breaks me out of my thoughts.

"Christie?" Ash's voice comes through the door. "Are you okay?"

I lower into the warm water and reply, "Yes, I'm okay."

"Your mom told me about the house news. I figured it would have hit you hard."

I push a wall of bubbles closer to my face for comfort. "It wasn't what I expected to hear after the meeting. It had to happen eventually, I guess."

"I can go with you tomorrow, if you want."

"You don't want to be around me at the house," I say in a wounded tone. "I'll be an absolute mess."

"I'd be there to hold you up and wipe away your tears."

I sigh hard at the sincerity in his voice. "When I'm out of here, I could do with your magic hug."

Ash's quiet laughter muffles through the door. "You got it."

"I'll be okay tomorrow. It's a family thing, and I need to be with my parents."

"I understand. I'll leave you to relax."

"Thank you."

I place a washcloth over my eyes and rest my head against the ergonomic lip at the bath's edge. With camomile and lavender scents, and the earthy music, my thoughts disappear.

When I get out of the bath, I'm a prune. Somehow, I lasted two hours.

I dry my hair, slip into pajamas, and tie a robe around me. Ash is still at dinner or perhaps in the theater. I move into my bedroom, ready to hit the pillow. I was almost asleep in the tub. The headache-inducing thoughts have led to monster exhaustion.

Lying in bed isn't easier than lying in the tub. Every time I shut my eyes, an ugly image sends my eyes open. I pass the time by reading on my phone, but my eyes sting, and my vision blurs. I just want to sleep, but I fear what will happen inside my head.

When it nears midnight and the struggle takes its toll, I pull myself out of bed. I need Ash. His hug will make all the bad thoughts disappear. I move into the brightly lit hall and inch my way to his door. I lift a fist to knock but hold it midair as I hear him inside.

Ash's tone is hurried and irritated. I listen in, concluding he's on the phone.

"Why did you lie to me?" his voice aggressively interrogates someone.

The room is silent except for the dull thumps of his pacing.

"No, no. I've heard all those excuses before. Just own up."

I move away from the door as confusion scrunches my face. Who lied to him? Is he talking to his family or someone from school?

The heat in his voice penetrates the door. I move back to my room, avoiding being caught in the crosshairs.

I sit on the edge of my bed, my heart pounding. The anger in his voice was palpable. Just like when he yelled at his dad. Just like when he talked about his mother. Just like when he met me.

I have to believe the real him is the sweet guy who takes me on dates. Why does this aggressive side keep reappearing?

The rest of the night was excruciating. I slept in and missed Ash before school. A horrible way to start the day. At least I have both my parents by my side. Dad's hugs are a nice consolation prize.

Mr. Ashworth's driver, Roger, takes us via limo to our former home. I rest my tired eyes on the hour-long journey, careful not to fall asleep. As we emerge into our former neighborhood, I'm beyond squeamish.

It's like the vehicle is in slow motion as it creeps along our old street. It's excruciating to wait for the charcoal remains of our house to come into view. Even though I know it's coming, I'm still not prepared...

And neither are my parents. They collapse in on each other. My dad tries to be strong, but my mother wails like it's that flame-fueled night all over again.

It's like I'm gut-punched. At night it was horrific, but now, in the daylight, it's catastrophic. If I didn't know better, I'd presumed a bomb had exploded. A firefighter described it that way. The heat and the pressure inside the house acted like a bomb.

I shiver at the sight, and soon, my parents' arms wrap snugly around me.

Dad kisses the top of my head and whispers, "You're such a brave young lady. I'm so proud of you."

"I'm not that brave."

"You've picked yourself up after the worst chaos of our lives," Dad continues. "You've grown stronger. You're my little hero."

I hug them both tighter. "Thanks, Dad."

"I don't know if I can walk through it," Mom says, sniffing back her tears. "It looks too ghastly."

"There's nothing left," Dad replies. "Whatever investigators found is waiting for us at the police station. You only need to walk through it if you need the closure."

I take another look at the house. "I might step outside."

"I'll go with you," Dad says.

"You two go," Mom says, cowering. "I can't."

Dad kisses Mom's cheek and whispers, "We will be back soon."

I snatch a cashmere throw by my seat and hand it to Mom. She thanks me, and I exit the limousine with Dad.

In the slight breeze, I stand tall and exhale gradually. Dad moves toward the house and steps into the burned remains. Parts of the foundations still stand. It's the same Swiss cheese effect I remember, although more has tumbled down since we left.

It's surreal we used to live here. Life at Ashworth Estate has been easily adaptable. I don't even recognize the girl who called this home.

She was covered in ash and soot, and a boy met her with disgust. A boy who mourned his family and believed he had no room in his heart for anyone.

I believe I now take up residency in his heart.

I shiver in the breeze and notice the doubt bubbling inside me.

That angry boy still exists. I heard him mere hours ago. The condemnation he uses when people are beneath him or have wronged him.

That boy scares me. I never want to hear him talk like that again. If he tells me who was lying to him, maybe I can defuse his temper. Maybe I can suggest a less hostile way to express his emotions.

Dad exits the fire-ravaged house. "Did you want to go inside?"

I shake my head. "I don't need to see it."

Dad nods and throws his arm around me as we walk back to the limo. Next stop, the police station.

"Hello," Dad says, approaching the sergeant's desk. "We are the Kleins. Detective Murdoch is expecting us."

The police officer nods and picks up his phone. He relays the message and puts down the phone.

"Murdoch will be out in a minute," the officer says. He turns around and collects something wrapped in plastic. "Here are the items recovered from your home," the officer says, placing it on the desk. "I apologize, it isn't much."

Dad replies, "Don't apologize. We weren't expecting anything."

Dad takes the items confined in plastic, and a tentative smile dashes across his lips.

"Mary," he says softly. "Look at this."

Mom steps forward, and upon seeing the items, she gasps and runs a hand to her mouth.

I edge close and see a metal picture frame. It's only the front frame with no backing or photograph remaining, but I remember what it held. It had Mom and Dad's wedding photo. They engraved the metal frame with their names and anniversary date. Beside the frame are two glass

239

goblets. They drank wine out of them on their wedding day.

"Thank you so much," Mom says with a sniff. "It's like getting a piece of home back."

"I'm glad it can make you smile," the officer replies kindly.

I slip between my parents and hug an arm around each. "That's fantastic. It's a good omen that they survived."

"That's right, kiddo," Dad replies

Five minutes later, Detective Murdoch greets us in the foyer and shows us to a private room.

"Thank you for coming down to the station," Murdoch says. "This news is better delivered in person."

"Isn't the investigation into the fire over?" Mom asks anxiously.

Murdoch shakes his head. "No, but we can tell you what caused the fire."

Mom uses her hand to shield her eyes. "I left something on in the kitchen, didn't I?"

"Mr. and Mrs. Klein," he says gravely, "the fire was deliberately lit. It was arson."

"Arson?" the three of us say in unison.

Whatever the detective says next doesn't register with me. It's muffled white noise as my heart rate slows and my sluggish blood drains through my body.

As I come back to life, I hear, "The case isn't resolved. We have a list of suspects, but we can't give you any further information at this time."

My chest rapidly rises and falls as my mind retraces the events of that horrid night. No sooner after we first spoke with the police did they notify us that Mr. Ashworth had sent a car. It always felt suspicious that he arranged it so soon.

Could he...?

Could he have arranged the fire?

But it could have killed us...

"Someone purposely set the fire?" I blurt loudly.

Mom's and Dad's fearful eyes fall on me, and Detective Murdoch replies, "I know this is a scary prospect."

"We could have died!" I exclaim. "Someone tried to kill us!"

Mom places a hand on my shoulder with heavy pressure.

I look at her with a narrow gaze. "It's true."

"We are close to nailing this guy," Murdoch says. "You have my word."

Is it possible the way the fire was lit gave us time to get out? Is Mr. Ashworth power-hungry enough to give someone these orders?

I rub my temple furiously as my brain goes haywire.

Dang. I really need to sleep.

The entire journey home, my brain fixates on Mr. Ashworth's orchestration of our house fire. The implications make me sick to my core. When I shiver inside the limousine, my parents worry it's because I saw the house, but the wreckage no longer haunts me.

It's the twisted way my suspicions are coming to life.

We ate dinner at a diner on the way home. It was wholesome and unpretentious, reminding me how sweet our life was before Ashworth Estate. I've adapted to life in a mansion. I no longer feel weird about Claudia doing my hair. I accept it and, dare I say, expect it.

I'm used to asking Murphy to help me with the perfect midnight snack. I walk around the halls, forgetting the enormity of the building. Somehow it has felt like home.

Have I lost who I really am?

Did I allow myself to fall into the Ashworth family's trap?

Ash told me his mother arranged my transfer to Ashworth Academy because it bolstered her interests. And she's still running the society events from another continent.

I'm glad to be back inside the manor, simply to find a bathroom and hurl my guts up. The burger at the diner was insanely delicious, but my mixed emotions and speculative theories have wreaked havoc in my

241

body.

"Hey, you're back," Ash says, meeting me in the hall outside my bathroom.

The pressure on my insides releases at the sight of him. I move in for a much-needed hug.

"Rough day?" he asks, rubbing my back and smelling my hair.

I don't have the strength to answer him.

"This isn't the best time to bring this up," Ash says, and I sense a strain in his body. "But I need to tell you something."

The tension in his body sends me into uneasiness. I pull out of the hug with trepidation and ask, "What?"

"It's about the benefit. I think it's best if I take Meghan," Ash says.

"What?" I splutter, assuming I heard him wrong.

"It will be the right thing to do."

I rub a thumb between my eyebrows and squint at him. "Since when?"

"She's been through a lot, and it would make her happy."

"But what about us?" I say in a whisper, searching the floor for answers. "Aren't we...?"

Ash steps forward and strokes my arm. "You're still my girl. I'll only be with Meghan as a friend."

I frown hard, unable to look at him. "But you're my boyfriend."

"Exactly," Ash replies. "Don't you trust me?"

Is he for real? I just returned from the wreckage of my house. We learned someone deliberately set it ablaze, and the first thing he mentions is wanting to date another girl?

"Why don't you want to go with me?" I mutter in a feeble voice.

"We'll have a good time together. Meghan will just feel better walking in with someone."

"Her family will be with her," I protest.

"Yeah, but Hope will be with Luke, and her parents are hosting."

"So I'll be alone instead?"

"No, I'll be with you at the benefit."

"But you're going with Meghan? Without me?"

"Is it really so bad?"

"I just don't understand. Is this normal for you to date one girl and escort another?"

"I'm just trying to make it up to Meghan."

My brain goes into overdrive, trying to make sense of his words. "Make up for her fall? That wasn't your fault. She's sick."

Ash fidgets in place. "I know. Ugh, I'm not explaining myself well."

"I don't understand why you'd want to be with her instead of me."

"I don't."

Tears prickle my eyes as my emotions frazzle. "Then why are we having this conversation?"

Ash chews his lip and shrugs. "I was too negative about Meghan before."

"I thought you hated her."

He looks away. "It's complicated."

My insides cramp. "Do you want to dump me for her?"

Ash's eyes lock on mine with an irritated glare. His voice is harsh when he asks, "Are you questioning my feelings for you?"

I step back, feeling one inch tall.

He sighs and softens his body language. "I'll be by your side at the benefit. Meghan just wants someone by her side when she enters."

My voice breaks as I ask, "Then why did you ask me to be your girlfriend?"

Ash holds his hips and stamps a foot. "Do you seriously think I want to break up with you?"

"It's the only thing that makes sense."

"I've been more honest with you than anyone else."

My frustrations boil over. "Then why aren't you being honest about your sudden one-eighty with Meghan?"

Ash exhales hard. "Stop giving me those judgmental eyes."

"Huh?"

"You're looking at me like you did when we first met. Deciding my motives without the whole story." He turns his back on me and mutters, "How could I think you'd ever stop judging me?"

The hurt leaves me crushed. "What? That's really what you think I'm doing?"

He spins back around, hand on heart, and says, "I've never in my life cared about dating until I met you. My number one priority is getting my family back together, and all this girlfriend crap is taking my sights off it."

"Girlfriend crap?" I say as a tear spills down my cheek. "Is that how you really feel?"

"I knew he planted you here as a distraction, but I was a blind fool anyway," he seethes. "How could I be such an idiot to play my dad's games?"

"As if. You're the one who played me," I fight back. "You used me just the same as your family has used my family. You probably knew about the plan to burn my house down."

Ash's face grows tense. "What are you talking about?"

"I should never have dropped my guard," I say, mid sob. "You were always the same arrogant and selfish brat."

"If that's what you think," Ash says in a steady voice, "then fine. We're through."

I stand tall as Ash leaves down the hall. I don't shake, fidget, or stammer.

Yet I feel every excruciating break of my shattering heart.

Shard by shard.

Twenty-Four

I cried myself to sleep last night. I cried myself awake at three thirty after dreaming of Ash burning in flames.

Never did I expect to experience worse pain after escaping the house fire. I didn't think it'd lead me to making my first friend. A friend I'd fall head over heels for. A friend I'd open up to, and who would leave me heartbroken.

Why couldn't he let me be invisible?

I didn't want this. This pain of trauma and love is intolerable.

Love.

Is that what it was?

He wanted to be with Meghan, despite my feelings.

It wasn't love.

I mistakenly fell asleep one more time. I had another nightmare, but there was no fire. It was a little girl with pigtails and wearing a party dress. She appeared sweet and innocent, but then she pointed at me and threw her head back with menacing laughter. Hope's laugh. Dread, torment, and angst filled my being. It was like being ripped apart from the inside out.

I wake up sitting. Sweat drenches my skin, and my chest heaves. I look at the wall separating me from the boy who, less than twenty-four hours ago, I called my boyfriend.

I'm alone in my misery. The rampant sobs have made my eyes crusty and my throat inflamed. I wish I'd never met Thomas Ashworth III. I wish I'd never learned I could feel better than this. Because it was all a lie.

I take a deep breath as I enter the dining room this morning. I exhale with relief when it's only Mom at the table.

"Morning, sweetheart," Mom says brightly.

"Morning," I say, taking my seat.

"Oh dear," Mom says. "You look like you haven't slept a wink. Have you been crying? I knew it was a mistake taking you to the house."

I wave off her concern. "No, Mom, I'm fine."

"You look dreadful."

I roll my eyes. "Thanks."

"Don't you want to talk about it?"

"Not really," I mutter as Murphy places a bowl of muesli, yogurt, and fruit in front of me.

I glance at the door, wondering how long I need to be on edge.

As nonchalantly as I can, I ask, "Has Ash already eaten?"

"Master Ashworth dined earlier and took the limousine to school."

I drop my spoon, and it clunks against the china bowl. "What?"

"There will be a Town Car to take you to school," Murphy adds.

"Ash didn't tell you he was leaving early?" Mom says, her concern still on red alert.

I shrug and pick at my breakfast. "I don't care when he leaves."

246

"Did something happen between you two?"

"Nothing worth talking about."

The iciness from my tone freezes Mom. We sit in silence for the rest of breakfast until I leave for school.

It stings that Ash left without me. The Town Car is a shiny black sedan with a driver I've never met. I remember the awkwardness of my first drive to school with Ash. Now the silence is deafening. What will school be like when Ash is ignoring me? Will other students ask about our breakup?

Ash told me it wasn't a regular occurrence for him to go to school. I pray he chooses to skip school.

What do I care what he thinks, anyway? He finally proved me right. He's a selfish brat without a shred of compassion. How dare he tell me his plans to date another girl after my house ordeal? He is so self-involved that my pain didn't even register with him. He'd decided what he wanted and went for it.

His dad will go ballistic after I tell my parents we need to move out. No way can we live with a man who arranged for our house to burn down.

It had to be him. It all lines up.

Mr. Ashworth wanted me occupied with Ash, my mom occupied with the ritzy service inside the manor, and my dad occupied with his new higher position at the company. Well, I'm done being his stooge.

Mr. Ashworth can't play with my family anymore. As the car pulls up at Ashworth Academy, my fingernails dig into my palms. I'm so done with this school and everything it stands for. I don't want to mingle with these elitists and pretend to fit in. When I get home today, I'm asking my parents to transfer me to a public school or let me homeschool.

I walk into Ashworth Academy with my head down. It's an easy glide up the steps. I lift my gaze and notice students stepping out of my way as if Ash were in front of me. I grip the straps of my backpack and walk inside, avoiding eye contact.

In everyone's eyes, Ash and I are still a couple. That must mean he's not here.

I'm not hanging out with anyone and breaking the news. If my nights are back to nightmares and insomnia, my days are reverting to libraries and solitary.

None of my classes had Ash in them. For my benefit, he had sat in on some in the past, like history. Not having him around made it better. The ugliness of yesterday faded to the background. I sketched in my notebook to escape my troubles.

Thankfully, I avoided Hope too. She called out to me at lunch, but I hightailed it to the library. No doubt, she wanted to gloat about Meghan's successful conquest of Ash.

Hearing Hope's laughter echo in the halls reminded me of the maniacal little girl from my dream. I swear I've seen her angelic features and golden pigtails before. Her appearance cued my body to enter into a shame spiral. Why did a little girl riddle me with fear and self-loathing?

On the way home, I stare out the window at the main street of Victoria Falls. The cafés I'm yet to dine in, the clothes I'm yet to try on, and the art shop I can't step foot in. Not that I ever need to. I have one of everything back at the manor.

Ash buying me all that stuff was off. I never believed that he could really like me. It was another ploy to buy me off.

My eyes well with tears, and I drop my face into my hands.

I sob, enduring an internal war. It was real. He did like me. I did like him. Sticking by each other in school, playing board games and swapping secrets, stargazing and a private dinner.

It was all real.

I loved him.

An avalanche of sobs thunders out of me. I tumble forward as the horrendous entirety of my emotions crashes over me. Why didn't he want to be with me anymore? Why wasn't I enough?

"Miss?" the driver says awkwardly. "Can I do anything for you?"

248

I wipe my face, and in a croaky voice, I reply, "Just speed home."

When we arrive at the manor, I race inside and bound up the staircase, hoping my mother is in her suite.

I bang on her door and turn the doorknob. As the door opens, Mom reaches out and scoops me into her embrace.

I collapse against her, panting.

"My goodness, Christie," Mom says with wild concern.

My eyes fill with tears as I admit, "Ash and I broke up."

"Oh, honey," Mom says, wounded. "I'm so sorry."

"That's awful news, kiddo," Dad's voice emerges with comfort.

I look up from Mom's shoulder and watch Dad approach from the bed.

"Dad?" I question. "You're home?"

He nods with an apprehensive expression. "I wasn't as brave as you today. I couldn't go to the office after what happened yesterday."

I move from Mom and into Dad's hug. Is he home because he suspects foul play from Mr. Ashworth, too? My heart pounds because I'm so close to being proven right.

"What happened between you and Ash, dear?" Mom asks, stroking my hair.

I move out of Dad's hug and sit on the bed. Mom sits beside me, and Dad takes the desk chair.

"I'm really confused about the whole thing," I explain. "Last night, he said he wanted to be Meghan's date for the benefit. He didn't seem to understand that this hurt me."

My parents' confused expressions fill me with relief. I had wondered if Ash's plan was normal and I was the crazy one.

"Anyway, we got into this big fight. He got so mad that he told me we were through."

Mom rubs my back, and Dad reaches out to take my hand. They both say they are sorry, and it does feel nice. With all the talk of game playing between Ash and me, I'm tempted to ask my parents about their arson suspicions. But it's too overwhelming to accuse the billionaire who gave us shelter.

"Have the nightmares come back?" Mom asks fearfully.

I nod and see the anguish writhing in my parents.

"I've dreamed about the fire two nights in a row," I tell them. "Last night, I had a different dream. It was weird but just as scary."

"Can you tell us about it?" Mom asks.

"There was this little girl with pigtails laughing at me," I reply. "I can't get her out of my head. She feels oddly familiar."

Dad leans forward, unnerved. "It sounds like Tina."

"Tina?" I question.

"Your kindergarten best friend," Dad replies.

"Oh my gosh," Mom says. "I'd forgotten about that girl."

"Wait," I draw out the word. "I had a childhood friend?"

"You don't remember Tina either?" Dad asks. "Well, I'm not surprised. When she chose to play with other kids, you were devastated. We were called to the school to console you."

"Why don't I remember this?" I mutter, forcing my brain to find a trapped memory.

"You never forgave Tina for cutting you out," Dad continues. "And we couldn't seem to encourage you to make more friends." He wraps his arms around me. "You were our skittish little girl. We didn't want to push you."

When Dad lets me go, my mind is blank until an image of Ash appears.

"Maybe that's why my subconscious brought her up," I suggest. "I've been going over how horrible my experience went with Ash, who I consider my first friend. I thought Meghan might be a friend too, but she's betrayed me. This is a pattern. I should stay alone."

"No, Christie," my parents say in unison.

"We've never seen you happier than when you were with Ash," Mom says. "And you had so much fun shopping with Meghan. You can't shut people out again."

Dad nods in agreement. "We won't allow it."

Ash was convinced something in my childhood made me standoffish about making friends. How did he know? Although, I'm not surprised. All that boy did was see me.

Then why did he break my heart? Why didn't he comfort me after seeing my house and visiting the police station? Why did he talk about Meghan instead of showing concern for me?

How can I not think he's a selfish, arrogant jerk?

"I won't isolate myself," I tell my parents, "but I do need to go to the art studio. I haven't started the artwork for the benefit, and Mrs. Fisher is counting on it. The painting will help me work through all these yucky feelings."

"If it gets too overwhelming," Mom says, "come back downstairs and find us."

I nod and kiss both my parents on the cheeks. "I will. Thank you guys so much. I love you."

"We love you too," they both say in their own sappy ways.

I say goodbye to my parents and leave the room. I make my way to the staircase, which leads to the third floor, when Ash approaches from the opposite direction.

I halt, wanting to avoid another heated argument. I can't ignore his face. His sunken eyes, messy hair, and even the collar on his shirt is askew. If one word was to sum up the person standing before me, it would be devastation.

Ash walks into a room, slamming the door behind him.

Happiness bubbles inside me. The cruel side of me revels in his sadness. But it fades. He said he wanted to date Meghan, and now he has the green light. Why is he moping around the mansion?

I press on and make it into the art studio. As I plonk down on my stool in front of the blank canvas, I'm wrecked. How many more personal revelations can come up in twenty-four hours?

How can a weekend of stargazing and making out catapult me into a week of Dante's Circle of Hell? I grab a mixing board and squirt on some colors. Grays, greens, and blues fit my mood, and I paint jagged, slanted, and aggressive angles on the canvas. The view of mountains from the helicopter filters into my mind. On the canvas, I haze them with fog and drizzling rain, symbolizing the constant sadness clouding my every thought. My vision blurs as tears obscure my view. My chest is heavy, and my posture is rigid. Even though the room is spacious, I feel cramped as I paint. My focus is insular, and everything besides the painting disappears into a vibrating hum.

My eyes clear, and my lungs relax, allowing me to breathe without the weight of anxiety. The painting comes to life with darkness and grief. Now that I stare at my emotions in front of me, I become unburdened. For the first time in days, I feel free.

At dinner, I feel like snoozing in my soup.

"Tom," Dad says with surprise as Mr. Ashworth enters the dining room. "I didn't think we'd see you this evening. Without me prodding you to come home for dinner, I figured you'd burn the midnight oil."

"I had to come home early," Mr. Ashworth says, walking to his seat at the head of the table. "I've been thinking about the police getting back to you all day."

I glare at Mr. Ashworth as he walks behind my parents' seats. He came home to see if we found him out.

"We haven't heard anything yet," Mom says, and as if on cue, Dad's phone rings.

As Dad fishes for the phone in his pocket, Mom nervously says, "Imagine if that's the police."

Dad retrieves his phone, and when he views the screen, his mouth falls open.

He turns to Mom and says, "It's Detective Murdoch."

Mom grows pale and whispers, "Answer it."

Dad skids his chair back, gives Mr. Ashworth an apologetic nod, and moves out of the room as he takes the call.

Mr. Ashworth's eyes follow my dad out of the room. It's the moment of truth, scumbag. Now we find out who you really are.

Mom fidgets with her linen napkin, and Mr. Ashworth clears his throat.

"A tense phone call, I presume," Mr. Ashworth says.

Mom nods. An anxious noise whispers out of her, and she politely replies, "Yes, indeed."

A few more tension-fueled moments later, Dad strides into the room.

"You will not believe this," he says animatedly. He is loud, and his hands fly about his head.

My heartbeat booms in my ears, and my gaze moves from Dad to Mr. Ashworth. Geez, why didn't I warn Dad? I should have told my parents about my suspicions. It will come to heated blows at the table. Look at all the knives and glass! This is a nightmare!

"What happened, Peter?" Mom asks, anxiety level set to extreme.

Dad sits beside her, resting his hand on her shoulder. "They've arrested the arsonist."

I'm not breathing. I can't breathe. I've forgotten how. Seriously, how do I make these lungs work? I'm choking!

"He was a repeat offender. That's why Detective Murdoch was so confident they had the right guy in their sights," Dad explains. "He lights houses ablaze as part of a sick fantasy. He enjoys watching a fire grow and has no regard for human life. Our survival wasn't a factor to him because he's devoid of empathy. Murdoch says he expects the man to be sent to a mental health facility for insanity instead of a prison."

"No," Mom says, red lines framing her eyes. "This was a game to this man? For his own twisted pleasure? This is revolting. We could have died."

I pant over my place setting, drawing in much-needed oxygen.

"Christie?" Dad asks.

I clear my throat and cough loudly.

"I'm okay," I say hoarsely. "Did this guy work alone?"

"Yes. We are the sixth house he has attacked."

Dumbfounded, my eyes land on Mr. Ashworth, who radiates warmth and kindness.

He didn't do it?

He was just being nice to us?

He genuinely likes my dad?

Is that really the full story? There's no greater mystery behind this guy?

Well, aren't I the grade A scumbag?

Mr. Ashworth clears his throat and calmly says, "Peter, Mary, I hope you know your invitation here is indefinite. You and your daughter are welcome here as long as you like. It's been a joy having you here. Plus, considering I'll now oversee a project in a different division, it'll be nice to still have cocktail hour with you, Peter."

Wait. Mr. Ashworth won't be hovering over my dad anymore?

Gratitude inflates Mom and Dad.

"Thank you, Tom," Dad says. "But we will get our own place."

"All I'm saying," Mr. Ashworth says with a happy smile, "it's a big house. You three don't take up much space."

"That means so much to us, Tom," Mom replies. "I'm sure we aren't in any rush to leave."

"Splendid," Mr. Ashworth says. He snaps his fingers. "Murphy, where's my son?"

"Master Ashworth has left for a friend's house this evening," Murphy informs us.

I slide down in my seat. Sitting next to Ash would be insufferable awkwardness. Yet I'm disillusioned.

"I could have guessed he'd skip out on dinner," Mr. Ashworth says and takes a sip of wine. "He's been upset since his mother informed him she's extending her stay in Switzerland."

"Oh, that's too bad," Mom says. "I was hoping she'd be back for the benefit this weekend."

Mr. Ashworth replies solemnly, "It's not in the cards."

I take in the sincerity in his eyes and then glimpse Ash's empty seat. Did his mother break this to him while we were visiting our old house? Or did I overhear him yelling at his mother and calling her a liar? Is this disappointment what caused him to lash out at me?

When he brought up Meghan, he turned the conversation into blaming me for taking his focus off his family. Did he think escorting Meghan to the benefit would please his mother, and she would return home?

I'm just making up stories to feel better. Trying to erase our breakup argument out of reality. The fact is, he's not here. He doesn't want to be anywhere near me.

I finally got what I wanted.

I'm invisible to him.

Twenty-Five

Over the next two days, Ash continues to skip school. He leaves his bedroom early and comes home late. The avoidance cripples my heart. I don't know what he does all day. Maybe he spends his time with Meghan. *Shudder.* Gosh, I hope not.

Last night, I finished the final touches to my auction piece. It's the day of the benefit, and my stomach won't stop flipping. At Mrs. Fisher's request, a courier arrives to deliver the artwork to the event hall. I don't know why we can't take it. Mom and I are leaving soon to oversee the flower arrangements.

"Miss Klein," Murphy calls. "The courier needs you to verify the painting before he leaves."

Murphy and the courier worker walk toward me in the hall, and my heart stops.

"No, not that one," I blurt.

"Oh?" he says, looking down at the artwork.

I'm panting as the artwork I painted for Ash, with the bench seat, flowers, and constellations, is held in front of me.

"It was the forest scape on the other easel," I say, my body burning with embarrassment.

The courier turns around as Ash enters the hall behind him. My fists curl, digging my nails into my palms as Ash views the piece. His eyes droop, and his pale face grows a pink hue. His shoulders tense, and he shifts in place, examining it from top to bottom.

"I…" It's barely audible. I want to say, "It's for you," but I can't.

My heart pounds out of control, and sweat greases my back.

He hasn't taken his eyes off it.

Does he like it?

He hasn't smiled.

Does he hate it?

The courier excuses himself to retrieve the correct piece. He walks past Ash, leaving empty space between us.

I open my mouth, trying to get the words out.

A red line frames his welling eyes, and he blinks hard.

I clear my throat, looking away. I keep my head down as his footsteps move away from me.

With a trembling hand, I rub the ache from my chest. I blow out a hard breath and smooth down my dress. I need to find my mom. I need to get out of this place.

Mom let me be quiet on the drive into Victoria Falls. She gave me a job when we reached the event hall and let me work solo. I appreciate her quiet understanding that breakups suck.

I gently part the delicate flowers in the centerpieces, ensuring they are evenly spaced. As the catering staff places the china, silverware, and glasses, the tables come to life.

"Why didn't you tell me?" a voice calls out.

I turn around and watch Meghan hurrying toward me.

I freeze, gripping a nearby chair and gritting my teeth, ready for the imminent attack.

Meghan stops in front of me and throws her hands in the air, exasperated. "What gives?" she says. "I thought we were friends."

"Wha... Wha...?"

"Christie," Meghan says delicately. "Why didn't you tell me you and Ash were so hot and heavy?"

I splutter more half words.

"You let me go on and on about my crush when you were dating him," Meghan says. "Why didn't you shut me up? If you had said something, I would have backed off."

Is she after an apology? "Sorry."

Meghan giggles and ropes me into a hug. "You don't have to say sorry, you silly girl. I'm the one who's sorry."

We pull out of the hug, and I cautiously fold my arms across my middle and eye her with distrust.

"Is it true you and Ash broke up?" Meghan asks, pouting. "Did I cause it?"

My stomach flips, and I swallow hard. "It was a mixture of things."

Meghan gestures to the chairs at the nearby table. "Can we sit for a minute?"

I accept because my knees are knocking. As I sit with Meghan, I'm torn. She still seems so sweet. But everyone says she's a devil in disguise.

"At the last benefit meeting," Meghan begins, "the one where I embarrassingly collapsed..." She pauses, clearing her throat. Her hands fumble with the tablecloth, and her gaze stays low. "I told Ash the truth about something I'd covered up. That's why he wanted to escort me to the benefit. He'd kept a grudge against me over something I didn't do."

I lean forward, curious. "What were you covering up?"

Meghan blows out a slow breath. "Before I got sick, I hung out with Hope and Vanessa. Vanessa was mad at her parents. They were breaking up but not being direct about it. She had a theory that her mom was having an affair."

"Oh geez."

Meghan nods, continuing the story. "Ness stalked her mom after a parent-teacher conference and snapped photos of her and a teacher. It got so crazy. Ness created posters, and she stuck them on school lockers. She wanted the teacher to confess." Meghan shakes her head in disbelief. "Vanessa wanted the school to call her mother and confront her with the images. The affair was all in Vanessa's head. Mr. and Mrs. Ashworth were falling out of love. It's super sad, but Vanessa took it too far."

"How did you get involved?"

Meghan chews her lip. "Vanessa wanted to save face. She knew if anyone found out, it would ruin her reputation. I took the fall because I was leaving school."

"Ash told me he hated you for that," I say. "Why did you take the blame?"

"Because Vanessa was my friend," Meghan says with a shrug. "At least, I thought she was. The plan was for the school to point blame at me. I was sick, so it wouldn't go any further. You know, the whole charity case thing. Vanessa promised she would tell her family the truth. I believed Ash knew I wasn't behind it. It wasn't until you told me that Ash said we didn't get along that I realized Vanessa hadn't come clean."

I sit back in the chair as remorse washes over Meghan. This is why it was painful to believe she was evil. My first impression of Meghan was right.

I scoop up her hand, and our eyes meet as I give her a warm smile.

"I got so paranoid I'd slip up," Meghan says. "Vanessa was adamant no one could know the truth. I'd go into a deep panic. I shut out my friends and boyfriend because I didn't want to lie to them. I kept thinking about how bad it would be for Vanessa if the truth slipped out."

"Vanessa shouldn't have done this to you."

"It's okay. I chose to go along with it."

I chew my lip as I think over my fight with Ash. "Ash told me he wanted to escort you to the benefit to make it up to you. It makes sense now."

Meghan nods. "I never would have asked him if I'd known you two were together."

"Well, we're not anymore, so he's all yours."

It's like I gut-punched myself.

"No way," Meghan says enthusiastically. "I'm devoted to getting you two back together."

"Why? You like him."

Meghan giggles and shakes her head. "No, I like the stories Hope and I concocted. Once Vanessa left town, I realized how isolated I became. I couldn't go to parties and lost my closest friends. Hope would tell me gossip, trying to boost my mood. It wasn't until she started talking about Ash that I felt better. Soon, we were creating fantasies about him. It all started with real stories, but then we turned them into fairy tales for my enjoyment. Soon, I wanted him for real, and Hope vowed to help me."

"So... You're not in love with him?"

Meghan giggles and sits back in her chair. "I'm in love with love."

"That means you two didn't kiss—?"

"No," Meghan blurts. "When did you think we kissed?"

"Ugh. I have a very imaginative brain."

"Ash and I are only friends. If you can even call it that. He wants you."

"Ash and I said some nasty things," I say. "I don't think we can come back from it."

"Ash is arriving in a limo to pick me up at my house this evening," Meghan says, clutching my hands as her eyes widen. "You should get ready at my house, and when he arrives, you can surprise him at the door."

"No, no. I can't do that."

260

"Sure you can," Meghan says with an excited jolt. She bounces in her seat, and her grip on me tightens. "Please, please, please. Let me help you."

I giggle at her enthusiasm and then say, "I don't understand why you want to help me."

"Because I like you, silly. Plus, you've always been nice to me."

I sigh and look at my lap. "I heard stories about you. Things that painted you in a cruel light. I believed them. I'm so sorry."

Meghan yanks me into another hug. "It's okay. It means so much you believe me now."

"I do. I couldn't understand how someone so bubbly and kind could also be the girl in those stories."

When we pull out of the hug, Meghan admits, "Of course, I've done bad stuff. I was in awe of my sister and her friends. I wanted to be like them. I've teased kids, and I've pulled pranks." She gestures around the room and singles out her fabulous portrait. "Karma got me. Now, I want to be nice to everyone."

I frown. "You don't really believe you got sick because you did some mean things?"

Meghan shakes her head. "I know it was a freak thing. But I see things differently."

"I'm still stunned that Ash's sister betrayed you like that. How could she not come clean?"

"I don't know. She obviously feels immense guilt and shame because she followed her mother halfway around the world with her tail tucked between her legs."

I nod, putting the last piece together. "She went with her mother as her own way of making amends."

"These Ashworths are a little screwy," Meghan jokes. "Like your boyfriend. He thought a date with me would be cool when he already has a gorgeous girlfriend."

"If I had known the whole story…"

Meghan smirks. "My point exactly."

"Ugh. I know. It's just… Ash and I were only starting up when I met you. I didn't know what I was to him. It was too awkward to blurt out to you."

"He is infatuated with you," Meghan says with a proud smile. "He looked ghastly the last time I saw him. I kept pestering him about what was wrong, and he admitted that you and he had broken up. Imagine my shock when I didn't know you were an item. He assumed you'd told me because he knew we were friends."

"He doesn't want to see me again."

"Umm, yes, he does," Meghan says with a hint of sarcasm. "He's shattered. Heartbroken. That means he was in love."

I choke. "In love?"

Meghan grins, avidly nodding in response.

I laugh with surprise and hide my face with my hands. "I do want him back. I want to make things right. But where do I begin?"

"You begin by letting me help," Meghan says, pushing her chair back. She stands and holds her hand out to me. "Come on, gorgeous. Let's get your man back."

I was a dizzy, befuddled mess on the way to Meghan's house. As she paraded evening dresses in front of me, my vision blurred. Life had become more complicated than I could ever imagine from suspecting my dad's boss of burning our house down when he was only being compassionate. Next, thinking my friend was an evil mastermind and stole my boyfriend when she was only trying to be honest. And topping it off with accusing my boyfriend of acting selfish and lacking empathy when he was hurting over his broken family.

Ash called me judgmental.

My gosh, he's totally right.

I believed Meghan was cruel.

Maybe I was cruel for believing hearsay.

"You need to calm down," Meghan's makeup artist says as she

applies powder to my face. "You're going all red."

"Christie, are you okay?" Meghan says from the other makeup chair.

A silk robe drapes around me, and I puff and pant at my reflection. "This will never work," I whisper, frowning. "He won't want to see me."

"Yes, he will," Meghan says, thrusting her fist in the air to cheer me on. "Trust me. The boy wants you."

My eyes flick to her reflection, and the honesty in her eyes renews my spirit.

"You really think so?" I say faintly.

"When I spoke to him, it was obvious his mind was elsewhere," Meghan replies. "I've dealt with enough high school boys to know when their minds are on another girl. Unfortunately, that's why I could tell Cody and Wendy would hook up."

I wince. "I'm sorry."

Meghan smiles and shrugs. "They're better together."

"I'd love to help you find someone at tonight's event."

"Aw, that's so sweet. I just want to have fun tonight. And I want you to focus on your relationship."

"I'll give it my best shot."

I take my phone from the nearby table and call Murphy's line at the manor. After several rings, he finally answers.

"Murphy, hi. It's Christie. Look, I know I messed up, but I need your help... Can you do me a massive favor? You know the painting the courier took by mistake...? Can you take it and hang it in Ash's bedroom?"

Murphy didn't give me convincing responses. However, he has always helped me whenever I've asked. He knows everything that goes on in the manor. He knows I hurt Ash, and hopefully, he wants to see me make things right.

After hair and makeup, I dress in a raspberry-pink floor-length gown. A much brighter shade than I would usually wear, yet dressing boldly is a power move I need to make. It has spaghetti straps, a fitted bodice, and a draping A-line skirt. A total Sleeping Beauty dress.

Meghan giggles and claps in front of me. "Yay! He's almost here."

"Oh my gosh, I'm gonna puke."

"No," Meghan gasps. "Deep breaths. In and out. Don't panic."

Ash's voice enters my head. *"You don't need to panic."* He'd always say it to me. He always meant it. He won't let me panic tonight.

After a long breath, I nod at Meghan. "I'm ready."

Hope enters the room and looks me up and down. "You look pretty."

"Thank you?" I respond.

Hope sighs. "Ash was happy with you. I truly hope you get him back."

"Okay," I say, guarded. "Thanks."

"I mean it," Hope replies. "My sister is backing off. I have no reason to stand in your way."

I smile. "Thanks, Hope. You look beautiful, by the way."

Hope points behind her. "Game faces on. Ash's limousine was pulling up as I passed the foyer."

My stomach quivers, but I pull it together before it flips. "Wish me luck," I mutter.

"Good luck," the sisters say in unison.

I glide out of the room and toward the foyer. I spy Luke ahead, mid-conversation. I steady my nerves, continuing toward them as Luke leaves in the opposite direction.

As I approach, Ash comes into view. His expression drops, and his lips lack a hint of a smile.

Twenty-Six

"Uh…" Ash utters, motionless.

I stop before him, clasping my hands in front, and ready to apologize for every unkind word I said to him.

A grin brightens Ash's face. "Whoa," he murmurs. "My dream came true."

I almost lose balance on my heels. "Come again?"

"I never expected you to be here," Ash says, brushing my arms. "But I was wishing hard that you would be."

My heart swells, and I'm mesmerized by those big brown eyes. "Really? You don't hate me?"

His smile grows more handsome by the second. "I could never."

I lift onto the balls of my feet, raise my hands to the sides of his face, and press my lips against his. Ash's hands run along my waist and rest on my back. His kiss melts me to my core. Comfort nestles every cell inside my body. I'm weightless as if our kiss has sent us floating.

We pull out of the kiss, breathless. Ash holds me close, resting his forehead against mine as he says, "I'm sorry. I didn't mean to push you away. I couldn't stop the words coming out of my mouth. Before I knew it, I was walking away."

"Don't apologize. I was already on the offensive. It was a long day, learning about the arson attack."

"My dad told me the news. I should have been there for you. You are right. I am too self-involved."

"No, I'm too judgmental. I actually thought your father hired someone to burn down our house."

Ash laughs out of surprise. "Huh? What?"

"I know, it's dumb. I let my suspicions get the better of me."

"Let's just promise to tell each other what we really mean," Ash says and kisses my cheek. "The misunderstandings aren't worth being apart."

"I wholeheartedly agree."

"It's been hell without you," Ash admits. "I wanted to knock on your door so many times. I left things in a mess. I assumed you didn't want to see me again."

"I was mad. But every time I didn't see you left me disappointed."

"Thank you for the painting," Ash says, clasping my hands tightly. "When I saw it earlier today... I was stunned. It reminded me of everything we've done together. I thought it was for me, but I didn't think I was worthy of your time."

"Since we met, you've taken up all my thoughts," I gush. "Painting is the only true way I know how to express myself."

"You are crazy talented, and it was so thoughtful." Ash grins. "When Murphy brought it to my room, I needed to find you. I banged on your door and was so confused when you weren't there." He laughs, shaking his head. "I'm so freaking glad you're here."

I lean into him. "Me too."

He kisses the top of my head. "I hope we have many more memories you can paint."

"I'm all for that."

"So what's the plan tonight?" Ash whispers, looking beyond the foyer. "Is Meghan...?"

"Meghan is going stag," I reply. "She's decided she wants to do a grand entrance on her own."

"I'm sorry I ever suggested going with her instead of you," Ash says, wrapping his arms around me. "I was all messed up. I'd just learned how Vanessa lied to me and left me humiliated. My mom doesn't want to come home. I wanted to do something, anything, to bring them back. I was hurting and lashed out."

"We both had intense emotions fueling us," I say, caressing his cheek. "I just hope we can stick to loving emotions from now on."

Ash blinks and then backs out of the foyer, tugging me with him as we exit through the front door.

"Okay, that's one way to leave the house," I joke.

Ash keeps me in his arms as his adorable grin grows. "I didn't want to stay in the Fisher house for this."

His smile is infectious, and goose bumps prick my limbs.

"Christie Klein," he says, inching his lips closer to mine. "I love you with all my heart."

I breathe him in and sigh dreamily. "Thomas Ashworth the third, I can't get enough of you. I love you so much."

Every kiss with Ash has gotten better, yet I can't imagine this one ever being topped. Fireworks explode inside me. Even on tippy-toes, my toes curl. My right hand slides down his neck and into his collar. My left hand runs into his luscious brunette hair. For a solid moment, I black out. The passion and lust dominate my senses. Desire and strength pump through his arms as he holds me.

This is enough to sustain me all night. Although, we have a party to attend. Luckily, I have the best-looking date to walk in, arm in arm.

"Shall we?" Ash asks, rubbing my lipstick off with the back of his hand.

I giggle a yes and follow him to the limo.

We arrive at the benefit, and Ash waves to those who call his name. I wave too, surprised kids and their parents say hello to me.

I'm so glad Ash isn't a fan of mingling, either. We find our table and join my parents.

"Great job with the flowers, Mom," I say, giving her and Dad a kiss and a hug.

"Thank you, sweetheart," Mom says. "You look sublime."

"Radiant, kiddo," Dad adds. "And Ash, very dashing in your suit."

"Thank you, Mr. Klein," Ash replies. "Just trying to measure up to Christie's beauty."

Mom and Dad are in awe as I try not to die from blushing.

"We're so glad to see you two back together," Mom says with a sappy smile. "You were both too mopey when solo."

"I completely agree," Mr. Ashworth says behind us.

When Ash and I turn around, Mr. Ashworth gathers Ash in a hug.

"I'm sorry if you ever felt neglected by me, Son," Mr. Ashworth says, patting Ash's back. "You and your sister are my world. I will also try harder with your mother."

"I appreciate it," Ash says as they pull out of the hug. "I'll lay off you. Well, I'll try."

Mr. Ashworth gives his son a wink. "We're Ashworths. When we put our mind to it, we can achieve anything."

Ash picks up my hand and kisses it. "Like being a more attentive boyfriend."

"Okay, now I have to work harder," Mr. Ashworth jokes, "if my son is beating me in the romance department."

My parents laugh, and Mr. Ashworth rounds the table to join them for champagne.

Ash gestures to the dance floor. "Want to give dancing another try?"

I grin, holding back a mischievous laugh. "Only if it means we can wander to the edge and make out instead."

"I'll take that deal," Ash says and takes me by the hand to the dance floor.

On our way, *oohs* and *aahs* encircle us. I try to find the source and soon land on Meghan, radiant in her dark purple evening gown. Her bronze tiara enhances the dazzling color of her hair. Her eyes are smoky and her lips dark. She looks ready for a glossy magazine cover.

I kiss Ash's cheek, and whisper in his ear, "Are you sure you didn't want to walk in with her instead?"

"And steal her thunder?" Ash jokes. He pecks my lips, and says, "I'm already with the most beautiful girl in town. Why would I look elsewhere when I already hit the jackpot?"

I retch mockingly. "Could you be any sappier?"

"I'm just feeling lucky," Ash says. "So lucky, in fact, I bet I'll win my favorite thing in the silent auction."

"What are you bidding on?"

"An artwork by Christie Klein."

I chew my lip and then say, "You don't want it. It's depressing. All my breakup energy went into it."

"Exactly," Ash replies. "It'll remind me to never be stupid again."

I hug my arms around his neck and rest my forehead against his. "I appreciate you so much. You don't need the reminder. Being happy together will be enough."

"I still want to bid on your work," Ash says. "What if I buy it and donate it to the hospital or something?"

"A depressing artwork in a hospital waiting room?"

Ash laughs. "Fine, whatever. I'm still buying it. Maybe I'll ship it to my mom as a subtle reminder."

"It might depress her enough to send her home," I reply. "Now, come on and dance with me."

"Admit it. You can't get enough of these lips."

"Believe me, they are just the cherry on top. I need all of you."

Ash takes me to the dance floor. Like our night under the stars, our steps are small.

Meghan is the belle of the ball. She reunites with long-lost friends, especially Wendy and Cody, and they introduce her to a boy I recognize from my history class. He has jet-black hair, piercing blue eyes, and a tall, strong frame. He escorts her to the dance floor, and they make a small circle near Ash and me.

Just like the night at the observatory, everything around us disappears into a hum.

I have Ash. Strong, kind, handsome, and loving Ash.

My heart is full, and I promise, this time, I'm never letting go.

Epilogue

One Month Later...

My parents still say we are buying a new house. Even though they now have the insurance money, they are yet to speak with a real estate agent.

Dad and Mr. Ashworth don't work together anymore. Dad has a new office closer to Victoria Falls. He has a new flashy car and drives himself every day. He is always home for dinner.

I can't believe I'm saying this, but I enjoy attending school now. For my whole life, I've felt unwanted and unseen. But now I have friends in class and out. I never dreamed starting over could feel this good. Especially now that I haven't had a single nightmare in a whole month!

When Ash and I declared our relationship official, our parents became concerned. It's highly unusual for a boyfriend and girlfriend to live under the same roof. Plus, the fact we share a wall made our parents antsy. The solution—Ash is moving into a larger suite a few doors down from my parents. I'm still in the kids' wing and am told I won't be alone long because Vanessa will return home.

I'm not holding my breath.

"I might come back here for the balcony," Ash says, collapsing his telescope. "It was such a good view."

"My parents' balcony is huge," I reply. "I'm sure you'll find a good angle in your new room."

Ash kisses my nose, hugging me close. Maybe I'm just looking for excuses.

"Don't worry, I'll get lost plenty of times on the way to my parents' room," I joke.

Ash kisses the top of my head and smells my hair. "It'll be weird not to share a wall with you anymore."

"I know. But maybe we will feel like a normal couple now."

"Normal couples live together."

"Not in high school."

"At least we go to the same school."

"And you actually go to classes now."

"I just need to kick that bad habit of failing assignments on purpose." Ash sighs, exiting our hug and picking up a box. "I guess I'd better get moving."

"I thought Murphy was assembling maintenance workers to move your gear."

"He is," Ash replies. "But certain things need to be handled with care."

I pick up his telescope and smirk. "Aka, your star nerd gear."

"Admit it. You think it's sexy."

I giggle. "Yeah, I kinda do."

Ash and I leave his bedroom, carrying the gear when a voice greets us.

"You're not leaving on my account, are you?"

I bump into Ash when he halts in place. "Ness?"

I place the telescope down and step beside Ash. I pivot between Ash and the stunning beauty standing before us.

Vanessa Ashworth is back.

Ash dumps the box and hurries toward his sister. He scoops her in a hug, asking, "When did you get back?"

"Just now. I chartered a plane," she replies.

Of course she did. How else does a rich kid get home?

Ash pulls out of the hug, wincing. "Does that mean Mom didn't come?"

Vanessa frowns. "Sorry, bro."

Ash wipes his brow and then gestures to me. "This is Christie, my girlfriend."

"Hi Christie," Vanessa says, stepping toward me with a welcoming hug. "I can't believe my brother is dating. You must be someone special."

"Thanks. It's so nice to finally meet you."

Vanessa smooths down her golden hair and sighs, "I'll leave you two to it. Jetlag is sinking in." She eyes her brother with a sincere smile. "I'm making up for things. I promise to be here for you."

"Thank you." Ash grins. "I can't believe you're back."

Vanessa smiles and leaves for her bedroom.

I pull Ash into a hug. "Another piece of your family back. I'm so happy for you."

"Why couldn't Mom come back?" Ash grumbles.

"Stick with the positive," I whisper.

He kisses my cheek, and replies, "You're right. Thanks for the reminder."

"You two will have a lot to discuss."

"Once she wakes up," Ash replies. "Right now, I want to test out my new bedroom. I don't know how it feels to make out with Christie Klein in there."

I giggle. "We need to get on it immediately."

Thank you for Reading

If you enjoy this book, please consider leaving a review! Reviews help other readers discover new books. Just a few short sentences about why you liked the book is truly appreciated.

You can leave a review on Amazon, as well as websites like Goodreads and Book Bub.

www.goodreads.com
www.bookbub.com
www.amazon.com
www.bookdepository.com
www.hcpbooks.com

Thank you, again!

Get Ash's Chapter

Scan the QR code to get a FREE chapter from Ash's perspective. This chapter picks up after the breakup in chapter 23.

You will also get a bonus behind the scenes look into how Milly Rose created a mystery and where she plans to take characters in the future.

Shy Girls Can't Date at Christmas

Look out for the next book in the *Shy Girls Sweet Romances* series.

Shy Girls Can't Date at Christmas is a high school bully, second chance romance. It will give you all the cozy holiday feels while tugging at your heartstrings.

I can't wait for you to fall in love with Ava and Beau!

Find it now on Amazon!

About the Author

Milly Rose is an animal-loving romance enthusiast with a swoon-inducing book formula. Shy girl + hot guy + first kisses. Her YA sweet romance books will have you falling in love every instalment. Milly Rose is the quintessential shy girl, who you can contact via her mailing list and reply to her monthly email blasts! Milly spends her days vying for her cat's affection, dreaming up her next book boyfriend, and writing a fun meet-cute under candlelight with a lovely brewed cup of tea.

Join Milly Rose's Mailing List Here

By joining the newsletter list you get a free ebook, exclusive deals, and are first to know about new releases.

Follow the Author

Follow author **Milly Rose** in the following places:

Website
www.hcpbooks.com

Amazon
www.amazon.com/Milly-Rose

BookBub
www.bookbub.com/authors/Milly-Rose

GoodReads
www.goodreads.com/MillyRose

Follow along on Instagram & Tiktok
@shy.author.milly.rose

CPSIA information can be obtained
at www.ICGtesting.com
Printed in the USA
BVHW040349300822
645822BV00021B/603